"I don't give autographs."

Oh, for God's sake, Jacelyn Ross thought to herself. It's not as if the man standing in front of her was a Nobel prizewinner or a famous author or a scientist who'd discovered the cure for cancer. He was a *football coach*! A *silly ball player*! "Look," she said. "I know you don't usually give them out. But I'm asking on behalf of my son. He really wants your autograph."

Mike Kingston looked her up and down—it was a very male perusal, but not a very friendly one. "Yeah, I'll believe that when snakes walk upright." He started to move away. "Y'all have a nice day."

She grabbed his arm. "My son is a staunch fan of yours. Since I teach here at Beckett, I said I'd try to get your autograph for him."

"No can do, babe."

"What if it was your son asking for something?"

His expression softened. "I'd do anything for my little guy," he replied. "Gimme something to write on."

Before he could change his mind, she handed him the program of the Bulls' summer training camp. He took it, scribbled on it and thrust it back. Before she could say anything more, he was gone.

She looked down and smiled. She'd gotten the Ki~~~ autograph. Kyle was goin~~~

Our Two Sons
Kathryn Shay

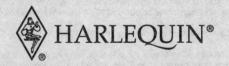

TORONTO • NEW YORK • LONDON
AMSTERDAM • PARIS • SYDNEY • HAMBURG
STOCKHOLM • ATHENS • TOKYO • MILAN • MADRID
PRAGUE • WARSAW • BUDAPEST • AUCKLAND

ISBN 0-373-71253-7

OUR TWO SONS

www.eHarlequin.com

Printed in U.S.A.

ABOUT THE AUTHOR

Kathryn Shay has been writing for as long as she can remember. She began by keeping diaries from the time she was thirteen. At fifteen, she started writing fiction. The youngest of four girls, with a baby brother ten years her junior, Kathryn longed to escape the hustle and bustle of growing up in a small house in Corning, New York. Writing gave her that escape.

For much of her adult life Kathryn has been a teacher. It's a profession she's loved, and she's combined it successfully with her career as a writer. *Our Two Sons* is Kathryn's eighteenth Harlequin Superromance novel. She has also written mainstream novels for the Berkley Publishing Group. Her books have won numerous industry awards and have appeared on bestseller lists at Waldenbooks and *Amazon.com*.

This year Kathryn has retired from teaching to write full-time. She still lives in upstate New York with her husband. They have two grown children, April and Ben.

Books by Kathryn Shay

HARLEQUIN SUPERROMANCE

659—THE FATHER FACTOR
709—A SUITABLE BODYGUARD
727—MICHAEL'S FAMILY
760—JUST ONE NIGHT
774—COP OF THE YEAR
815—BECAUSE IT'S CHRISTMAS
871—FEEL THE HEAT
877—THE MAN WHO LOVED CHRISTMAS
882—CODE OF HONOR
908—FINALLY A FAMILY

948—A CHRISTMAS LEGACY
976—COUNT ON ME
1018—THE FIRE WITHIN
1066—PRACTICE MAKES PERFECT
1088—A PLACE TO BELONG
1123—AGAINST THE ODDS
1206—THE UNKNOWN TWIN

Don't miss any of our special offers. Write to us at the following address for information on our newest releases.

Harlequin Reader Service
U.S.: 3010 Walden Ave., P.O. Box 1325, Buffalo, NY 14269
Canadian: P.O. Box 609, Fort Erie, Ont. L2A 5X3

CHAPTER ONE

THE HEAVY wooden door to what used to be Jacelyn Ross's office whipped open just as she raised her hand to knock on it; out barreled two hundred pounds of pure male flesh—right into her. The man said, "Oops...damn." His fingers grasped her shoulders to prevent her imminent fall.

Totally unbalanced, Jacelyn pitched forward into his hard chest, smacking her nose against it; the contact actually *hurt.* "Ouch."

He chuckled, gentling his hold on her. "Sorry."

As she drew in a steadying breath, she lifted her gaze. "No, it's my fault," she told him, her voice husky.

The man's face was all angles and planes. Short hair, a bit darker than honey, accented his features. Eyes the color of warm gray suede were alight with mischief. And he smelled so good. "Not that I mind." He glanced down at her shirt and those eyes narrowed. "What are you doin' up here, darlin'? This area is off limits for Beckett students. Or are you a Buckland fan?"

A small liberal arts school in Rockford, New York, Beckett College had recently implemented a Sports Studies major, where students could pursue all the business aspects of sports—such as management, finance, marketing and law—and apply them to the sports industry. To coincide with the new program, the Buckland Bulls, a professional football team in upstate New York, had moved their summer training camp to Beckett and would be part of the course of study. The team shared this space with the new staff, which was why no one was allowed up here in the summer.

But her, a fan? Oh, please. She was forty-three years old. She had a PhD and was head of the Business Department. She'd been married and had a nineteen-year-old son.

"I'm not a fan." Self-consciously, Jacelyn tugged down the blue T-shirt she wore with white shorts. She'd come to the campus today to clean out her new office and a very odd request from her son, Kyle, had brought her here. Despite her casual attire, and her utter embarrassment about doing this, she tried to maintain some dignity. "I work at Beckett."

Abruptly, the man released her and stepped back. "Whatever you say." He circled around her.

She called out to him. "Wait, I'm looking for one of the Bulls' coaches, Mike Kingston. Is he inside?"

Halting, the man turned back around and folded his arms across his chest. "You got him right here, little lady. What can I do for you?"

"Give me your autograph." She couldn't fathom why Kyle wanted this man's John Hancock so badly. Jacelyn knew people coveted sports stars' signatures for resale, but she was sure her son wouldn't do that. There must be more to his reasoning, but he'd been vague and evasive when she'd pressed him to tell her.

Kingston's eyes turned flinty and his posture stiffened. "I don't give autographs."

Oh, for God's sake. Though Kyle had warned her of this, she was still mind-boggled. It wasn't like he was a Nobel Prize winner or a famous writer or a scientist who'd discovered the cure for cancer. She'd been told he held numerous records and had earned many accolades as a wide receiver for the Bulls before becoming a coach, but the fact remained that he was just a silly ball player. "I know you don't give them out. It's why *I'm* here. The signature is for my son."

He looked her up and down—it was a very male perusal—but not a friendly one. "Yeah, when snakes walk upright." Again, he started away. "Y'all have a nice day."

Reaching out, she grabbed his arm. It was all steely muscle. "Honestly, it is for my son. He's a staunch fan of yours and is dying for your autograph. Since I work at the college, I said I'd try to get it."

"No can do, babe."

Darlin'? Little lady? Babe? Kyle had told her Kingston was from the South, but did men really call women those things these days? "What if it was your son who asked you for something? Wouldn't you want a stranger to help you get it?"

His face blanked. "I'd do anything for my little guy."

She hadn't known he *had* a son. Still, she capitalized on the knowledge. "I would, too."

Which was exactly the truth. After her ex-husband, Neil, had left her and Kyle for a more prestigious job and a younger woman, Jacelyn had promised herself that she'd compensate Kyle for his father's absence.

She'd even come up here like some groupie to beg on Kyle's behalf.

The words stuck in her throat, but she got them out. "Please, Mr. Kingston."

Sighing, he shook his head. "Gimme something."

Before he could change his mind, she handed him the program that outlined the daily agenda for the Bulls' summer training camp. He scribbled on it, and thrust it back. She gave the paper a quick peek. "Could you address it to Kyle?"

"You gotta be kidding me."

"Excuse me?"

"Where I come from, Kyle is a girl's name."

"Not—" But before she could explain, he pivoted and stalked away.

"Well," she said staring at his retreating back. "That was rude." Jacelyn looked down, then smiled and shook off her irritation. She'd gotten *the King's* autograph, even if it wasn't personalized to Kyle.

Swallowing her embarrassment, she headed for the steps.

WHAT THE HELL was this world coming to? Mike thought as he banged out of Basil Hall and strode toward the sports complex. People lying to get a few scribbles on a piece of paper? Go figure. He'd stopped signing autographs because he was told they were selling on eBay for tons of money, then he'd found out his boycott only made his signature worth more. Like hell this one was for that woman's son. She was dressed as a student, and her hair was in a ponytail, but he supposed she could be around thirty. She might have a kid, but he didn't believe her story for a second.

Walking through the quiet paths of the campus calmed him. Beckett College had been chosen as the new site for the Buckland Bulls' summer training camp for many reasons: they'd outgrown their old facilities at a neighboring state school; the Bulls' director of development and marketing had been a Beckett graduate and had an "in" with the college president; and Mike himself had recommended a look-see at the campus. One of his three older brothers had gone to school here and Mike had enjoyed visiting when they were both still in college. Even then the grounds were real pretty with their ivy-covered stone buildings and a springtime so green it took his breath away. He also liked the fact that the campus was out of the city but close enough to get to restaurants and theaters. So when the choices had been knocked around, and the powers that be had asked his opinion, he'd thrown Beckett's name into the hat.

He passed people pitching tents, vendors checking out concession sites, the workers who were renovating dorm rooms for the team carrying in air conditioners and huge air beds. Set-up for the camp took a couple of weeks, and was almost done. The low rumbling of voices and occasional hammering livened up the solemn campus.

"Hey, Coach, how you doing?" One student in a group sitting at a picnic table called to him as he walked by. Beckett usually had two summer-school sessions of five weeks each, but the college had canceled the second one because it would overlap with the Bulls' arrival. There were a few special seminars taking place, though, before the team got here.

"Great, guys. You?" He kept walking. Not that he didn't enjoy the contact, especially with kids. But he was hoping to get a run in before meeting with the team's administrator in charge of the camp. The guy wanted to talk about the parade coming up next weekend. The fanfare was necessary, but if Mike had his druthers, he'd have passed on most of it. He was the team's wide receiver coach, however, and he had responsibilities. One of them was to carry the ball on PR stuff until the head coach, who had had a family emergency, could get to Rockford. Another, that he looked forward to more, was as team liaison with the college Sports Studies program. He'd just been appointed last week and was hoping to use his brain, as well as his body, in that venue.

Before he knew it, he was at the site. He hustled through the huge red helmet serving as the camp entrance into the tent that would be the activity center. Once outside again, he jogged over to the practice field. In the year preceding the camp's move to Beckett, a new field house and two playing fields had been built. Leaving on his light nylon jacket, even though it was seventy-five degrees and humid, Mike began to cover the gravel path around the field at a slow jog. Running helped clear his mind, so after a few laps he was feeling pretty good mentally. He noticed some people sitting in the bleachers, and a couple of guys by the fence, watching him. He blocked them out. Suddenly something snagged his attention— a bright-blue T-shirt, a ponytail and long legs. Most of the time, he steered clear of women who hung out by the fields—too dangerous—but today, his interest was piqued. It was the girl from the office, the one who'd stolen his signature. Hell and damnation! He kept running, and forced himself to think about something else.

Tyler. That little guy always brought a smile to his lips and tugged on his heart. His son was now living with him permanently. Six months ago, Tyler's mother Trudy had called to say she was going to Europe with an Italian soccer player. *Once a groupie, always a groupie,* Mike had thought at the time and then had felt bad for his unkind sentiment when she didn't come back. Both she and the guy had been killed in a car accident. Mike had flown out to Ohio to be with Tyler, who'd been staying with Trudy's parents. With the Bulls in the middle of playoffs, it was decided his son would finish school there and come up to live with Mike in New York at the end of the year.

In the last six weeks, Mike had spent time with the boy, and was stunned by how much he'd loved being a full-time daddy to Tyler. But during that time, the normally quiet child had been even more subdued. And he'd had bad nightmares. So Mike had decided to bring his son to training camp instead of leaving him with his own parents for the rest of the summer as had been the plan. They'd keep him for a week while Mike got settled, took care of some details for the camp and found somebody to watch Tyler while he worked.

He could still see the fear in Tyler's big brown eyes when Mike said he'd be leaving for a while. His son's misery had eaten away at his insides and he wanted badly to ease it…

"I'll see you in a few days," he'd told Tyler.

"Okay."

Brushing the thick brown hair from his child's eyes,

Mike's chest had tightened. "Honest, Champ. I promise."

Tyler had only nodded. He was insecure because his mother had gone away and never come back. Mike knew that had to be traumatic, and he was determined to fill the void now that he had custody. He wanted to; hell, he loved the kid!

In a better mood, he picked up speed on the tenth lap. He'd gone a fair piece when he saw the blonde again; she was with the two guys by the fence. And was hugging one with…enthusiasm.

Figured. She had a boyfriend—was the autograph for him? That thought made Mike mad all over again. He ran harder; eventually he shed his warm-up jacket.

He wished he could shed the freakin' fan scene just as quick.

"HEY, MOM. You *got* it?" Kyle stared down at the signature of the King and grinned, despite his embarrassment. He knew he was acting like a kid, but he really wanted the autograph.

"Oh, ye of little faith." He looked up to see his uncle Eric grinning. "Your mom can do anything she sets her mind to." Eric let go of Kyle's mother, whom he'd greeted with a customary hug, then held out his hand. "Let me see it."

"Be careful." He gave the program to his uncle.

His mother rolled her eyes. "You guys. It's just an autograph. I don't get why it's such a big deal."

"It's the King's autograph," Eric told her.

She sighed the way she did when she didn't understand some guy thing. Jacelyn Ross was one terrific mom but she didn't get the male perspective some-times. "Why's he called that, anyway?"

Eric—who was two years older than Kyle's mom—studied the autograph with respect. "Because he's the king of wide receivers. When he stopped playing in 2002, he held the NFL records for most catches, con-secutive games with at least one reception and most re-ceiving yards. He still holds the top spot for most seasons with fifty or more receptions."

Kyle jumped in. "Since he rarely missed a catch, the crowd used to yell, 'King me,' when they wanted the quarterback to throw him a pass. They named an award after him, it's given every year. And he was voted Man of the—"

Jacelyn held up her hands. "Enough."

"How'd you get her to do this, kiddo?" Eric asked. "I know my sister. She'd eat ground glass before she'd willingly have contact with athletes."

Kyle blushed. He'd resorted to wheedling the way he used to when he was little…. *"Please, Mom. You're the only one who can get the King's autograph. He refuses to sign them for the public. And no students are al-lowed near the sports office. I put in to work for him this summer, but a lot of kids did so I probably won't get the job. A teacher could get near him, though."*

"But, Kyle, why do you even want it?"

He hadn't told her the truth. The autograph was for Kay, the gorgeous, smart and funny girl he'd fallen for during his freshman year. An athlete herself, she was a huge Buckland fan, particularly of the King. Next week was her birthday and he wanted to surprise her with it then. But he couldn't tell his mom how serious he was about his girlfriend or she'd have a million questions and give him more advice than he wanted. So he'd flashed her an indulgent look. *"If you weren't such a sports snob, you'd know why I want it."*

"I'm not a sports snob." She'd lied with a perfectly straight face.

He'd laughed and hugged her, already taller than her five-seven. *"Yeah, you are. But I love you anyway."* He'd hooked his arm around her neck. *"Please?"*

She'd finally conceded. *"All right…"*

Kyle told his uncle a shortened version, leaving out Kay. Smiling, he tucked the paper into his backpack. "I gotta go, Mom," he said giving her another hug. He liked how she always held on a little longer than he did. "I got that meeting to see about my summer job with the team."

His mom scowled.

"Hey, I need a job. And the Beckett students get first pass with the Bulls' training camp. Which is totally cool."

"I know. But I wish you'd reconsider taking that seminar at Hochstein instead."

He forced himself not to stiffen. As far as anybody besides Kay knew, Kyle was enjoying his music studies at Beckett and at the prestigious Hochstein School of Music, where he took private piano lessons. Everybody thought he was still excited about his chances of getting into Julliard for grad school. "The seminar didn't pay money, Mom. Besides, I want to do something different." He started away. "See ya."

He could feel his mom watching him. He hated not telling her where his mind was at these days. The two of them had always been tight. But things were changing now, and he had to follow his own path. He just hoped she'd be okay with it.

"I'D RATHER be anywhere but here," Jacelyn remarked to her brother as they pulled up to President Cavanaugh's house and got out of Eric's car. Located a few short blocks from campus in the prestigious suburb, the house sprawled like a Southern mansion with its three stories, wraparound porch, peaks and gables and even a widow's walk. It overlooked the canal.

"Careful, Jacey baby, your biases are showing."

Nervously, she smoothed down the gauzy yellow sundress she wore with strappy sandals. The outfit was casual and summer-cool, but sophisticated enough for tonight's affair.

The event was to honor the staff of the Buckland Bulls, along with the star players who'd driven up for the party. As if that wasn't bad enough, it was also to welcome the entire Sports Studies faculty to their first year at the college. A double whammy.

"I wish we could have stayed home with Kyle."

"Kyle would much rather be alone with Killer Kay."

"Killer Kay?"

"Yeah, I hear she's a wild woman on the lacrosse field."

As they followed the brick path to the back of the house, Jacelyn shook her head. "I'll never understand the penchant for nicknames that sports people have."

"Hey, you're talking to the former Ross the Boss."

Jacelyn didn't respond. A breeze off the canal ruffled her hair; she tried to enjoy the balmy night, but couldn't.

"Honey, it's okay. I can talk about those days."

"I know. But it still makes me feel bad that you got hurt."

He slung an arm around her. "My biggest fan. Even in high school, when I got all the attention and they ignored you."

She leaned into him. "I loved watching you play." He'd never know how bad she felt at her parents' dismissal of her own achievements in favor of Eric's. They'd been dead for several years, but she still thought about their favoritism. Yet, she loved her brother unconditionally. "I just wish you could have your dream."

"Look at it this way. If I hadn't blown out my knee on the soccer field, I never would have met Lily. She and my four girls are my life."

"I know. Are you sure it's okay you're doing all this stuff with me this week?"

"Yeah, Lil knew how much I wanted to experience the hoopla for the camp."

"Well," Jacelyn said as they reached the back of the house, "let the games begin."

Though to be fair, this wasn't a circus. The yard was tastefully decorated in blue and white, the team's colors. Music wafted out from a quintet Jacelyn recognized as the college's jazz ensemble. She wondered why Kyle wasn't playing with them. All around the perimeter of the manicured backyard were food stations. The aroma of spicy food and breads mixed with the rich scents of the earth and water.

At the food stations were jocks. Lots of them. Their brawny stature separated them from the academicians who mingled among them. Well, some of them mingled. Others distanced themselves. "Good old Hal's over there, sis," Eric quipped, derision lacing his tone. Her brother wasn't crazy about the colleague Jacelyn dated.

"Be nice."

"Always. But, jeez, you should be able to find something better with all this prime beef here tonight."

"I'm not looking for something better, Eric."

"You should be." He grasped her shoulders and turned her to face the crowd. "Humor me. Don't any of those broad shoulders, washboard abs or sinewy chests call to you?"

She remembered a sinewy chest from this morning. And nice shoulders. Though the encounter still mortified her, she could appreciate those attributes of the King. "Yep. I can hear them call out forty-three, twenty-four, hupp." She mimicked, or tried to, the huddle noises.

Eric laughed. "Let's get something to drink."

"I have to say hello to some people first."

"Oh, well, you're on your own. I'll head over there." He nodded to where Millie Smith stood with a few colleagues. As a close friend of Jacelyn's, Millie knew Eric well. "I'll talk to Mil until you're done with the PR thing."

A waiter passed by with a tray of drinks; she snagged a glass of wine. "Okay. See you later."

Eric grabbed a beer and winked at her. "Maybe I'll get to meet the King."

"Lucky you."

As her brother strolled away whistling, Jacelyn watched him. Though he spoke lightly of it, she knew he'd been devastated when he'd gotten hurt in his sophomore year at UVA and couldn't play Division One soccer anymore. Then he'd lost his scholarship. Then his interest in school—which had never been great—had evaporated completely. Rockford East High's Athlete Most Likely to Make the Pros was now a car salesman.

Who's happier than you, she told herself. Sighing, Jacelyn scanned the crowd. Hal was deep in discussion with Lew Cavanaugh. She headed toward them.

"Well, there she is." Hal pivoted and touched her arm. "We were just talking about you."

"Good things, I hope." As she sipped her wine, she studied Hal. He was medium height, thin and dressed in teacher garb. Oxford shirt, tailored blazer. He headed Beckett's renowned Science Department, noted for the award-winning faculty. Hal himself had been voted one of the top ten department chairs in small colleges across the nation.

He was smiling at her. "Everybody always says good things about you." Nodding to the crowd, he added, "We were just discussing the new program in your department, Jacelyn. Think you can handle all these athletes?"

"Handle them?"

Lew answered. "Well, the three Sports Studies profs come from athletic backgrounds. And then there's the team, who will be involved."

Involved, as in lecturing, participating in a speaker series and some even might be adjuncts and teach a course or two.

Hal threw her a conspiratorial look. It said, *we agree on this one*. In truth, she did agree with Hal, and about a third of the faculty who resented the athletes' disruption of their quiet summer campus. They'd also objected to the addition of a program to their curriculum for what many thought were political reasons as opposed to sound academic decision-making. If, indeed, Jacelyn was a snob, at least she was honest about it.

But she tried not to take part in the catty comments a few of the other teachers had bandied about...

From an English professor: *Can't you hear them bumbling through a lecture...?*

From a math associate: *They'll probably have to resort to taking off their shirts and flexing their muscles to keep the kids interested....*

And of course, from the Education Department: *Teach here? What are their qualifications? Half of them probably took courses like basket weaving—and got Cs in it.*

"Jacelyn, I asked if you'd met with the team liaison yet?"

"Um, no. Last we heard, he hadn't been appointed yet."

"He was. Last week. And he's heading right toward us."

Jacelyn pivoted to see none other than Mike Kingston approach them. His stride was confident, his big, rangy body encased now in nice-fitting khakis and a tucked-in black silk shirt with the sleeves rolled up his forearms. It accented his sinewy chest even more than the clothes he'd worn this morning.

When he reached them, he nodded to Lew. "President Cavanaugh." They shook hands.

Lew pivoted toward her. "Mike. This is Dr. Jacelyn Ross, our Business Department chair."

The King's mouth literally dropped.

Jacelyn couldn't keep back the condescending smile. "We met, earlier today." She arched a brow. "We were discussing my son."

"Kyle?" Hal asked. "The boy wonder of the music department?"

NOT MUCH surprised Mike these days. Hardly anything embarrassed him anymore. But he'd jumped the gun on this one, and felt his face flush like some first-year rookie fumbling the ball. "You're Dr. Ross?"

Her blue eyes sparkled with humor. It made them about as pretty as a Georgia sky in summer. "Yes, Mr. Kingston, I am. And this is Dr. Harrington."

"I don't like formalities, ma'am. Make it Mike or Coach."

Harrington choked on his cocktail but covered it with a cough. "I can't imagine Dr. Ross ever calling you Coach."

"Mike, then," he said, frowning. He faced Jacelyn. "Listen, I apologize about this morning."

Now her complexion reddened. "No need. An honest mistake." Her frigid tone said there wasn't a chance in hell she meant it.

The science professor caught on. "What happened this morning, Jacelyn?"

"Nothing of import, Hal." She dismissed Mike with a glance and focused her gaze on the other men. "I need to find Eric. I just wanted to say hello to you two."

"Don't forget to set up a meeting with Coach Kingston before you leave," Cavanaugh reminded her.

"For what?" Mike asked.

"As team liaison, you'll work with Dr. Ross on the Bulls' inclusion into the Sports Studies program."

"I thought I'd be workin' with Jake Lansing." Mike had met the teacher he'd been told would direct Sports Studies.

For some reason, that got Dr. Ross's back up, almost visibly. "Jake's a teacher in my department, and though he set up the curriculum, I'm in charge of the major. I'm the Business Department chair. Everything has to be run by me."

Hmm. "Run by you or approved by you?"

Cavanaugh slapped Mike on the back. "Technically, approved, but I set the parameters with Lansing for what we're planning this fall and spring myself, and Jacelyn is in agreement with them."

Delicate shoulders stiffened even more. Though tense, they looked great in the sundress she wore. "Of course. Now, if you'll excuse me. Want to say hello to Eric, Hal?"

The man's smile was smug. "I'd like that." He nodded to Cavanaugh. "Lew." Now a smirk. "Coach."

Mike watched them go. They walked close, like a guy strolling with his best girl. Mike faced Cavanaugh. "Don't look like they're hankerin' to have the team on the campus, President Cavanaugh."

The president was frowning. "There's been flak about the Sports Studies program. My faculty is divided. Some think it will be an easy major, and was instituted for purely political reasons. Their attitude has carried over to the Bulls' camp." He sighed. "Sometimes colleges and universities are ivory towers, Mike. The inhabitants can't always see that change is good."

Mike was well acquainted with that attitude. "Why'd *you* want us here?"

"The team or the program?"

"Both, I reckon." Though the team being here was a no-brainer.

"Well, the team making us their summer home breathes life into the campus. Creates jobs. Gives us national exposure."

"Dr. Ross doesn't understand that?"

"She's more concerned about the academic advisability of having athletes give talks and perhaps teach in the Sports Studies program."

Mike stiffened at the implication that guys who played sports were stupid. "When will we be talkin' about our staff doing some teaching?"

"You and Jacelyn should decide it soon."

"Can't imagine that'll go real smooth." He took a beer from a passing waiter.

"Jacelyn's fair. Honest. More open-minded than some." Like Professor Hal, Mike bet. "She does have a couple of stumbling blocks about the Sports Studies program—one deals with the Outreach Program for disadvantaged kids that she heads. It provides a great deal of scholarship money for students who can't afford our steep tuition."

"Don't you have a financial aid office to take care of that?"

"Our official aid comes through that office, but it's limited because we're a private institution and we depend mostly on endowments. Jacelyn's garnered a lot of support from the community, from the Alumni Association, from grants and has managed to get many more students here than the college could without her Outreach Center."

"So what's the fire in her belly about us?"

"Well, first, we gave the Sports Studies guys and your team her Outreach office."

"Why'd you do that?"

"Her needs were small for such a big space."

"She got a place for her project though, right?" He didn't like the idea of booting out a charity group.

"Yes." Cavanaugh glanced at the crowd. "There's more, but I don't want to go into it now." He stared at Mike. "She's a good department chair and an excellent teacher. And she's brilliant, so that helps. A little sweet-talking wouldn't hurt, though. From what I hear, you Southern gentlemen are good at that."

He bet Dr. Ross wouldn't like Cavanaugh's comment. After the president was pulled aside by someone else, Mike scanned the area and saw her across the way eating from a small plate and smiling at the man she'd been hugging earlier at the field. Probably her husband. Since he believed in the old sports adage that the best defense was a good offense, he headed toward her. "Hi, y'all," he said, summoning some of that Southern charm.

"Mike." She glanced at the other guy. "This is Eric Ross. My brother."

"I'm a big fan, Coach."

Well, that would help. "Of the team?"

"Yeah, and of you. Jacey's son and I followed your college and NFL career religiously."

Now there was a shocker. A little devil pushed inside him. "You, too, Dr. Ross?"

Eric chuckled. "Nah, Jacey here doesn't know a first down from a penalty."

"That's a bit of an exaggeration." She smiled sweetly—too sweetly—at him. "Though I would rather read a good book than waste an afternoon zoning out in front of the TV."

He was insulted by that but tried not to show it. "Me, too. Don't think Bulls fans ever zone out, though."

Eric laughed aloud. Clearly *Jacey* didn't get it. "What?" she asked.

Mike grinned. "The Bulls Brigade are a might rowdy. And active."

"Yeah, remember the time you were mobbed after you caught that seventy-yard pass and took it into the end zone just as the clock ran out?"

"Against the Broncos. Man, that made my heart stop."

Mike listened while Eric recounted a few more stories; stealing a glance at Jacelyn, he could see she was more than bored. But she was pretending she wasn't. For her brother. It made him like her. He thought of his own brothers. Though he'd always felt inferior to them intellectually, he loved them and would do anything for them. Because of that, he said, "I think your sister's eyes are glazing over."

"Don't stop. Eric loves professional sports."

"You live here?" Mike asked the guy.

"Yeah, across the city."

"Wanna have a beer sometime? We can shoot the breeze about sports then."

Soft approval shone on Jacelyn's face. It made Mike's gut feel funny.

"Don't get me wrong, that would make my day." Eric grinned. "But we may be seeing a lot of you anyway, and your son."

Jacelyn cocked her head. "I don't understand."

"Didn't Kyle tell you?"

"No, I haven't seen him since we were at the field today."

"He's one of three students up for a job with Coach here, for his summer assignment." Eric nodded to Mike. "The Coach is interviewing him tomorrow to take care of his seven-year-old son."

Now Mike was confused. "No, there's gotta be some mistake. I'm fixin' to interview somebody named Worthington. My assistant picked him and two others for me to talk to from a ton of résumés."

A huge sigh from Jacelyn. "That's my son. Kyle Worthington. He has his father's last name."

"You don't?"

"I'm divorced." She faced him. "Your wife won't be watching your son, Mr. Kingston?"

"I'm not married."

"I see." Her tone was indifferent. Not the usual reaction he got from attractive women when they found out he was single.

But of course, she was more than attractive. She was *brilliant*. And she obviously considered him and his cohorts dumb jocks.

Not much bothered him at this point in his life after the success and financial security he'd achieved, but being considered a no-brain athlete still got to him. It had been his Achilles' heel since the first time he'd picked up a pigskin and found magic between it and his hands. Though he loved football, he hated being considered a stupid athlete and had worked hard in high school, and especially in college, to thwart that image. Still, it had been hard to unring that bell.

Damn it, he'd thought this issue was dead and buried. He hadn't expected to encounter it in a place where he hoped eventually to teach.

CHAPTER TWO

PRESIDENT CAVANAUGH'S office overlooked the southern part of the campus, which was tree-lined and verdant, typical of July in upstate New York. The stately interior sported hardwood floors covered by antique carpets, and walls displaying every president of Beckett since 1907 when the college had been founded by an order of Basilian monks. Jacelyn had been here many times and appreciated the aesthetic ambience and collegiate atmosphere; the rest of the campus reflected that—or at least it had before the arrival of the Bulls. Even though the camp hadn't opened yet, there was a buzz of activity around the school reminiscent of an amusement park.

"Jacelyn, sorry to keep you waiting. I was at lunch with the mayor." Calm and composed, Lew Cavanaugh strode confidently into his office. He was a tall man with a shock of white hair and a wise face.

"No problem." She'd taken a chair opposite his desk and he sat behind it. She liked his professionalism: he always wore a suit, no matter what the time of year, he positioned himself behind his desk at a meeting and, though he was friendly and congenial, he rarely shared anything personal with his staff. It just didn't fit with…

"What are you thinking? You just frowned."

She smoothed down the skirt of her pinstripe suit. "May I be honest?"

"Of course."

"I was thinking about your professionalism. You have a reserved formality that suits you and the college well."

Gray brows knitted over shrewd eyes. "Is that a compliment?"

"Yes, of course."

"Then why the scowl?"

"Your attitude, your old-school demeanor, doesn't fit with what's happened on campus this year."

"A good segue into why I asked to meet with you today."

"Really?"

"You've made no secret that you disapprove of the Sports Studies program I pushed for."

"You asked—"

Lew held up his hand, palm out. "Let me finish. You voiced your objections, but when you were overridden by me and two-thirds of the department chairs, you gave in gracefully. I respect that. Unfortunately, you're the one working with these guys, and you bear the brunt of our decision."

"I told you then that I won't let personal feelings interfere with doing my job."

"Nothing less than what I expect. Still, I wish I could convince you that this is in the best interest of the college." He steepled his hands. "Did you know tours for prospective students are up fifty percent?"

"No, I didn't know that. It's quite a jump."

"And early-decision applications rose by almost half, too."

"I realize the training camp gives us national visibility."

"Not all those declaring majors are in Sports Studies."

"I'm glad you were right on this." Her smile was genuine. "Truly. I want Beckett to grow. I love this college."

"You graduated from here, didn't you?"

"Yes."

"Came here on an academic scholarship, if I remember."

Jacelyn crossed her legs. "It's why I'm so enthusiastic about the Outreach Center." Watching him, she asked, "Lew, why did you want to talk to me today?"

"Well, not all the news is good. The final numbers for next year are in. Enrollment in some of your business courses is down."

"Really?" Her heart rate speeded up. Enrollment was a huge deal. It meant a department was flourishing or stagnant. It meant a chair was successful or not. It meant loss of income for faculty.

"I'm surprised. Last year we had more courses than we could handle. We had to hire two adjuncts."

"I know." His gaze was searching. "You're blaming this on the Sports Studies program."

"Yes, I am. Do you see any other reason?"

"Actually, no. There's always some shifting when we put new programs in place. It evens out in a few semesters. I'm not worried about it."

"You'll have a difficult time convincing the teachers who lose their full load that it's no big deal."

"I have meetings today with everyone who's affected." Lew drew in a breath. "Look, I didn't want this to happen. But it has. We'll deal with it."

"You wanted the Sports Studies program to happen."

"Yes, I did. Not at the expense of your traditional business courses, though."

"What about other departments? You expected they'd benefit by teaching electives for Sports Studies."

"That did happen. Millie Smith's not only teaching Sports Psychology, but has two sections. Theo's Ethics of Sports is a go. Hal's Anatomy and Physiology is overflowing." He leaned over and braced his arms on his desk. "I know it's a blow about the numbers. But this is all going to shake out in the end."

"So you keep saying." Jacelyn settled back into the leather chair, struggling to be fair. "Maybe you're right. I've seen fluctuation in the courses before. And other departments have gone through this. It happened when we instituted the teaching degree."

"I'd like to hear that this turn of events won't further alienate you. I need your support of the program."

Anger sparked inside her. "I'll do my job."

"Of course you will. But we both know department chairs wield a lot of power. I'm fully aware Hal Harrington opposed the nutrition course that would have been perfect for Sports Studies."

"Eating to Win?"

"Yes. He roadblocked it by subtly influencing his people to discourage their advisees from taking it. Consequently, enrollment was down too low to offer it to the Sports Studies majors. I've spoken with him about his actions."

Hal hadn't told her. Oh, she knew he didn't want the

course to be part of his curriculum—he thought it su-
perficial and foolish—but she was shocked that he'd
sabotaged it.

"I wouldn't want that to happen in your department,
since the Sports Studies major is under your auspices."

"This shift in numbers won't affect my professional
deportment." She felt her face flush. "I have to say I resent your implication that it might."

He gave her a wry smile. "Well, that puts me in my
place."

She startled. "I'm sorry, Lew. I didn't mean to be dis-
respectful of this office."

"No, of course not. In any case, it's my job to address
difficult topics. If my remarks have offended you, then
I, too, apologize."

Jacelyn came to the edge of her seat. "Is that all?"

"Yes, for now. I'll want to go over sections and teaching assignments with you soon." He checked his calen-
dar. "How about tomorrow afternoon? Same time."

"Fine." She stood.

He watched her as if deciding something. "Jacelyn,
how's Kyle doing?"

"Good. Why?"

"He's working for the training camp this summer.
I'm surprised. So is Paul Hadley." Kyle's music advisor and mentor.

"You have kids, Lew. Ever try to steer them toward
what you'd like them to do when they have their hearts
set on something else? Especially when they're approaching twenty."

He chuckled. "Give him my best."

"I will. I'm meeting him right after I check in at

the Outreach Center. *He's* meeting with Mike Kingston now."

Lew shook his head. "Should be an interesting summer."

"In more ways than one. Goodbye, Lew."

The president's comment about Kyle bothered Jacelyn as she hurried down the stairs to the ground floor of the faculty building where her Outreach Center was now located. She hoped Kyle didn't get too involved with Mike Kingston, especially if he got the job watching the man's son. Kyle needed to practice several hours a day, and he had some recitals scheduled at night.

She made a mental note to talk to him about the time constraints working for the Kingstons would impose. She wasn't sure that "Coach" would be a very good influence on her son.

SOMETHING REALLY NEEDED to be done about the Outreach Center's new office. The custodians had cleaned it up as best they could, but the hardwood floors were scarred, the walls a dingy gray and the windows filmy, making for poor lighting. Jacelyn had gotten an order to replace the windows, and sand and refinish the floor, but the rest was on hold.

The office that had been taken away from them was spacious and bright and pleasant. And it now housed the athletes.

"What's the scowl for?"

Jacelyn turned to find her part-time secretary, Lucy Jones, looking up from her computer toward Jacelyn's desk, which was by the window opposite Millie's. "This space is pathetic."

"Not very inviting, I know. Though the eucalyptus and potpourri you brought in make it smell great." Lucy looked around. "When are the windows and floor going to be done?"

"The end of this week."

"That'll help." She peered over thick glasses. "It's hard not to resent them, isn't it?"

"Yes." Jacelyn nodded to the numbers Lucy was crunching on her own computer. "How's next year's budget looking?"

"About the same as this year's if the alumni come through again."

"They have for four years. They will again."

"I hope so."

"Me, too." She drew in a breath and glanced around. "But I have a feeling we're going to be on our own sprucing the rest of this place up."

"I'll volunteer to help."

"That would be great."

Lucy stood. "I have to go get my son from Vacation Bible School. Anything else I can do before I leave?"

Jacelyn checked her watch. "No, I'm meeting Kyle in a few minutes, too. Thanks for coming in today."

"You're welcome." She studied Jacelyn. "You okay?"

"Yeah, why?"

"You seem distracted."

She *was* distracted—thinking about losing the office space, about the decline in numbers for her courses, about Kyle wanting to baby-sit Mike Kingston's son. "No, I'm fine." She looked out the window and stood, too. "It's too nice a day to be indoors. I'll walk you out."

Chatting about their kids, the two women left the office. Jacelyn wished Kyle was still young enough for
Vacation Bible School. She wished he was as amenable
to her suggestions as he used to be. At one time, she'd
wished he was older, more self-reliant, and then it
wouldn't be so hard being a single mother.

She reminded herself of the old adage, *Be careful
what you wish for.* For years you encouraged your kids'
sense of independence and ability to think for themselves. Then they grew up, and ambushed you with
their independence and ability to think for themselves.

THE BALL flew through the air, spinning at fifty miles
an hour at least. Mike leaped off his feet and twisted; it
landed with a thunk in his hands. He had to remind himself this was a jugs machine mechanically pitching the
ball to him, not Ace McCabe, the quarterback who had
led the Bulls to three Super Bowls; this was a sleepy college campus, not Bulls Stadium; and he was thirty-six
and a coach, not some hotshot young player up for
MVP of the game. Still, it felt mighty fine to catch the
pigskin again. He missed putting his body on the line.

He glanced around the area. The activity was picking up for the camp, as the players would be arriving
Friday. Some kids were tossing a ball up on the embank-
ment that surrounded the field; the ball had already
come across his playing area once and Mike had thrown
it back. Couples strolled along that grassy knoll, which
sported a walking/biking path. Beyond that, a group of
coeds lazed under a tree. Mike could hear the tinkle of
feminine laughter, reminding him of his own college
days when he flirted with his girl in the warm summer

air. The outdoors in upstate New York had that green-earth smell that no place else in the country could match.

He'd caught a couple more throws when he heard clapping from the bleachers. Turning, he found a dark-haired, broad-shouldered boy watching him, applauding. A shy grin split the kid's face. "Nice catch, Coach," he called out.

Mike took a good look at the spectator. This must be the kid he was meeting. "You Kyle Worthington?"

"Yes, sir."

Jogging across the short distance that separated them, he smiled at Kyle. His dark-eyed gaze reminded Mike of Tyler. "Ditch the formalities, okay?"

"Sure." Kyle eyed the ball. "You haven't lost your touch."

Jacey's son and I followed your career religiously.

"Your uncle said you were a football fan."

With sham alarm, the kid looked from left to right. "Shh, don't tell anybody."

Gripping the ball, Mike dropped down on the bleachers. "Why's that? Your mama was with us when he said it and she didn't freak."

"It's not my mom that I'm worried about." Obviously wanting to change the subject, Kyle nodded to the ball. "I read an article in *Sports Illustrated* that said your father used to practice with you every night when you were little."

Mike pictured Jim Kingston out in the backyard tossing footballs even when he was tuckered out from a hard day teaching adolescents at the high school and tutoring afterward to make ends meet. His shoulders would be slumped like an old man, but he never let on how exhausted he was. Mike's brothers weren't into sports, but his dad was, and it had become an interest they shared.

"Yep, he did that."

"Neat."

There was something about the kid's tone. "Your daddy play with you?"

"My dad did music with me."

"Huh?"

"I'm a musician. My father recognized my budding talent—his words—when I was three. He made me practice hours a day."

"When you were *three?*"

"Don't get me wrong. I loved it." The boy stared off into the field. "He was…so interested in me then."

"What do you play?"

"Piano."

"Hey, my son likes to tinker with a keyboard."

"Yeah?" Mischief lit Kyle's face. "If you pick me to watch him this summer, I could give him lessons."

"Which was the point of this meeting." Mike held out his hand. "Nice to make your acquaintance, Kyle Worthington."

"Same here, Coach Kingston." The boy had strength in his long slim fingers—just right for piano-playing. Or for catching a football.

"So, you wanna watch Tyler?"

"Yeah. I put in for it."

"Why?"

"I love kids, and since I never had brothers or sisters, I thought this would be fun. And it'd sort of make me feel part of the team."

"You play sports?"

"Only in my mind."

"What's that mean?"

"My dad wouldn't let me sign up for any teams when I was little. When he left…well, it's a long story. Now I make a great fan."

Mike wondered what was wrong with parents. Some of them ought to be horsewhipped. "Sorry your daddy and mama kept you from the games."

Kyle laughed out loud. "Not my mom. When she found out I'd hidden my interest from Dad, she tried to get me into stuff, but it was too late. By then, I was a klutz." He got a faraway look in his eyes. "That didn't stop her, though. She took me to every game—soccer, football, basketball—I wanted to go to. We even saw a few Bulls games when you played. It was a while before I figured out she was bored to tears."

Score one for Dr. Ross. "I got the impression she isn't a sports enthusiast."

"That's for sure. Anyway, Uncle Eric had daughters, and they're into ballet. So we started to do stuff together to spare Mom the agony of watching a game."

"Hmm." Mike stood and situated himself in the gravel that surrounded the field. He didn't like sitting still too long; it made him jittery. He tossed the ball up in the air. "So, if you took care of my son, what would you do with him?"

"I don't know. Find out what he likes to do, first."

Mike saw Kyle watching the ball, so he pointed about ten feet down the gravel. "Go over there. I'll toss this to you."

The expression on Kyle's face was like a child's at Christmas. "You kidding?"

"Never kid about my pigskin, boy."

"I told you I was a klutz."

"I wanna see for myself."

Bolting up from the bleachers, Kyle jogged about ten feet down. Mike threw him a light toss. He caught it easily. As they threw the ball back and forth, they talked more about Tyler, his likes and dislikes and Mike's views on discipline. All the while, Mike interspersed directions…. "Here, hold it where the stitching is…flick your wrist like this…that's it, a little more pressure in your fingers."

"What kind of kid is Tyler?" Kyle asked.

"He's shy."

"*Your* son is shy?"

"I know. Don't that beat all?" Mike scowled. "His mama died not too long ago, and he's still holding everything in."

"I'm sorry. Jeez, I don't know what I'd do without my mother."

Mike threw another pass. Backed up a step. "Tyler's into board games."

"Mom would love him. She blackmails me into Scrabble all the time."

"Oh, God. My worst nightmare," Mike joked.

A few more tosses, then Kyle asked, "What does he like to eat?"

Mike appreciated Kyle's questions. "Fancy stuff. His mother always cooked new things. We reverse roles when we go out; I get a hamburger and French fries and he orders Caesar salad."

"Mom taught me to cook." Kyle caught a toss that should have gone over his head.

"I do believe you been playin' possum on this, buddy. You're real good."

"No way."

Despite his denial, Mike could tell the kid was pleased by the compliment. "You live at home during the school year?"

"Nope, on campus. Mom said the independence is good for me."

"Your mother sounds pretty darn smart. You like having her teach here?"

"Yeah, sure, why wouldn't I?" His eyes twinkled. "She got me your autograph, didn't she?"

Much to Mike's chagrin, he recalled the encounter. "She tell you I thought she was lyin'? That she was a fan?"

"Ohmigod, did she faint on the spot?"

"No, why should she?"

They tossed some more passes, and widened the distance between them to a point where conversation wasn't possible so Mike never got his last question answered.

After a while, somebody came into Mike's line of vision. He stopped the play. "Looks like your mother's here, boy."

Kyle turned and held up the ball. "Hey, Mom, did you see? I can catch the football."

She came closer, out of place on the field in a suit and white heels—though they did great things for her legs. "Yes, I saw." And wasn't happy, if her tone was any indication. "Watch out for your hands, honey. You don't want to jam a finger before your concert with the Philharmonic next week."

"Oh, yeah, sure."

"It's okay." The lines around her mouth softened. "Just be careful."

Mike crossed to Kyle from the opposite direction that Jacelyn was coming from. They reached him at the same time. "Hi, Dr. Ross," he said.

"Mr. Kingston."

"We were just talking about me watching Tyler this summer, Mom."

"The secretary at the sports office told me your interview was out here."

Kyle nodded.

"If you're not done, I can wait at the car."

Mike spoke up. "No, we're done."

Kyle's face blanked. Then it revealed the same emotions Mike used to see in the mirror before every game. Hope. Determination. The desire to win.

"The job's yours, kid. We'll have to sit down and hammer out the nitty-gritty but I think you and Tyler would be a good match." He winked at Kyle. "Besides, I already checked out your résumé and references."

"It's mine?"

"Yep."

"That's great. Really great."

"I think so. But before you decide for sure, you should know that you'll have to watch Ty at odd hours, maybe even an occasional overnight." He shook his head. "I'd like to enroll him in some kind of camp, too, so he'd get some playtime with other kids." He looked at Kyle. "Then you could have mornings off, to compensate for the unusual hours."

"My girlfriend Kay is working at a summer camp. We could check it out for Tyler."

"Super." Mike faced Jacelyn. "This all right with you?"

"Yes, it is." She gripped the strap of a navy purse she carried. "When does Tyler arrive?"

"Two days from now. I can't wait. I'm just finishin' his room in my house."

"You're not living in the dorms with the players?"

"No, I rented a house because of him." And took a lot of grief from management because of it. Still, he'd held out for Tyler. His son was first and foremost in his life these days.

"What are you doing to his room?" Kyle asked.

Mike rolled his eyes. "He wants it blue and white."

"The team's colors." The boy's eyes sparkled. "Need some help?"

"What?"

"I could help you paint. Move in stuff."

"I'd be downright happy for the help."

Kyle looked at his mother. "It's okay, Mom, isn't it?"

"Sure."

"Thanks, Coach." Kyle held out his hand.

"You're welcome."

The boy turned to his mother. "Do I have time to run over to the Cyber Café and tell Kay? She's waiting there to hear how the interview went."

"You can call her on your cell."

"Mo-om."

"Okay. Meet me at the car in ten minutes."

"Fifteen," he called out as he jogged away.

"Nice kid." Mike looked after Kyle. "He doesn't drive? He'd need to for this job."

"My car's in the shop. He's driving *me* today."

"I like him."

She drew herself up. "He means everything to me. I wouldn't want to see him hurt." Hell, Ms. Frigid was back.

"You mean his hands?"

"Partly. If he injures his hands doing something athletic and can't play the piano, he'll miss out on all the concerts and music activities he's got planned this summer." She crossed her arms over her chest. The jacket she wore had two strategically placed buttons. Closed. Some little navy thing peeked out from beneath. "I'm not sure your influence…" She seemed to think better about completing the statement.

Mike felt his temper heat. Deadly calm, he crossed his arms over his chest, too. "You don't like me much, do you?"

"Excuse me? I hardly know you."

"That's what I was thinkin'. So I don't get why the temperature drops fifty degrees when you have to say a few words to me. If it's because of the comments I made outside the Sports Studies office that day…"

"It's not that."

"Is it because you lost the office? President Cavanaugh said we ousted you."

She smoothed back her hair. It was pulled off her face, and tied up in some fancy do at her neck. It looked nice. "I can deal with that. Other things…"

"Jacelyn, is that you down there?" Mike glanced at the raised path. On it was good old Professor Hal walking a beautiful black Lab.

She waved to him. "Hi, Hal. Just waiting for Kyle."

Hal frowned at Mike, who gave him a little salute. The professor called out, "Well, I'll see you tonight at eight."

"Yes, of course."

When Jacelyn turned back around, her face was flushed. Not from the sun. He was reminded of a couple of smart girls he'd tried dating in school. There was one in particular whom he'd really liked. Oftentimes, when she was out with Mike, she avoided being at places where her *other*—read smarter—friends frequented. With more slice in his voice than he'd intended, he asked, "You embarrassed to be seen with me, Dr. Ross?"

"No, of course not. You're team liaison to the Sports Studies program, which is part of my department. We have reason to be together."

Mike stared hard at her, offended by her attitude. "Well, in case you are, we could always meet in your office to take care of business."

Jacelyn raised her chin. "Regardless of where, we do need to discuss some issues," she said stiffly.

"It'll have to be soon." He checked his watch for the date. "Tyler comes day after tomorrow and practice starts at the end of the week."

"We certainly wouldn't want to interfere with practice."

Hell, the woman was prickly. "You don't want us here, do you?"

"Us?"

"The team."

She faced him fully. "No."

"Why?"

"It totally disrupts the campus. The second semester of summer school was canceled because of it." She nodded to the tent. "The whole place transforms into a circus."

Something made him ask, "What about the Sports Studies program? You like that any better?"

"As a matter of fact, I don't."

"At least you're honest."

"I am. I haven't made a secret of my views. But the college went ahead and did this…" she indicated the stadium and field house with a sweep of her arm "…so I'm making the best of it."

He nodded in the direction Kyle had gone. His tone softened. "Doesn't help to have your nose rubbed in it, does it?"

"Because he loves it all?"

"Uh-huh."

"It comes second to music, of course, but still…" She rolled her eyes. "I won't let what I think of all this interfere with any communication you and I have."

"It already—"

"Coach, heads up."

Mike was used to balls flying at his face. So when he looked up and saw one coming right at them, he didn't panic. Until he heard an "Oh, my God!" from Jacelyn Ross and saw the ball take a slight spin. Being all too acquainted with that kind of spin, he knew it was headed right for her.

He leapt up. His body blocked the ball; it glanced off his shoulder—hurting like hell as the point jutted into a tendon—and upset his balance. But he'd already reached out to protect Jacelyn, so he took her down with him into the gravel path.

JACELYN SAW the big dark thing flying through the air and thought it was a bird. She cried out as it came right for her head. Suddenly Mike's body was there, blocking hers. She tried to grab his shoulders just as he grasped her.

She hit the ground hard, and the world dimmed. Her breathing was cut off.

"Jacelyn. Oh, God."

She opened her eyes; spots swam before her in the sun.

"Are you all right?"

"I—I can't…breathe."

"Got the wind knocked out of you."

She nodded. "Heavy. You," she managed.

"What? Oh, damn." He rolled off her.

She drew in ragged breaths.

Kneeling over her, Mike rubbed her arms. "Can you sit up?" His voice was gruff.

"I think so." She started to rise and the world spun. "Oh."

"Wait. Don't try and get up, darlin'. You're dizzy."

Jacelyn stayed where she was for a few seconds. Her vision cleared and she took the opportunity to study Mike up close. His eyes were gray with a thin band of black around them, which matched his pupils. Right now they were filled with concern. A beard bristled along his chin and jaw, around a frowning mouth. "Better?"

"Yes. Let me try to get up again." With his arm supporting her back, she eased to a sitting position. Her stomach pitched but she stayed upright. "I'm all right."

"Jeez, Coach, we're sorry."

A vein pulsed in Mike's neck. He looked past her to find the boys who'd thrown the ball. "You shouldn't be tossin' that willy-nilly, guys."

"I know," the youngest one, about twelve, said. "I overthrew. Sorry, lady."

"It's okay. Be more careful next time."

Mike picked up the ball next to him and tossed it to them. They rushed off.

He transferred his gaze back to her and gave her a wry smile. "Along with the autograph thing, this gives 'starting off on the wrong foot' new meaning."

Jacelyn chuckled. "I'm fine." She glanced down. Her stockings were ripped, and a big bruise had already begun to form on one of her knees. "I'm a mess, though." He was staring at her hair. She reached up to it. "Looks awful, right?"

"No, mussed is all." His eyes darkened a bit. "Let me help you up." Standing, he reached out a hand and took hers. His was warm, solid and strong. Bending her knees, tucking her feet under her, she started to rise. When she put weight on her left ankle, she faltered and would have fallen if he hadn't grabbed her. "Oh… ah…damn."

He glanced down. "Hell. Your ankle."

She could feel it swelling and saw it was already bulging.

"Kick off the shoe."

"What?"

"That heel. Take it off." Under his breath he mumbled, "Silly things."

She raised her foot to remove her shoe and cried out.

He scowled. "Let's get you to the bleachers." Before she realized his intent, he scooped her off her feet. Jacelyn couldn't remember a time anyone had carried her anywhere.

"Wait, Mike, I…"

"Hush, now." He covered the few yards to the bleachers. Her face was brushing his chest, and she could smell him again, as she had the first time they met. The scent was combined with sweat. He still smelled good. Really good. She must have taken a hard knock on the head if she was noticing that and not her throbbing foot. When he set her gently on the first bench seat, she groaned. His gaze was downcast. She tracked it. Her skirt had ridden up and a navy-blue garter belt peeked out. "Oh, dear." She tugged the hem down.

A smile claimed his lips. "Hmm," was all he said and knelt in front of her. He removed her shoe, making her moan again.

"I've got more training than most nurses in this kind of thing. All right if I see what's going on here?"

"Yes, sure."

"Um, it'd help if you could take off the stockings." He fought back a grin. "Seein' as how they'd be right easy to remove."

She felt her face flush and swallowed hard. She hated wearing panty hose in the summer so she indulged in other lingerie. Reaching under her skirt, Jacelyn undid the front of the garter belt. Awkwardly, she slid her hand beneath her leg, and released the back. Bending over, she tried to unroll the stocking, but the angle was difficult.

"Let me finish." Big, masculine hands grasped the nylon at her calf. With a touch gentle enough for babies—or lovers—he rolled the stocking the rest of the way down. As Mike drew it off, he cleared his throat.

With just as much care, he began palpating her foot.

She gasped. "Sorry." Still he examined it and sighed. "It looks and feels like a sprain. Nothing broken, would be my guess." Kneeling before her, he raised his eyes to her. "Wanna go to the doctor?"

"I'd rather not. Especially if you think it's only sprained."

"I do, but you should check this out. The infirmary here might be a good choice."

"They were open for the first summer session. They're closed now."

"Hmm." Mike thought a minute. "Our trainer might still be around. I know he came up yesterday. Where's your cell phone?" When she told him, he retrieved her purse, got her phone and punched in a number. "Susan, is Gage still in?" He shook his head. "Catch him, will you?" A pause. "Yeah, hey. I got somebody with a sprained ankle here I'd like you to look at. Oh. Listen, as a favor to me, could you hold on a piece? No, I'll bring her there. My guess is we'll need ice." Another pause and a very male smile. "Yeah, stuff it, Garrison." He clicked off.

"What?"

"He said to come over." He nodded across the campus. "He's in the Sports Office in Basil Hall."

Biting her lip, Jacelyn sighed. "I don't think I can walk that far."

"No need. I'll carry you."

"Oh, Mike, no. I'm too heavy."

He scoffed. "You're kiddin', right? You ever see our drills? Us jocks are strong, ma'am." He leaned over. "And I can still sprint the length of a football field."

"It's quite a ways to Basil."

Deep male laughter. "Hey, it's a tough job, but somebody's got to do it."

She laughed, too. Once again she was picked up and nestled against his chest. "Hmm," he said starting toward the faculty building. "I could get used to this."

Without her mind's conscious consent, Jacelyn buried her face into his chest.

He took a few steps then gripped her tighter. "Uh-oh," he said. "Second team's coming in."

"What?"

He nodded across the field.

Jacelyn followed his gaze. Heading toward them were Kyle with Kay…and Hal with his dog.

As they got nearer, she could see the scowl on Hal's face and the stunned expression on Kyle's.

When they reached each other, Kyle said, "Mom, what *happened?*"

Hal gave Mike a furious look, then transferred it to her. "What the hell are you doing with this man, Jacelyn?"

CHAPTER THREE

MIKE'S HEART beat a touch faster as he watched his dad's car pull up to the little house on Canal Drive. He could just make out the tip of his son's head; the seven-year-old was belted into the back seat of Jim Kingston's sedan.

Quickly Mike strode from the garage to the car. He whipped open the door and barely gave Tyler enough time to free himself and climb out before Mike crouched down and had him in a bear hug. "Hey, Champ. Man, I missed you." It was true. Having been with Tyler continuously for several weeks, Mike had found the seven-day separation very long. It was hard to believe he'd gone months at a time without seeing the kid. No way could he tolerate that now.

Tyler held on and nosed into Mike's chest. Though shy and reserved, he took affection easily. Trudy had done some things right. "Hi, Daddy."

Instead of letting him go, Mike stood, hefted the boy up and held him on his hip. Ty was small for his age and easy to lift. Circling the car, he hugged his dad with his free arm. "Thanks for bringin' him, Pa. And for keeping him this week."

"Are you kidding? Your mama cried when he left."

Natives of Georgia, his parents resided in Buckland

every summer and fall to be with Mike and watch him play football and then coach the team. Two years ago, he'd bought them a nice little patio home near the stadium. During the worst of New York State winters, they returned to the South, where two of his brothers lived. Logan, the oldest and technically his half-brother, never stayed put, so they didn't see him often. Ironically, Mike was closest to him.

"How come Ma didn't come with you?"

Having laid his head on Mike's shoulder, Tyler relaxed into his father's hold. Mike could smell soap and licorice. "Nana's sick."

"Nothing serious, is it?"

"No," Jim said. "She sprained her ankle jogging." Mike's mom was sixty going on sixteen.

"Seems to be a lot of that going around." He kissed Tyler's head. "Can you stay a while, Pa?"

"I'll have coffee, but I gotta get back. That woman will overdo it if I'm not around to keep her down."

Briefly, Mike wondered if Jacelyn was staying off her sprained ankle, too.

The three Kingston men settled together in the sunny kitchen at a scarred oak table that had come with the partially furnished home. Warm July air drifted in through the window; sounds from the canal—ducks quacking and an occasional boat buzzing by—also floated in. After Mike got coffee for him and his dad and juice for Tyler, Jim Kingston asked, "How're things going up here for you, son?"

Mike shrugged. "Just gettin' my feet wet."

"Good. You got a lot to offer in the way of knowledge gained through experience."

Mike stirred his coffee. "I think so. The Business Department chair is not a big fan of athletics, though."

You don't much like us bein' here, do you?

No.

Jim shook his head. "What's that got to do with anything?"

"I love coaching, as much as I loved playing, Pa. But I need something more." He ruffled Tyler's hair. "And I gotta think about the future now."

"Money-wise, you're set for life."

"Yeah, but not up here." He tapped an index finger on his temple. "I need a challenge. I think I'd like to do some teaching in the Sports Studies program that's having its rookie year at the college."

His pa sighed and sat back. "You always did want to do more with your mind. Remember how the teachers at school used to tick you off when they assumed you *couldn't* do the math or write those long papers?" He scowled. "Made me pretty damn mad, too."

"Yeah. I liked sports more than academics, but I hated being stereotyped as a dumb jock." Especially since his brothers, Luke and Nick, were in Honor Society, on the debating team and got into good colleges.

As if reading his mind, his dad said, "Despite the other boys' accomplishments, I never saw you as dumb, Mikey."

"I know, Dad. And I appreciated that as much as the support I got from you and mom about football."

"We loved your athletic success, and you did decent enough in school."

"I never really applied myself, though."

Tyler, who had asked for paper and markers, sat happily drawing next to Mike. "I like school, Daddy. Mrs. Shank said I'm smart."

"Course you are, boy. Don't ever let anybody convince you different." He'd be damned if his kid suffered any kind of negativity.

When Jim Kingston left, with a promise to come up for the opening day of camp and the parade, Mike said to Tyler, "Wanna see your room?"

Big dark eyes filled with guarded pleasure. "Yeah, sure."

"How 'bout a ride?"

Tyler nodded enthusiastically. He scrambled onto the chair and stood. When Mike did the same and turned his back, the boy hopped on. "Ugh. You're getting big, kid."

"Nana says I'm growing like a weed."

Making a game of it, Mike took the boy on a tour of the small A-frame he'd rented. First they checked out the ground floor, then Mike trundled up the curved staircase to a loft which accommodated two bedrooms and a bath. To the right, he stopped in a doorway. He felt his son freeze. "What's wrong, Ty?"

"This for *me?*"

"Yeah, I fixed it all up myself, with a little help from somebody who's gonna be your good buddy." True to his word, Kyle had come by to paint and move in furniture. Mike and the boy had had a good time working and shooting the breeze about football and other sports. Now *that* guy was smart. Just like his mother.

"Is that…is that my bed?"

Tyler's openmouthed reaction was understandable; the bed was in the shape of a football, and the headboard actually looked like a pigskin, complete with stitching. Mike had paid an arm and a leg for it. He let the boy slide to the floor then squatted down to face him. "Do you like it?"

"Yeah, sure." He crossed to the bed and examined the quilt on top. "Holy cow, Daddy. All these guys are football players."

Mike couldn't resist. "Check underneath the pillow, son."

Tyler followed instructions. "That's *you.*"

"Yep, I made the cut." When Mike had sought something special out on the Internet for Tyler's covers, he'd been surprised and pleased to find his own face on the bedding.

"Can I sit on it?" Tyler asked.

Mike placed his hand on Tyler's shoulder. "You can even jump on it if you want, Champ."

The child's smile rivaled the sun on a hot day. "Honest?"

"Honest. Nobody's here but you and me, so if I say you can jump on it, you can."

It was a weak little bounce that damn near broke Mike's heart. The kid seemed to expect so little, take so little for granted. From the time he'd been Tyler's age, Mike had had sports to boost his self-esteem and give him high expectations in life. He needed to help his kid develop that.

Mike sat on the floor and watched Tyler explore the room. There was a good-size closet which Mike had filled with the boy's summer clothes, a low window taking up the back wall faced the canal, and the dresser was decorated with a football lamp and a boom box. He didn't want Tyler to have a TV in here.

After Tyler made the rounds, he faced his father. "Thanks, Daddy."

"You're welcome."

"Who helped you?"

"Huh?"

"You said somebody was gonna be my buddy."

"That I did." He patted the floor beside him. "Come sit here." Tyler flopped down next to him. Close, which tickled Mike. "Remember we discussed that I'd be busy at camp, but I wanted you here with me?"

"Uh-huh. You *gotta teach those guys how to catch a ball.*" Mike smiled at Tyler mimicking his words.

"Well, I got somebody to watch you."

"Okay." He pointed to a crate where Mike had stacked some toys. "Can I play with these?"

"Yeah, they're yours."

Tyler picked up a miniature fire truck. "What's she like?"

Where I come from, Kyle's a girl's name. Man, Mike had almost blown it with Jacelyn. But he'd redeemed himself Monday by taking care of her foot. He still remembered how good she'd felt snuggled up to his chest when he'd carried her. All soft and feminine and womanly. Not that he was thinking along those lines about Jacelyn Ross. Well, maybe it had crossed his mind because of the unsnap-me-please garter belt that spiked his blood pressure when it had peeked out from her skirt.

"Daddy?"

"It's a he. His name is Kyle."

"I got a boy baby-sitter?"

"Well, I'm hopin' he'll be your friend."

"Is he nice?"

"Right nice."

"Rummm." Tyler took the truck across the floor and bumped into Mike's leg. "Oops."

Mike smiled.

"When'll I meet him?"

"How 'bout today?"

"Okay."

"Tyler, stop playin' a minute."

The boy obeyed immediately. Owl eyes stared up at him.

"I promise we'll spend time together. I just can't watch you all the time. Camp gets real busy, especially the second half. And there'll be a couple of nights when I'll be away."

"I know. You gotta work."

"I signed you up for a morning summer camp so you'll have kids your age to play with. Kyle's friend Kay works at it."

"Okay, Daddy."

"Just so we're straight. You're my priority."

"What's that mean?"

"That I love you and you're the most important thing in the world to me."

"More than *football?*"

Mike kissed Tyler's head. "Yeah, Champ, more than football."

Drawing back, Mike fished in his pocket for his cell phone; he found Kyle's number in his speed dial and punched it out. They'd arranged to get together sometime today so Kyle could meet Tyler.

Mike wondered whether he'd get to see Kyle's mother, too.

"MOM?" KYLE COVERED the phone with his hand as he walked out into the backyard. His dark hair and shirt were a bit damp from the heat. "Is it okay if Coach comes over here now so I can meet Tyler?"

Jacelyn shifted uneasily in her lawn chaise. Stretched out with her foot elevated as she'd been ordered to do, she looked up at her son. "Honey, you don't have to stay with me. You can go over to their house."

"Nope. If I do, you'll start walking on that again." He nodded to her foot. "Like you did yesterday—which is why you're laid up, *Mother.*"

"All right."

While he spoke into the phone, Jacelyn privately admitted her son was right. After she'd gone into school yesterday to meet with Lew about staffing, then put in some hours at the Outreach office, her foot had swelled badly again. Still, Kyle didn't have to stay with her, and she didn't really want to see Mike Kingston. For one thing, she was embarrassed at having been carried all over campus by him.

Hal had had a fit about that….

"Jacelyn, what were you thinking? Do you have any idea what it looked like?"

She'd winced in embarrassment. *"Hal, I couldn't walk."*

"He could have gotten a wheelchair from the infirmary instead of playing out the caveman thing."

She remembered thinking the "caveman thing" had felt pretty good at the time…

"Mo-om." Kyle was off the phone. "Where'd you go?"

"No place. I'll have to get changed if the Kingstons are coming over."

"You look okay."

Glancing down, she frowned at her yellow T-shirt and flowered capris. She'd been bored so she painted her toenails and fingernails a bright red. "I suppose I do."

Kyle left, saying he'd told Coach to come around back, and he'd watch for them from his room upstairs.

Jacelyn picked up the *Cosmopolitan* magazine her friend Millie had brought her, with an admonishment to relax for a change. Millie had even done Jacelyn's hair in an updo, like the cover model's. Leafing through the pages, Jacelyn's mind went back to Monday.

She'd been flustered when Mike had caught a glimpse of her garter belt and smiled with masculine interest. And she'd been in pain, not thinking clearly, or she wouldn't have let him carry her halfway across campus. Then there was the encounter with the trainer who'd checked out her foot, which was indeed just sprained.

Gage Garrison had been flirty and fun. "Well, this is the end of a perfect day," he'd said, picking up her foot and examining it. He, too, was big and broad-shouldered, with a shock of thick gray hair and a friendly smile. "Usually I get to check out hairy skin and stinky feet." His hands slid up her calf. "Hurt here?"

"No."

He wiggled her toes. "Here?"

"A bit."

After a few minutes, he'd declared she was okay. "It's sprained. Let's ice it here, then you need to do the same at home." He gave her specific directions. "Stay off it for a day or two. If you wrap it, it'll feel better when you put weight on it. But you aren't gonna do any dancin' for a while, sweetheart."

"Oh, dear. I love to dance."

Gage had smiled back. "So do I."

She'd sent Kyle off to walk Kay to her car and bring his around, and had sat in the trainer's office and sipped water from their fridge. Gage had wrapped her foot and he and Mike waited with her for Kyle. It was fun listening to their banter—so different from the teachers' conversations at social events.

Jacelyn focused back on *Cosmo,* which lay open to a picture of a short-haired blond man with bulging muscles. The caption read, Why We Like Those Jocks!

Rolling her eyes, she closed the magazine and reached down to pick up a textbook from the stack on the patio. She was thinking of changing texts for her Macroeconomics course and had narrowed her choice to two. When Mike arrived, she was still reading.

"Hi," he said easily, calling her attention to the fence. He stood at the back gate, dressed in a black T-shirt with beltless jeans and sandals. He looked fit and…virile.

She sat up straighter. "Hi."

"Kyle told us to mosey on back, that you'd both be here."

"Yes, I know. Come on in."

He unlatched the gate and stepped into the yard. A small boy clung to his leg. Mike circled his arm around Tyler's shoulders and led him across the grass to the patio. The child was beautiful, with huge brown eyes and dark hair. Kyle had told her Tyler's mother had died recently, and her heart went out to the boy. "Who is this?"

"This is my son, Tyler Kingston. Tyler, this is Dr. Ross. She teaches at the college where we're holding camp. Her son is—"

"Hey, Coach."

Mike turned and smiled warmly at Kyle. "Hey, Kyle." He glanced down. "This is Tyler. Ty, this is Kyle Worthington."

Jacelyn watched Kyle cross to them. He grinned as he knelt down. "Hi, there. You like to be called Ty or Tyler?"

Tyler nosed his face into Mike's waist. Mike locked a hand at the boy's neck. Jacelyn had a flash of Neil moving away from Kyle when he was little and got clingy.

Tyler said, "I like it when my daddy calls me Ty."

Mike's brows arched. "I didn't know that."

Kyle said, "You want me to call you that?"

"Kinda."

"I hear you like board games."

Tyler nodded.

"I dug out all my old ones." Kyle glanced at Jacelyn. "I've got lots from when I was little."

Kyle's manner was coaxing, tender. Again Jacelyn had a memory of Neil, rolling his eyes at Kyle's demonstrativeness. Later, when she'd mentioned it, he'd barked at her that he wasn't the touchy-feely type.

"Kyle plays the piano, Ty."

The little boy's eyes widened. "I like the piano."

"So your dad said. I'll play for you if you want." Standing, Kyle held out his hand. "Come inside to the living room with me."

Tyler edged closer to Mike. For several seconds, he stared at Kyle's hand, then grasped it. The two headed into the house.

"That's right nice," Mike said.

"Yes, it is. I've never seen Kyle in that role. As the adult in a situation."

"He's going to be good with Tyler." Mike shrugged. "Ty, I guess."

"I'm sure they'll get along. I hope this job is good for him. He gave up an important music seminar to do it."

"Well, he'll be back in school before you know it."

Jacelyn felt irritated by his dismissal of her concern, even if she did partly agree.

Casually, Mike dropped down into a chair across from her. "How's the foot?"

"Okay."

"Still keepin' it raised?"

"I overdid it yesterday. It was sore again today."

"Ah, cardinal rule of sports. Don't go back into play when you're injured."

"Oh, really? I hear stories all the time of athletes playing with broken hands and sprained ankles."

"That's nuts. I'd kill one of my guys if he did that."

Jacelyn realized she knew very little about the world of professional athletes. "You never did it?"

"I—" The full rich tones of the piano drifted out from the house. Mike halted in midsentence and his mouth dropped. After the song, "Claire de Lune," finished, he said, "I'm speechless. I...that was indescribable."

"Kyle's gifted."

"That's an understatement."

A children's song came next. Then the William Tell Overture. Jacelyn never tired of hearing her son play, so she sat back and let his music wash over her. But Mike's reaction was distracting. He clearly was in awe.

When the impromptu concert was over, the two boys came back out.

"He's really good, Daddy," Tyler said.

Mike addressed Kyle. "You knocked the wind out of me, Kyle. I felt like I'd been tackled."

Her son blushed. "Thanks." He looked down at Tyler. "Want to play one of those games now?"

Tyler looked up at his father. "Can I?"

Glancing at his watch, Mike hesitated. "Well, it's near five. We don't wanna spoil their supper hour."

"Stay and eat with us," Kyle suggested. "I'm cooking. It's okay, isn't it, Mom?"

"As you said, you're cooking." She smiled and nodded to her foot. "Got one more day of loafing."

"What are you making?" Tyler asked.

"Chicken crepes."

"What are they?"

"You'll love them. Come on, you can help." Kyle caught Mike's attention. "I can throw a burger on the grill for you, Coach, if you want."

Mike smiled. "No, I think I can handle some of them crepes."

Kyle and Tyler headed for the kitchen. Jacelyn heard Kyle say, "This is fun."

It was. They had a nice meal at the umbrella table outside. It was only six and the sun hadn't set yet; the air was warm but a mild breeze drifted around them.

Tyler really loosened up and talked. Jacelyn learned
he'd lived in Cincinnati with his mother and had just
moved here to be with Mike. Though they were different, Tyler clearly idolized his father. He latched onto
Mike's every word and gravitated toward him physically. And Mike never missed an opportunity to cuddle
him close.

The men cleaned up as Jacelyn limped back to her
chaise. When they were done, Mike suggested they toss
a football in the yard. Jacelyn watched the three of them
with undisguised interest, until she noticed Tyler lagging.

"Hey, Ty, want to play Perquacky with me?"

The child left the two guys and ran over. "Yes,
ma'am."

So, as Kyle's grunts and the low cadence of Mike's
comments surrounded them, Jacelyn set up the board
and played with Tyler. It was pleasant—until a boom-
ing voice came from the left. "Kyle Worthington, what
the *hell* do you think you're doing?"

Jacelyn turned to the fence to see her ex-husband,
red-faced and stiff, poised at the entrance to the yard.

His father always blindsided him, so Kyle shouldn't
have been surprised. As he watched Dr. Neil Worthington, eminent professor of musicology at Ithaca College, come through the back gate, he remembered some
of the other times his father had cut him off at the
knees….

*I've enrolled you in that summer music program on
Canandaigua Lake; you're old enough to be away from
home for six weeks.* He had been eight.

I've changed my mind about letting you go camping

with Millie Smith and her boys. They'll be canoeing and waterskiing. I don't want you to get hurt. He had been ten.

And then, when he was eleven, the big bombshell… *I'm moving out, Kyle. When you're older, you'll understand.*

Now, in the bright sunshine, his father approached him—his gait confident, his slight frame covered in expensive-looking dress slacks and a beige polo shirt. Kyle glanced at Coach Kingston, who stood stone-faced and still, waiting—Kyle guessed—to see what would happen. From the corner of his eye, he saw his mother awkwardly trying to get out of the chaise where she'd been playing with Tyler.

"I asked you a question, young man."

Kyle shrugged. "Just tossing around a ball, Dad."

Jamming his hands on his hips, his father straightened to his full height of five foot eight. Kyle had been taller than him for a long time. "Just tossing around a ball. Do you have any idea what that *thing* can do to a musician's fingers?"

"We were taking it easy."

His father's face flushed. It used to scare the hell out of Kyle when that happened. Tonight, it irritated him.

"Hey, man, no big deal. Nobody got hurt." Coach Kingston had come to stand beside Kyle.

His father's gaze was heated. "Who are you?"

Coach held out his hand. "Mike Kingston."

Neil studied Coach. He didn't offer his own hand. "Kingston? Why does that name sound familiar?"

"You follow football?"

The look on his father's face would have been funny

if he wasn't about to insult Coach. His light complexion reddened even more. "Football? You're joking, right?"

"Guess you don't follow the game. I played for the Buckland Bulls and now I'm a coach."

"Ah, I get it. You're part of that public relations nightmare at Beckett and that ridiculous Sports Studies program they just instituted."

Kyle's mother joined them. "That's enough, Neil. You're insulting our guest."

His dad turned to face her. Immediately Kyle moved to her side, paltry armor against his father's wrath.

"And where the hell have you been during all this?" Neil swept the backyard with his hand. "Isn't it bad enough that your son is working for that team instead of attending Hochstein's music seminar? Paul Hadley's very disappointed. His phone call today is why I drove a hundred miles to find out what the hell's happening up here."

"Dad, I went to the seminar you told me to take in summer school. But I didn't want to be in classrooms all through August."

His mother's gaze narrowed on his father. "Kyle e-mailed you about that."

"I've been skimming my e-mails for vital information. I'm putting together that Labor Day Music Festival at the college and have been up to my ears in arrangements."

Translation: *I didn't have time to read my own kid's e-mails.*

So what else was new? Still, the old familiar hurt welled up inside Kyle, threatening to drown him. For a minute, he couldn't breathe.

His mother was staring at him. She knew how much it hurt. Now she'd try to work his father, get him to qualify his words so the neglect wouldn't seem so big. He glanced at Coach, whose expression told Kyle that he'd caught on, too.

A little blur raced up to them. "Daddy, why is that man mad?"

Distracted, Neil Worthington peered down at Tyler. "Who is that?"

"My son."

Maybe it was because Coach grasped Tyler around the shoulders in a way Kyle's father had never once touched him in his whole life, but something spurred Kyle to say, "I'm watching Tyler for the rest of the summer. That's my job with the team."

Fury flashed in his father's eyes. He directed it at Kyle's mother. "You allowed this? What the hell's wrong with you? First, you let the silly sports program into your department. Now you let your son associate with the players. At the expense of his music."

"Dad, don't—"

His mother held up her hand. "No, Kyle, let me." She straightened to her full height, though in the casual summer outfit, barefoot and with her hair up, she looked more like a student than a mom. "First, I opposed implementing a Sports Studies program at Beckett and you know it. Second, Kyle needs some downtime. His taking care of Tyler is fine with me. Third, you should apologize to the Kingstons for your rudeness. And last, don't you *ever* storm into my house and yell at my son or me again."

"He's my son, too."

That really sucked, so Kyle let go of his temper. "Yeah, Dad, you can start acting like a father any day now." Kyle looked down at Tyler. "Come on, Ty, I want to show you this video game I got." He started to the house, holding Tyler's hand.

From behind him he heard Neil Worthington's perpetually stern voice. "Now wait just a minute, young man."

But Kyle didn't wait. He kept going to the house. Mostly because he didn't want to start blubbering in front of Coach and his mom. But also because he was afraid that, in order to really blister his dad, he'd blurt out something he'd been thinking about since the spring semester and hadn't found the nerve to discuss with his mom yet. And since that decision would hurt his mother as much as his father, Kyle left the backyard.

CHAPTER FOUR

THE NEWSPAPERS had been filled with stories of the Buckland Bulls' arrival in Rockford for their first summer training camp at Beckett College. Everybody on campus seemed to be reading about them.

"Listen to this one." Craig Anderson, a business teacher who'd lost a course for the following semester, held up Rockford's paper, the *Democrat and Chronicle*. "It's by a veteran player about the *hardships* of moving the camp to a new location." His glasses riding low on his nose, Craig looked at his colleagues scattered around the room. "They have to be kidding, right?"

Jacelyn sat at a table, pretending to make notes in her Palm Pilot. She remembered showing the instrument to Tyler, and he had been fascinated by it. Kyle had brought Ty home a couple of times when Jacelyn had been there. She was always happy to see the somber little boy.

Millie, who taught psychology, was openly watching the show.

"Read the article aloud." Hal was obviously amused by all this. "Then I'll tell you about this one." He held up a piece that he'd cut out and apparently planned to pin up to the bulletin board, near where he stood.

Craig read, "All the familiarity—where's the ice machine, how far is it to walk to the playing fields, the route to the closest grocery story—is gone. It's going to take three or four years to learn the new setting. And nobody can help. In years past, the old guys told the new guys where to go, what to do. Not only do the players have to deal with the usual pain and anguish of not having any privacy, now they have no familiar escape routes to get away from the fans." Craig rolled his eyes and finished, "I just hope it doesn't affect the season."

"Poor guys." This from Millie, which surprised Jacelyn. She was a kind, sensitive woman who rarely put anybody down.

Craig rolled his eyes. "I know."

"I wasn't being sarcastic. If you were pulled out of your comfort zone for a month, Craig, you'd be nervous about it."

"They're in their comfort zone, Millie. They're playing football here."

She shook her head, but before she could say more, Hal interrupted. "My turn. This is from a player who thinks he's going to like it at Beckett. 'The weight room's a lot better than Fairview, where we had the camp before, and they say the food is going to be great.'" Hal skimmed down. "And listen to this. He says, 'I watch the soap operas. Most of the guys do, even if they don't admit it. Victor Newman on *The Young and the Restless* is an icon.'"

Breaking her silence because she was so surprised, Jacelyn asked, "Do you think they really watch the soaps?"

Hal laughed aloud. "Do you think they really know the meaning of the word *icon?*"

"It's an emblem or symbol of something good. In this case, Victor stands for the best of actors." Mike Kingston filled the doorway, wearing a rolled-up-at-the-sleeves blue-and-black checked shirt and a scowl on his face. His hands were tucked into the back pockets of black jeans.

Millie gave a little gasp. Hal and Craig exchanged looks. Jacelyn was mortified.

"Victor's all that and more," Mike told them, his chin jutted out arrogantly. "I guess y'all are just too busy figurin' out things like the theory of relativity to enjoy simple pleasures."

Church-like quiet pervaded the room. In the hallway, there was a bustle of traffic and conversation, but no one spoke in the lounge.

Finally, Jacelyn stood. "Mike, did you want something?"

"Yeah, I was looking for you. I was hoping we could move up our meeting time. The guys are all coming in and I wanna help them."

"Sure. Let's go to my office."

"I changed my mind. We'll keep it at four." His jaw was rigid. "I'll be back." He turned and stalked out.

"Wow…just like the Terminator," Craig said snidely.

"Put a sock in it, Craig." Millie's voice was irritated. "You and Hal were cruel."

"Why, because I'm telling it like it is? Hell, Millie, they play ball. They were carrying Nintendos and large-screen TVs into the dorm when I came up. They're just big kids with a lot of toys. Pardon me if I don't feel sorry for them being out of their *comfort zone*."

"You could be sorry you insulted one of them to his face."

"I didn't know he was here. This place should be off-limits to them."

Millie stood. "This is a damn lounge, Craig." She turned to Jacelyn. "Let's go get coffee somewhere else where we don't have to listen to this." She threw a disgusted glance at the guys. "Maybe we'll bump into a few players. I'll bet they're nice guys."

"Jacelyn?" Hal's tone was critical. Unfortunately for him, it reminded her of Neil's two nights ago. Mike had stayed after her ex left and told her to forget about Neil and just worry about Kyle.

"Millie's right, Hal. You're acting like children."

In defiance, he turned and tacked the article to the bulletin board. Craig rose and did the same. Jacelyn could see the headlines: Distraction of Camp Hard on the Bulls and The Rigors of Training Camp. Craig faced Jacelyn and pointed to the board. "This is ridiculous. They're a bunch of spoiled crybabies."

Without responding, Jacelyn strode out of the lounge. Millie was leaning against the wall in the hall waiting for her. "Their masculinity's threatened by the athletes."

Jacelyn nodded. "I know."

They began walking. Millie added, "Craig's livelihood is in question because of the Sports Studies program."

"I feel bad about that."

"It's the only reason I wasn't harder on them."

Jacelyn stopped when they reached the elevator. "I partly agree with them, Mil. How hard can it be to go away for a month to play ball? How hard can playing ball *be*?"

"It's physically exhausting. And we're talking pros

here. A lot's on the line. They could lose their jobs if they have a bad season."

"Just like the rest of us."

"I know. And they make bigger bucks."

Jacelyn shook her head. "Notwithstanding all that, it doesn't sit right constantly hearing them being put down."

"That's what I like about you, girl. You have your biases but can see past them to what's right."

They stepped in the elevator and Millie pressed four. Jacelyn pressed one. "Aren't you going to your office?" Millie asked.

"No, I'm going to look for Mike Kingston."

"Why?"

"I feel bad about what he just overheard. He's the team liaison to the Sports Studies program, so I don't want to alienate him. And he was kind to us two days ago when Neil pitched his fit."

"Neil and Hal and Craig—the Stepford Profs."

"Well, they're cut from the same cloth."

"Kyle talk to you about it yet?"

"No. He's angry, though." Jacelyn ran a hand through her hair. "Hell, so am I."

"I think it's good for Kyle to be showing anger. And you, too."

"Always the psychologist."

"Always your friend. Want me to come with you to see the King?"

"No, it's okay."

"He looked sexy as hell in those tight-fittin' jeans."

Jacelyn snorted.

"You know, Jacelyn, a summer fling might be good for you."

"I'm seeing Hal."

"Oh, God, no, not with him. With the King. I bet he's great in bed."

"Millie, I don't even like sports."

"I'm thinking of having one myself."

"With Mike?" The notion didn't sit well with Jacelyn.

"No, with one of those hunky trainers. His name is Gage Garrison. You met him when you hurt your foot."

"He's a doll."

"Yeah, we ran into each other at the new field house. My boys wanted to see it so I snuck them in. Gage was setting up things in there and showed them around."

"The team's only here for a few weeks." Jacelyn didn't want Millie to get hurt.

"Enough time. I'm not looking for anything serious." The elevator pinged. "You ought to think about it, too."

Jacelyn did. All the way down in the elevator. But she was no groupie. And it took her a long time to get involved with a man sexually. She hadn't even slept with Hal and they'd been dating several months.

Though the images of Mike's hands on her leg, of his covering her body when they fell, of the look in his eyes over the garter belt weren't…unpleasant.

The first-floor elevator opened in front of the Cyber Café, where she found Mike sitting at one of the computer stations provided for on-campus use. Even from a distance, she could see his face was set in stern lines. He was staring hard at the screen. Taking a deep breath, she wrapped her arms around the waist of her off-white dress and headed toward him.

"Mike?"

He didn't look up.

"I'd like to talk to you."

"I reckon that's not a good idea right now."

"I'm sorry about what you heard."

He didn't say any more.

She drew a chair over and sat down adjacent to him. "They shouldn't be trashing you like that."

"They?"

"I wasn't participating."

Mike was using e-mail; he typed something and sent it. Then he turned toward her. The blast of his gaze sent her leaning back against her chair. "So, you weren't participating?"

"No. I asked one innocuous question about the soap thing."

"Ever hear of silent consent, darlin'?"

"I told them after you left that they were acting like little boys on the playground."

Casually, he lazed back and crossed an ankle over his knee. His face was flushed and his gray eyes turbulent. "But you agree with them, don't you?"

"What do you mean?"

"You think my job is a piece of cake, that *we're* all spoiled little boys on the *athletic* field."

Remembering her comments to Millie, she hesitated.

He swiveled away. "That's all the confirmation I need, Dr. Ross. You know, I was beginning to think you weren't so bad—that you had hang-ups about things, but could get past them."

"Look, I've made no secret about my feelings regarding the team's disruption of campus life and the viability of a sports major."

He didn't say anything, just stared at the screen again. "But you're a nice guy, Mike, and I don't want to offend you. You were so understanding of what happened at my house Monday—you didn't—"

Again, he swiveled angrily around. "What? Give my opinion on that scene with your ex?"

His tone silenced her.

"Didn't ask you how you could let that jerk walk all over you?"

"He didn't walk all over me. I stood up to him."

He ignored her comment. "That I didn't ask what the hell kind of mother you are to let him hurt your boy like he did? Like he apparently *does* all the time."

She felt her face blanch. His opinion of her cut to the quick and tapped into her insecurities. And it hurt.

Carefully, Jacelyn stood and smoothed the skirt of her dress before slowly turning and walking away. It wasn't until she reached her office that she realized he'd done to her what she'd done to him—each of them had given their negative opinions of the other's life. Unfortunately, they'd both spoken the truth.

"HEY, COACH, where are you?"

Mike turned from the Porsche parked by the dorms and stared at the tall, good-looking guy in front of him. Marcus Stormweather—the fans had a field day with his last name—was one of his best wide receivers. He was also a nice guy. Not all of them were.

He waited to answer Marc's question because he'd been thinking about some stupid female who insulted him without even trying. He'd insulted her back, but good. And it made him feel like a slug. "I'm checkin' out your new wheels." He patted the hood of the black beauty. "Bet it's faster than greased lightning."

"Yeah. Bet it's faster than yours."

You think this job is a piece of cake, that we're spoiled little boys on the athletic field.

"Mine's red." Mike reached in and grabbed a box. "What's in here?"

"DVDs, man. I gotta do something at night, now that my honey's not with me." Marcus had recently married. Mike had been his best man.

"How's my favorite lady?"

"Singing your praises." Marcus picked up a heavy box as if it held feathers. "I'm jealous, man."

"Hey, that does my ego good." They walked toward the dorms. "And I need it."

"Why?"

He glanced around the formerly sleepy campus—now abuzz with activity. "We're not being welcomed here with open arms."

"Why the hell not? Jeez, the camp's gotta be bringing business into the city and giving the college lots of air time."

Mike nodded to the faculty building, tall and stately and covered with ivy. A perfect home for Jacelyn Ross. "The brains beg to disagree."

"Then they ain't so smart. We're good for Beckett."

"Yeah, we are. Still, we do turn them around some. Summer school was cut for the second session."

"Small price to pay."

"Guess there's just no reasoning with those academic types." They took the stairs to Marcus's room. When they reached it, Mike scanned the inside. "This is pretty near the Ritz, Stormy."

"Hardly. I'm gonna miss my foam bed. And o' course, Marissa."

"She coming up for the parade Friday?"

"Yeah." He studied Mike. "Your family coming?"

"Uh-huh."

Mike pushed aside a video-game player and set his box next to the big-screen TV. "Looks like you got all the comforts of home."

"Easy for you to say. You rented a house."

"For my kid, Marc."

"I know, Coach. How is he?"

"Better. He misses his mama, though."

"I bet he does. Poor little guy."

"There you are." Head Coach Tim Mason stood in the doorway.

Mike smiled broadly. "Hey, bossman. How ya doin'?"

Marcus greeted the coach, too.

"I'm doin'. Sorry I couldn't get here earlier."

"How's your mother?" The point man for the Buckland Bulls had been taking care of his mother, who had been in the hospital, so his arrival at camp had been delayed.

"Better. Think we dodged that bullet."

Mike shook his head. They were regular guys with regular problems. Too bad Jacelyn Ross couldn't see that.

"I need to talk to you." Mason addressed Mike. "Can we meet this afternoon?"

"I got some time in a bit. Later, I'm meeting with the Business Department chair on the Sports Studies speaker series. I think we're gonna decide who from our team's gonna participate."

Mason held up his hands, arrest-style. "Don't volunteer me. I ain't no teacher."

"I'm planning to volunteer myself," Mike said. "And to see who else she wants."

Marcus asked, "What's wrong, Coach?"

"Wrong?"

"You got that look on your face you usually get when I miss a pass."

"Nothing. I'm just itchin' to get to practice."

He made arrangements to meet up with Mason in a half hour. His cell phone rang as he was heading back down to the first floor. "Kingston."

"Hi, Daddy."

Just the sound of his son's voice warmed him. "Hey, how's my best boy?"

"Right nice." The kid was picking up his expressions. "Kyle said I could call you."

"I'm glad you did. Talking to you makes my day, Champ."

The boy giggled. "Can Kyle take me to the beach?"

"It's hot enough." He thought a minute; there was a lot he didn't know about his son. "Can you swim, Tyler?"

"Yeah. Like a fish, Papa says."

"Good. Let me talk to Kyle."

A brief wait. "Hey, Coach."

"Hi. You wanna hit the waves?"

"Yeah, there's this great place called Hamlin Beach about a half hour from here. Kay and I want to take Tyler there."

Mike hesitated. "Kay's going?"

"I won't take my eyes off Tyler, Coach. Neither will

Kay. She's majoring in education and phys ed. She had a CPR—"

"Whoa. Okay, you can take him. Be careful though."

"I will."

"Seat belts?"

"You already told me all this."

"Right."

"Great, now if Mom can just get a ride home, we're all set."

"A ride?"

"Her car's still kaput. And she's got a late meeting so I can't pick her up now."

Don't offer. "The late meeting's with me."

"Oh."

A meaningful pause.

"I can drop her off at home."

"Jeez, that'd be terrific."

Mike wondered if Dr. Ross would think so.

"I'll let her know."

"Put Tyler back on."

Mike said goodbye to his son, calling himself all kinds of a fool. He had no business offering Jacelyn Ross a ride home. Hell, she probably wouldn't even take it. She'd probably be embarrassed to be seen with him—afraid her colleagues might see her with the likes of him. More than ever, that notion was getting to him, big-time.

NERVOUS ABOUT her upcoming meeting, Jacelyn couldn't concentrate on the computer screen before her. So she was glad when Jake Lansing arrived. She liked the young associate professor who'd set up the Sports

Studies curriculum, except that sometimes he was overly enthusiastic and tended to sidestep protocol.

"Hi, Jake, come on in."

A small, wiry guy with lots of muscles, he'd played college soccer and had been on a semi-pro team for a while. "Hi, Jacelyn." He entered the office and scanned the room. "You had this painted."

"Yeah. Since there was no second summer-school session, I could let maintenance come in and disrupt everything." She nodded to the light-yellow walls with Degas and Renoir prints hung on them. "The color brightens it up. Now I just wish we could get the Outreach Center painted." Rising from her computer, she came around the desk. "Everything's over at the table. We can meet there."

"Coach Kingston isn't here yet?"

"Ah, no." She wasn't sure he'd even show up. She wasn't sure she wanted him to. Sitting down, Jacelyn reached for her notes.

Jake blurted out, "I heard about Craig Anderson's course."

"Did you?"

"Yeah. We're going to get blamed for it, aren't we?"

"We?"

"The Sports Studies program. They're going to say the enrollment's down in other business classes because of us."

"Well, that's probably true, Jake."

"Anderson's enrollment is down because he bores the kids to tears."

"How would you know that? This will be your first year teaching at Beckett."

"My sister's a student here. She and her friends talked to me about it. He reads from his notes, never uses multimedia materials and makes business about as tasteless as dry cereal."

She'd heard that, too. But Craig was tenured, and it was tough to do anything about his teaching practices.

"Can I be frank?"

Jacelyn leaned back and crossed her legs. "Sure."

"I hope you're not thinking about giving him anything from our program to compensate."

Oh, Lord. Wouldn't Craig love that? "What on earth could he teach in the sports program?"

"Maybe an accounting course or a statistics course. But they're supposed to be geared toward sports business. We've already got someone in the Sports Studies area to teach them."

A knock on the door precluded her answer. Both looked up to see Mike standing in the doorway. "Am I late?" he asked. He still wore the black jeans and shirt he had on earlier, though he was sweaty from the heat.

"Jake and I were just discussing the Sports Studies program. Come on in."

Mike covered the floor in a few long strides.

"You know Jake, right?"

"Of course." The men shook hands with obvious warmth. Mike sat down next to Jacelyn. His big shoulders filled up the space between them.

"How's the settling-in going?" Jake asked.

"I was helpin' out Marcus Stormweather. He wanted to take the stairs, so I'm plum tuckered out."

"Word has it you're in as good shape as your guys."

He certainly looked it, Jacelyn thought.

"I need to be to keep them in line."

"You keep them in line with your fairness."

"I think we're boring Dr. Ross." Mike faced her. "Should we talk about the purpose of today's meeting?"

"Jake?"

"The speaker series." He opened a notebook. "As liaison to the team, I was hoping you'd be part of it."

Jacelyn cocked her head. "I thought we were brainstorming possibilities today."

She felt Mike stiffen beside her.

"Not that I wouldn't want you to do this, Mike. I just thought we'd bat around ideas."

Mike glared at her. Hell, she was going to have to watch every word she said.

"Let's see what you already got set up." His tone was strained. "And decide who from the team could do the best job."

Jake handed her and Mike copies of a list. "We haven't confirmed all of them. But this is what we're hoping for, if we can get these people."

Mike skimmed the names. "Steve Wright's a nice guy and is a big supporter of education. Plus he can give you solid insight into Major League Soccer."

"You know him?"

"The sports world is small." He read further. "I know Frank Scarce from ESPN, too. I did some PR things with them. I can give them both a call if you want."

"That's great, Coach."

"The PGA guy is confirmed, isn't he?" Jacelyn asked, scanning the list.

"Yeah, he and Nancy Baker, the number one rookie

of women's basketball. Actually, she's going to head up a panel on women's sports."

"So you're missing the coaching angle," Jacelyn stated.

"Yep."

"Tim Mason's a good speaker," Mike said tightly.

"I'd rather have you. You're more accessible. The kids would love you." Jake ducked his head. "As a matter of fact, I was hoping to persuade you to do some teaching."

Mike glanced at Jacelyn. She held her tongue. Jake shouldn't be discussing this without her input. But she didn't want to make another wrong move with Mike.

"What course would you want me for?" Mike asked Jake.

"The one called Sports Stakeholders. We're going to examine the interaction with athlete, coach, owner, business and media. I thought you'd be perfect as you've been both coach and player. You also have connections to get speakers for the other parts."

Jacelyn felt her temper rise. "We haven't talked about staffing that position, Jake."

"Lew Cavanaugh wants one of the Bulls to teach it."

She drew in a breath. "In any case, before you make any job offers, we need to talk."

Mike's face was inscrutable.

"However, I do think asking Coach Kingston to be a speaker is a good idea. What do you say, Mike?"

Again, his face was tight. But he smiled at Jake. "I'd be glad to do it. Just let my assistant know where and when so we can schedule it."

"Fine."

After taking care of other details that concerned the team, Jake stood. "Thanks, Coach. I'll be in touch. And don't forget to contact those other two guys."

Mike stood, too. "I won't."

"Jake, could you wait a minute? I'd like to talk to you alone."

"Sorry, Jacelyn, I gotta pick up my daughter at the day care by five."

"All right, but come and see me tomorrow."

"Sure thing. I gotta run." He left the office.

She turned to Mike and smiled weakly. "Thanks for coming."

He gave her a quizzical look.

"What?"

"Didn't you talk to Kyle?"

"No."

"He was supposed to call you."

She glanced at her office phone. The message light was blinking. Crossing to it, she pressed play. "Jacelyn, this is Hal. I'd like to talk to you. I've tried your cell, too. Call me."

She shook her head, and listened for the second message.

"Mom, it's Kyle. Kay and I are bookin' for the beach with Tyler. Coach said he'd give you a ride home. Gotta go. Love you."

She drew in a breath.

"If you'd rather not be seen with me, you can call somebody else." He nodded to the phone. "Like Professor Hal."

Jacelyn stared at him. "I'm surprised you want to take me home."

"I don't."

"What?"

"I'm mad as hell at you, Dr. Ross. But your son asked for my help. You need a ride because he's takin' my kid to the beach."

"All right." Now she was feeling cranky. "Let's just do this."

She grabbed her purse and some books and headed for the door. Mike stood aside for her to go ahead of him, then took her books without asking so she could lock up. He didn't return them.

"I can carry those."

"Us dumb jocks like to do grunt work," he said nastily.

"I'll carry my own damn books."

"Not when I'm around."

"Fine."

Neither spoke as they headed to the elevator. The ride down was funereal. Outside, a blast of heat hit them. "It's hot," she said to break the silence.

He didn't respond.

They walked toward the parking lot. Several players passed them.

"Hey, Coach."

"There's the King…"

"New recruit, Coach?"

They reached the lot. Jacelyn was stunned as she glanced around at the cars. "The players drive Porsches and Mercedes?"

"Yeah." He continued on toward the first row.

"Must be nice."

He was ahead of her now. "Yeah, it is. Amazing, isn't it, that for guys so stupid we manage to make enough money for these babies?" He stopped at a red Ferrari and pulled out his keys. "Your chariot awaits, ma'am."

MAYBE SHE was right about him and his team being big kids. He was acting like a child, being a jerk. He was just so mad at her. She sat stiffly on her side of the car, hands folded in her lap. Her lightly tanned arms looked good in that dress. He hadn't noticed her appearance before. Of course, he'd been seeing red most of the time he was with her today. Still angry, he stepped hard on the gas pedal when he reached the main road.

"Please slow down."

He didn't. "I won't get a ticket. The cops love athletes." He winked at her; it wasn't a flirty gesture. "My license plate says The King so I'm all set."

She scowled. "You don't take Tyler in this car, do you? There's no back seat and he shouldn't—"

"Sit in the front because of the air bag. I'm not a complete idiot, you know. I rented an SUV for the month he's here."

The silence went on.

A few minutes later she flicked on the radio to some highbrow station that played opera. In Italian.

He gritted his teeth.

It seemed to take forever to reach her house. Pulling into her driveway, Mike stopped but let the engine idle. He had no intention of getting out of the car. "Here you go, little lady."

"Are you being intentionally obnoxious?"

He nodded to the radio. "Are you?" He flicked off the music.

She turned in her seat. A smile broached her lips. "We're behaving like teenagers having a fight."

He laid his head back against the black leather. It was cool and his temper began to calm. "I know."

"You were offended by the incident in the teachers' lounge today."

"Yep. So I struck back at you." He glanced across the seat. "I don't believe you're a bad mother. Kyle's a great kid. I just said those nasty things because of what happened earlier."

"I wasn't supporting their remarks, Mike. I'm sorry for what they said."

"I'm sorry, too. For what I said." He turned off the engine and swiveled toward her. "Jake Lansing was out of line today. He shouldn't have said anything without consulting you. I'd kill one of my players if they did something like that."

"I'm not happy about it."

"They all treat you that way?"

"Who?"

"The guys here."

"No, men in academics are pretty fair. It's just a few who drive me crazy."

"Are you sayin' it's because Lansing's in sports?"

"Please don't jump on everything I say. Jake's a nice guy. He's just eager to make the program work. And for the record, I wasn't objecting to your participation in the speaker series or teaching, Mike."

"That's good to hear."

She held out her hand. "Truce?"

"Yeah." Her skin was soft. Feminine. And her scent, when it wafted over him, reminded him of a dark bedroom and satiny sheets. Suddenly it seemed warm in the car, though cold air blasted through the vents.

She tilted her head to the side. "Want to come in for a drink? Maybe we can work on our social skills together."

"Okay. But before we do that, I wanna say something about that meeting."

"What?"

Man, this was a risk, but he was going to take it. He hoped like hell she didn't laugh at him. "I been thinkin' all along I'd like to teach in the Sports Studies program. I was gonna talk to you about it as soon as the dust settled. I know professors have to have advanced degrees, and I only have a BS, but it's in business. I'd like to try out teaching and being an adjunct would be a good way to get my feet wet and see if that's what I want to do."

"Won't you stay in coaching?"

"I'm not sure. Sometimes, I like it. But I need to do something with my brain—I have for a long time. And now that I have Tyler, I'm thinking of a different lifestyle. One less erratic. I'll have to decide soon, though. I'll be offered the assistant coach position when Smitty retires in a couple of years, and I'm not sure I want it."

"Would you consider going back to school so you could teach full-time at a college?"

Mike was surprised at Jacelyn's interest, and at the fact that she thought he would get more education, so he could actually teach at a college. Most of the women in his past would have been shocked at his proposal. "Yeah, I'd go back to school in a flash, but I'm not positive I want something full-time, either."

"All right, I'll think about the Sports Studies course."

"Now I'll have that drink."

She smiled, reached for her seat belt and released it. It snapped back and caught part of her hair. "Ouch."

"Sorry. The belt does that because of how the door opens. Here, let me help."

He leaned over. When he touched her hair, he reckoned it was the softest thing he'd ever felt—like the inside of a cornstalk. He didn't let go right away.

"Mike." Her voice was throaty.

His arm stretched across her chest, his shoulder grazing hers. The contact was intimate. He drew back a bit and looked into her face. Her cheeks were flushed. Her eyes were wide and sparkled like stars in the southern sky.

And suddenly Mike wanted to kiss her more than he wanted to win the Super Bowl. He might have resisted, though, given their circumstances, if her tongue hadn't come out and licked her lips just then. He lifted his hand to them, brushed his thumb over them. Still, he might have controlled himself if Jacelyn hadn't raised her own hand to his neck and anchored it there. His skin, already sweaty, heated at her touch.

He lowered his mouth. He pressed. She pressed. He inched closer. She moved toward him. Her hand tightened on his neck; he tunneled his fingers through her hair. She moaned; he ran his tongue over the seam of her lips. She opened them. He took the invitation.

His other arm wrapped around her; when she leaned forward, he pulled her closer. Through the summer dress he felt her curves, her heat. To get more of it, he left her mouth and buried his face in her neck. His hand moved down to her breast, cradled it in his palm, massaged it.

A car whizzed by, with a muffler that should have been in a junkyard. The noise jolted both of them.

"Oh, my God," she said.

He drew back, smiling. Her hair was a sexy mess, and he tucked a strand behind her ear. "Jacey, that was—"

"A mistake."

"What?"

"It was an unprofessional, foolish mistake."

"Hold on, darlin'."

"Let me go."

"What?"

"Let me go." She pushed on his chest. Mike drew back.

She reached for the door handle. Fumbled it.

"I'll get it." He started to open his door.

"No, don't get out. You're not coming in."

"I'm not?" Hell, he sounded like an idiot, but she'd put his body in overdrive and then slammed on the brakes. He was still reeling from the momentum. When she didn't answer, he barked, "Why the hell not? You kiss me like you're suckin' up the air I breathe and then you say I'm not coming in. What game are you playing?"

"Look, Mike, I can't do this. You and me, it's unthinkable."

"You didn't need to think about it a few minutes ago, sweetheart." Maybe that was the problem.

"No, I won't do this. I'm not some groupie. I—" She covered her mouth with her hands.

"Oh, I get it. It's beneath the professor to kiss a jock."

"I hardly know you. I'm embarrassed at my behavior."

"I see." He swore. "Get out of the car."

Jacelyn tried the handle again. "I can't—it's stuck."

Reaching past her, ignoring the brush of his arm against her, he thrust open the door. As though she was escaping a mugger, she bolted and ran up the driveway. He shook his head as he watched her scoot into her house and close the door.

She probably locked it. Against him.

What had he been thinking? She was a lofty professor and he was the dumb jock. He hit the steering wheel hard with the palm of his hand and swore at the pain. Both kinds.

CHAPTER FIVE

JACELYN WASN'T embarrassed. And she wasn't angry. Oh, she regretted having once again insulted Mike. But the overriding emotion swirling inside her this morning as she opened the door to the Outreach Center was excitement over what had happened yesterday in the car. Mike's body had felt wonderful pressing into her, his mouth on hers, his hand closing over her breast. "Oh, Lord. What am I *doing?*"

"I don't know, but I think I'd like to." Millie's voice came from behind her. Jacelyn turned to see her friend following her inside. "Want to talk?"

"Maybe." She set her things down on her desk. She was missing two textbooks and her Palm Pilot because she'd left them in Mike's car. Damn it.

"Come sit here." Millie dropped onto the tapestry couch that was stuck in between their desks in the crowded space. "What's going on?"

Jacelyn joined her. "I'm not in a good place."

"Professionally or personally?"

"Both. Actually, they intersect." She stared at the dingy walls, the filmy windows. "Remember how you said the other day...that it...well, I needed a ride home..."

Millie's laugh was low and throaty. "Spit it out, Jacelyn."

"Mike Kingston kissed me yesterday."

"Wow, that was fast."

"In his red Ferrari."

"He has a red Ferrari?"

"We were in my driveway in broad daylight."

"Was it good?" There was mischief in Millie's face.

"Of course it was good, or I wouldn't have lost my mind and gone at it with him right out in the open like that. God, anyone could have seen us."

"You *went at it?* Oh, be still my heart."

"This is not good, Mil."

"You just said it was."

"Not the kiss. Well, yes, the kiss."

"That's clear."

She swiveled in her seat to face Millie. "I liked the kiss, and everything else that happened. It's just that professionally, this is suicide."

"You worried about those jerks who were criticizing him yesterday?"

"Partly. I'll lose my credibility with them if I date a ballplayer."

"Who the hell cares? I can't believe you'd let that hold you back."

"He's going to be part of the speaker series for the Sports Studies program."

"So?"

"He wants to teach in the program."

"Ah, well, that could be an issue. You'd oversee him, then. Evaluations, that kind of thing."

"I know." She scowled. "Do you think he kissed me to get an in for the job?"

Millie laughed out loud. "You have to be kidding." At Jacelyn's sober look, she said, "Did you know *Sports Illustrated* named him football's most eligible bachelor last year? Kyle showed me a copy."

"No. But what does that have to do with anything?"

"There was an interview with him talking about jocks and groupies and affairs. He doesn't take those things lightly."

"He never married Tyler's mother."

"Maybe he was different years ago. But he sounded mature about his relationships with women in the article. Like he's choosy about whom he kisses. Does he strike you as being unethical?"

"No."

"Like he'd try to get what he wants by seducing you?"

"No."

"Another thing the article said was that he's now one of the most respected coaches around. He's accessible and the players like him. I think any college with a Sports Studies program would be lucky to get him."

"Probably."

"So he wouldn't have to kiss you to get an in for teaching."

Jacelyn shook her head. "Of course you're right."

"That should take care of one worry."

Because the conversation made her uncomfortable, Jacelyn glanced at her watch.

Millie asked, "Do you have to go somewhere?"

"No. I was supposed to have a meeting with Ed Dickinson." The Alumni Association president. "We were going to talk about donations to the Outreach Program. But he canceled."

"Do you think anything's wrong? Those funds account for half of our scholarship money."

"No, he's a busy man. He was making time for me and something probably came up."

"Well, *I* have to go. I'm meeting with my department to discuss numbers." She studied Jacelyn. "Want to talk about this thing with Mike more later?"

"I want to forget all about Mike Kingston."

"Ha! Fat chance." Millie rose. On close inspection, Jacelyn's friend and colleague looked different. Her hair was down around her shoulders and her pretty brown eyes shone. "Oh, by the way, Gage Garrison asked me to go to the parade tonight with him."

"Really? Now *that* was fast."

"Nah. As you said yourself, they're only here a few weeks." She gave Jacelyn a sly look. "Besides, I had drinks with him last night. We got to know each other pretty well."

When Millie left, Jacelyn stared after her. Millie didn't give a damn about what anybody thought; still, she was highly respected on campus. There was something admirable about that.

Jacelyn stood, crossed to her computer and called up the names of students who had already applied for aid for next year. The process began almost a year in advance so kids could make early decisions about colleges. But instead of concentrating on the screen, Jacelyn's thoughts returned to Mike. She wondered how he was doing. *What* he was doing.

TYLER HAD BEEN difficult all afternoon. Mike was spending a few hours alone with him before his parents arrived for the parade tonight and had hoped to enjoy their time together.

But the kid was being as ornery as a four-time-sacked quarterback. "I don't wanna eat lunch."

"Aren't you hungry, Champ?"

He looked at the peanut-butter sandwich. "Mommy never made me eat this."

"I'm sorry. You wanna go out for a burger or something?"

"Can we go see Kyle and his mama instead?"

Kyle's mama, Mike thought, who'd felt terrific under his hands yesterday. "She's workin' right about now, son."

"Can I see her tonight?"

"She'll be at the parade." As he nursed his coffee, he had a thought. "Tyler, it's okay if you miss your own mama. You can say so."

The boy broke crumbs off the bread before him and nibbled on them. "I like you."

Mike's heart twisted in his chest. "I like you, too. I *love* you. And we're getting to know each other right fine. But you can still like me and miss your mama."

"I can?"

Mike angled his chair. "Come here." He held out his arms and Tyler dived into them. He gripped his neck, making Mike's throat constrict. "It's okay, Champ." The boy began to cry. Mike soothed his back, smoothed down his hair. Just held on. Tyler's sobs dwindled to hiccups. Then he quieted.

When the doorbell rang, Mike kissed his head. "That's Nana and Papa, Ty."

Tyler pulled back. "Don't tell 'em."

"What?"

"You know…that I…you know."

"Ty, it's all right to cry."

Big, doubtful eyes challenged that statement and Mike was reminded of rookie players who questioned everything he said.

"My players cry."

"Not hardly." The bell again.

Mike stood, hiking Tyler up with him. "Yep, they do. Come on, let's go see your grandparents."

When he opened the door, Mike's own eyes widened. "Hell and damnation!"

"Hi, little brother."

"Logan, you SOB. What are you doin' here?"

"I came for the parade."

"From where?"

"I'll tell you all about it." He smiled at Tyler. "Hi, little guy."

Shy now, Tyler buried his face in Mike's neck. God, that felt good. From behind Logan, Mike saw his parents walking toward the porch. "Come on in, everybody."

Later, after chowing down on pizza for dinner, Mike's parents took Ty to get some ice cream and Logan stayed behind. His Pierce Brosnan look-alike brother gave Mike a knowing smile. "So, what's bothering you, Mikey?"

"Tell me about you first."

"Uh-uh. You spill it, then I'll tell you about my wife."

Mike sputtered Molson's all over himself. "You got married?"

"Yep."

"I gotta hear about the woman who snared Logan Kane."

He shook his head. "More the other way, boyo. Now talk to me." He studied Mike. "It's a woman."

"Nah, camp's a zoo. No time for women up here."

"I wasn't born yesterday."

"Nope, no woman."

"What were you thinking about during pizza when you totally lost track of the conversation—about eight times?"

Casually, Mike peeled the label off the beer. "Her name's Jacey."

"She a camp-girl?"

Mike snorted at the derogatory name athletes gave to women who pursued jocks at summer training camps. "Not hardly. She's the head of the Business Department here at Beckett."

"Smart, huh?" Logan sipped his own beer. When Mike just nodded, his brother said, "Your old nemesis."

"Hey, we all had our roles. You were James Bond, I was the dumb jock, Luke and Nick were the scholars, just like Mom and Dad."

"You never wanted to be the dumb jock."

"No. But people can't see beyond their expectations."

"Right. This Jacey doesn't?"

"Looks that way." He raked a hand through his hair. "She's driving me nuts."

"What happened?"

"I don't even know her that well. But we were parked in my car yesterday afternoon and she practically blew the top of my head off."

"You did it in the *car?* Goddamn, you lead an exciting life."

"Get your mind out of the gutter. Not much happened. Just what did—I'd go after her real good if she was willing."

"And she's not?"

"She says she isn't. It's just that…I don't believe her."

"This day and age, *no* never means *yes.*"

"I know." Mike stood. "You're right. I gotta put her out of my mind."

"I didn't say that."

"No, you're right. She's no good for me."

"Mike, I—"

"I don't need that crap from a woman."

"I—"

"Thanks, bro. I feel better."

Logan laughed and stood. "You're something else, Coach." He clapped his hand on Mike's back. "Now, don't you have to change for this shindig?"

"Yeah. Come up and keep me company."

"Like old times."

"You can tell me about your *wife.*"

As he listened to Logan's story about his new wife, Mike experienced the stirrings of jealousy. It was unfamiliar and unwanted. He never felt *like* this. He didn't like feeling like this. Damn that woman. It was her fault.

KYLE STARED at the man who Kay had teased was quickly becoming his idol. The night was warm and the air crackled with excitement. "Jeez, Coach, this is mad-cool."

"That mean you like it, kid?" Coach's tone was dry. He sat with Kyle and Tyler on the top of the convertible; in front of them were cars carrying the head and assistant coaches. Before them came a high-school marching band, which sounded pretty good. Behind Coach Kingston's vehicle were more convertibles carrying the players; bringing up the rear was a volunteer fire truck. The whole parade was headed down Main Street in the suburb of Rockford, where Beckett was located.

Kyle grinned at him. "You kidding? I never thought I'd be part of something like this."

Tyler leaned into Kyle. "Me, too, Daddy."

Coach waved to a group of college girls trying to get his attention. They yelled hello to Kyle, too. Coach ignored a few older women who held a sign saying, *King me.* "Lotta people here."

"There sure are. This is a big thing." Kyle scanned the crowd and listened to the clapping and cheering. "Hey, there's Mom."

Coach stared over and his jaw got tight.

"What's wrong, Coach?"

"Nothin'." He didn't acknowledge Kyle's mother, though.

Tyler did. "Hey, Dr. Ross." The boy waved enthusiastically. "Who's your mama with, Kyle?"

"That's my uncle Eric on the left, but the other guy's a teacher from school. He picked her up."

Kyle thought he heard Coach mumble something under his breath.

He saw Kay with a group of kids from school, and Tyler spotted his grandparents and uncle. The whole trip couldn't have been more fun, except that Coach didn't look too happy.

When it was over, Kyle met his mom and Kay and uncle Eric by the Hicks and McCarthy drugstore, as arranged. Coach came along since Kyle was taking Tyler home with him, but he stood back stiffly for some reason.

Kyle nodded to his mom. "Hey, Mom, Uncle Eric."

Uncle Eric greeted him and the Kingstons.

"Hi, sweetie." His mom looked at Coach, said a curt hello, then peered down at Tyler and gave his hair a tousle. "Hello, Ty."

Tyler moved in toward Kyle's mother, so she put her arm around him. "You guys have a good time?"

Kyle grinned. "It was awesome."

His uncle Eric turned to Coach. "Nice of you to take Kyle in the car."

"No problem. We still gotta have that beer, Eric."

"Anytime."

Professor Harrington cleared his throat. "Quite a production here."

"I know." Kyle was still flying over it. "What'd you think, Mom?"

She didn't look at Coach at all. Kyle noticed her face was tense. "I thought it was great."

"Just like conquering heroes returning from war." Professor Harrington's tone wasn't nice.

Uncle Eric frowned at the comment. So did Kyle's mom. After some small talk, his uncle left.

Coach said, "I gotta go, too, and meet my brother and parents. You sure you want to stay with Kyle, Ty?"

His mother raised her brows in surprise.

"I told Coach to go have a drink with his family and Kay and I would take Tyler home for a while."

"Oh, that's nice."

"I wanna go to Kyle's house, Daddy." Tyler leaned his head against Jacelyn's leg. "You coming, too?"

"I—" His mom stared down at the little boy. "Sure." She turned to Hal. "I'll just ride back to the house with Kyle."

"Jacelyn, we're meeting Craig and his wife for drinks."

"Oh, I forgot."

Tyler's eyes got really wide. She looked down, then knelt in front of him. "Did you really want me to come home with you, Ty?"

"Uh-huh."

"All right. How about if I go with Professor Harrington for a half hour? You go back to our house with Kyle and I'll meet you there."

"Can we play Scrabble?"

"Of course. Get the game set up."

Coach leaned over and swung Ty up to his chest. "No need to disrupt your plans, Dr. Ross."

"I'd like to spend time with Tyler," Jacelyn said coolly. She turned to Professor Harrington. "Let's go, Hal. See you in a bit," she told the boys.

The three of them walked to the parking lot. Coach settled Ty into the car, then faced Kyle. "Thanks for doing this. It wasn't part of the job description, you know. To watch Ty at night so I could *socialize*. Just when I had to work."

"I want to. Go have fun with your family."

"I don't get to see much of Logan, so I'll do that. But I won't be late."

"No problem. If Ty gets tired, he can go to sleep in the spare bed in my room."

"He has trouble sleepin' sometimes. But you can try it. Promise to call my cell if there's any problems?"

"I will."

Coach clasped him on the shoulder. "We hit pay dirt, getting you in our lives, Kyle."

"Thanks, Coach." The comment felt great. "My mom, too?"

"What do you mean?"

"You and her seemed mad at each other."

"Nah. Nothing to be mad about. See you in a while." With one last kiss for Tyler, Coach left.

Kyle hummed all the way home. Man, he was happy. What good luck to have gotten in with Tyler and Coach. He wondered if his mom felt the same. She seemed upset tonight. He hoped his father hadn't done anything to her. This was how she usually got when she was having man trouble.

JACELYN SLIPPED into a peach-colored tank top and flowered pajama bottoms and sank onto her bed. She was exhausted, not having slept much last night. She'd tossed and turned over a kiss that she couldn't get out of her mind—very different from the one that Hal had given her at the door just an hour ago….

"I don't like this, Jacelyn. You're spending a lot of time with those people."

"Let's not get into all that now, Hal. I've got to go inside. Good night." She'd tried for a quick exit before she said something she'd regret.

"Not so fast." Without warning he'd grabbed her and

kissed her. It wasn't pleasant. In the past she'd enjoyed his affection, even if it was somewhat lukewarm. Now, with the hot memory of Mike's mouth on her, his hands on her, Hal's attentions were unwelcome milquetoast. She'd wound down the encounter quickly.

Afterward she'd had a good time with Tyler and Kyle and Kay. Instead of Scrabble, they'd played a junior version of Wheel of Fortune that Kyle had bought for Tyler. The young boy and Jacelyn had challenged the other two kids and they'd all had fun. After an hour, when Tyler had begun to yawn, Kay left and Kyle took Ty to his room to watch a video. Jacelyn had peeked in on them, and found Ty asleep in one bed, and Kyle dozing in the other....

It was only ten o'clock and she wasn't ready for sleep. She picked up a book from her nightstand—one of the business texts Mike had returned via messenger. He was mad at her; she didn't blame him. Dropping the book to the floor, she got up and crossed to the wall of oak shelves she'd had a carpenter put in when she bought this small house after her divorce. They sported several different kinds of reading material. Some had been gifts from Kyle and Millie and Eric. She smiled at Millie's taste. To Honor and Cherish, A Man to Believe In, Everything I Want. Always the romantic.

Thinking about Millie, Jacelyn picked up the middle one. She wondered how her friend's date with Gage was going. She wondered what the players and coaches routinely did during their spare time, where they went, who they dated....

Oh, hell, truthfully, she wondered what Mike did, where *he* went, who *he* dated. Damn it. She opened the book. She was into the first chapter when she heard Tyler cry out. In seconds Kyle came to the door holding the boy; his legs were wrapped around Kyle's waist and his arms headlocked her son. "Mom, I don't know what to do."

"What's wrong?"

"He won't stop crying. He woke up calling—"

"Mom-my." Tyler's tone broke Jacelyn's heart.

Kyle came fully into the room and walked back and forth, soothing the boy's back. "Should I call Coach's cell?"

"Yes." Jacelyn pushed away the book. "Here, give him to me."

Kyle handed Tyler to Jacelyn and went for her phone. Tyler was small for his age. She took him onto her lap; he nuzzled into her chest and locked his arms around her, too. She soothed down his hair, whispering, "That's it, little guy. Shh. It's okay."

She heard Kyle in the background. "He's crying for his mother, Coach. Okay…sorry to cut your visit short…" He hung up and came to sit on the edge of the bed.

Jacelyn continued to croon to Tyler and in minutes, he quieted.

Kyle nodded to the small boy. "That's scary."

"Kids have nightmares, honey."

"Did I?"

"When your dad left."

Her grown son sat back and braced his arms behind him. "I was eleven, Mom."

"I know. You had them, though." She smiled when Tyler nosed into her more. Gently she rubbed his neck.

Though small, he felt solid. "Abandonment issues, I'd guess. Just like with Ty here."

"Yeah, well, Dad sure abandoned us."

"You haven't heard from him since the other night?"

"No. He probably won't come to my concert Thursday."

"Want me to call him?"

"Nope. I'm sick of begging for his attention." He stretched out at the foot of the bed and nodded to Tyler. "Coach is so close to Ty." Kyle picked at the Southwestern print quilt. "I'm jealous sometimes."

"Oh, Kyle…"

"Mom, you did a great job. You and me are cool, so don't sweat it."

"I hope so. I love you, buddy."

"I love you, too."

He seemed so old lounging there, a dark lock of hair falling over his forehead. She remembered how, as a child, they always lazed on her bed like this, talked, read books and sometimes watched a video. He couldn't get enough of her time. Now she couldn't get enough of his.

Looking around the room, he shrugged. "Um… there's something I want to talk to you about."

"Girls?"

"No. Kay and I are doing great. I like her a lot."

"I can tell. She seems to like you, too."

"I—" The doorbell rang downstairs. Kyle shook his head and rolled to his feet. "We can talk tomorrow." He left Jacelyn wondering what he'd been going to say.

She heard male voices on the first floor, rumbling on the steps. Then Kyle and Mike appeared in her doorway.

"Jacelyn, jeez, is Tyler okay?" Mike crossed immediately to the bed.

"Now he is. He woke up calling for his mother, Mike."

He ran a hand through his short hair. "Oh, hell." He scowled. "It's been tough for him. He had a lot of problems when he first came to live with me, but in the last month, he seemed to be acclimatin' better. Poor little guy." He glanced around. "Sorry to inconvenience y'all with this."

"I'm glad I was here to help."

"I'll take him now." Reaching down, Mike tried to draw Tyler up. But the boy's arms clenched around Jacelyn. She lifted him from her end, but he only clutched on to her tighter. And began to cry again, this time in his sleep. Mike let go. "Hell."

"Why don't I hold him for a while longer? We'll wait till he's in a deeper sleep."

"You're sure?"

"Yes. Sit down."

She was surprised when he dropped onto the edge of the bed. Kyle took the chair in the corner. They made small talk about the parade and the team. After nearly five minutes, Mike tried again to pick up Kyle, but he cried out even harder.

The phone rang—it was Kay. Jacelyn smiled as Kyle left to take the call in his bedroom. "He'll be on a while."

Mike stared after him. "I remember those days."

"Me, too. They were more carefree than I ever realized."

He stared hard at her. He seemed about to say something, but instead nodded to his son. "What's the game plan here, do you think?"

"Let's give him a little more time-out."

Smiling at her use of sports terminology, he shrugged off his dark-gray sports coat and tossed it aside. "Mind if I stretch out, then? I can't sit too long in one position."

She shook her head. "No, of course not."

He slid over to the other side and sprawled on her bed, crooking his elbow and resting his head on his hand.

She kissed Tyler's hair. "What was his mother like?"

Mike's forehead furrowed in thought. "She was real pretty." He reached out and traced Tyler's brow, his nose, the curve of his jaw. "He looks like her."

Jacelyn didn't say anything.

"She was a...fan of athletes. Picked them to have flings with, I think. I was a first-round draft choice."

Chuckling at *his* term, Jacelyn waited for him to say more.

"She was a pistol and I enjoyed her while it lasted."

"What happened?"

"The season ended, and she moved to Cincinnati. I think she traded me for a Red Skin."

Jacelyn frowned.

"I know what you're thinkin'." He nodded to Ty. "Is he mine?"

"I'm sorry. I didn't mean—"

"No, it's okay. I wondered the same thing. He is. I had DNA tests done. I paid all her expenses through the pregnancy and birth before I knew for sure, but after he was born, we did the test."

She thought about Neil. "Didn't you want to be with him when you found out he was your son?"

"Sure I did. But I didn't wanna marry Trudy. She

wasn't hankerin' to tie the knot, either, so I dropped back and punted. I saw Tyler as often as I could, but it was never enough. And to give her credit, she was a pretty good mother when she was around. Sometimes she left him with his grandparents to pal around with some jock, but mostly she was there for him." He brushed back Tyler's hair. "It's how she died. She followed a soccer player to Europe and they ran their car off the road."

"So you got him."

"Yes, ma'am. And this little guy is the best damn thing that ever happened to me. I'd do anything for him."

"I feel the same about Kyle."

They were quiet for a while; Jacelyn heard the trees rustle outside the open window. A car beeped in the road.

Tyler shifted, and moved in her arms. She loved the feel of him. The slow cadence of his breathing. "I miss this—holding a child."

"Did you want more babies after Kyle?"

She ran a hand over Tyler's silky hair—it was the same texture as Mike's, which she remembered vividly from yesterday in the car. "Not at first. When it was too late, I wished I had, though."

"What happened with Kyle's dad?" His tone was as gentle as the breeze wafting in from the window, and invited confidences. She'd turned down the lamp and it was dim and hushed in the room.

"Better job. Younger woman. We couldn't compete." The familiar wash of rejection welled inside her.

"His loss."

"He's brilliant. But he's cold. I'm not sure what I saw

in him." She smiled nostalgically. "He liked to dance as much as I do."

"So you told Gage." At her questioning look, he added, "When you hurt your foot."

She nodded.

"Finish tellin' me about Neil."

"After a while he didn't even want to go dancing." Jacelyn shook her head. "I guess his mind attracted me. His intellect."

"Can't have been all that smart if he gave up you two."

Mike's words brought a smile to her lips. "Anyway, one of my regrets *is* not having another child when we still loved each other."

"Why didn't you?"

"When I was pregnant with Kyle I was getting my PhD and teaching classes at the same time."

"Must've been tough on you."

"It was. The doctoral course work was murder, but I really wanted a permanent position in a college, so I tackled the program."

Mike didn't say anything for a while. He seemed to be thinking about something. "Do the professors here resent having people without PhDs work at the school?"

"Some do."

"Do you?"

"I thought I did. But I can see that we'd be lucky to get someone like you to tell the kids how it really is in the sports world."

"I guess I can see how teachers wouldn't cotton to guys like us. It'd be like bein' on a team without doing the practicing."

"I've thought about what you asked me yesterday. About teaching that course Jake suggested."

"Yeah?"

"It would be good—*you'd* be good—for the program. I need to talk to other department members, though. I don't like to make unilateral decisions."

He stared hard at her. "That makes me feel a whole lot better, Jacey."

The use of the nickname that he'd uttered in the car made the setting even more intimate—him stretched out on her mattress, the room itself with its muted lighting, the big bed and quiet atmosphere. Her voice was wispy when she said, "I know you felt bad about yesterday."

His jaw tightened. She adjusted Tyler on her chest as she waited for an answer. "I did. You seemed embarrassed that you kissed me. It kicked into some old insecurities I have."

"Oh, God, no, I wasn't embarrassed."

"What were you feeling?"

"Confused." She swallowed hard and captured his intense gaze. "Afraid."

Mike sucked in a deep breath. "Of me?"

"No, of what I was feeling." Before he could question her about that, Jacelyn asked, "What insecurities were you talking about?"

"The dumb-jock image has followed me around forever. I always hated it, but didn't seem to be able to rise above it, no matter what I did. And right now, I want more than that."

"You want to teach."

"Yeah." He bunched a pillow under his head and

turned onto his back, staring up at the oak ceiling she'd
had put in just last year. It was a while before he said,
"I was hurt thinkin' you were ashamed of kissing me."
He gave her a sideways glance. "And turned on as hell."

She smiled.

"You said you were confused. About what?" he
asked.

She bit her lip; she wanted to be honest, but didn't
want the wall to go back up between them.

"Tell me the truth."

"My first thought was that you kissed me so you
could sway me about the teaching job."

Mike flipped back to his side abruptly. *"What?"*

"I'm sorry. I know that's insulting."

"It's ridiculous. Jacey, darlin', any man in his right
mind would want to lap you up like this morning's
cream."

She laughed aloud. "I doubt that."

"Take it from me, it's true." He shook his head.

She warmed to the comment. To the hot look in his
eyes.

"Seems like we both got insecurities." He watched
her. "Was that your only objection?"

"No. It gets complicated. If you want to teach at
Beckett, I can't possibly…see…date…kiss you again."

His wheat-colored brows furrowed. "You never
kissed good ole Professor Hal?"

"He doesn't work in my department. I wouldn't be
responsible for hiring him, or evaluating him."

"Aw, hell. I never thought of that."

She lifted her chin. "So no matter how interested I
am, it can't happen like that between us."

"Are you? Interested?"

She nodded. "Yes, Mike, I am." She felt herself blush. "I haven't done anything like that since I was a kid."

"What? Neck with a guy in the front seat?"

"Don't forget it was broad daylight."

"I won't forget anything about what happened in that car."

"I'm afraid we have to."

Again a thoughtful silence. Longer this time. "What if I don't go for the job?"

"Jake Lansing's determined to have you. He talked to me about it again today."

"I—"

"And you said you want to teach. We're the only Sports Studies program in the area. You couldn't do this somewhere else close enough to the team's hometown, where you've settled with Ty." She paused. "Pretty high price tag for just a few weeks together."

"I guess." His gray eyes were made deeper by a gun-metal shirt tucked into nicely pressed black slacks. "You sure this isn't an excuse, Jacey? That you're not usin' it to get rid of me?"

She shook her head. "No, Coach. It's not an excuse. What you said about yesterday? About being turned on?"

"Yeah, darlin'."

"So was I."

"Well, that's good to hear." Mike shook his head. "This is a fine kettle of fish."

"We could be friends, couldn't we? I hate the sniping and misunderstanding between us."

"Me, too." He reached out and encircled her wrist with

his fingers. Slowly, he rubbed up and down her forearm.
"I'd rather have this. But if I can't, okay. We'll be friends."

When he didn't remove his hand right away, Jacelyn
closed her eyes and sighed.

He groaned.

And then Tyler woke up.

CHAPTER SIX

THE BALL SOARED through the air, fast and furious. From the sidelines, Mike judged it to be going about seventy miles an hour. That new second-string quarterback was good.

Near the ten-yard line, Marcus Stormweather leaped off the ground like a ballet dancer. Catching the ball, he landed gracefully, turned and ran into the end zone.

"It'd be a touchdown," Mike yelled, cupping his hands around his mouth. "Good goin', Stormy."

From behind him, he heard mumbling. Johnny Turk, a first-round draft choice whose place on the team was still up in the air, was mouthing off again. The late-morning sun was brutal, making the day over eighty and humid. And making tempers flare. The first week of camp was always a bitch. And Mike had about had it with the rookie. The kid didn't even know how green he was. "All right, Turk, you're next."

"'Bout time."

Mike gripped the clipboard and pivoted to take a bite out of the Turk's ass when he saw Tyler, Kyle, Jacelyn and Eric watching from the box reserved for the family of players and coaches. Thousands of fans had come today and cheered enthusiastically as they

watched each group of players practice. Nothing unusual about that—except Dr. Ross was among them. He
hadn't talked to her since that night on her bed. Seeing
her and the kids, though, he rode herd on his temper and
said only, "What was that, Turk?"

"Didn't say nothing." Turk ran out to the field.

Marcus jogged off. Mike swatted his behind with the
clipboard. "Lookin' good."

"Thanks."

They stood together after Marcus got water. Mike let
Turk take a few tosses, then blew the whistle. "We'll try
it with the line." He jogged over to the defensive backs'
coach. "Ready to combine, Coach?"

"Sure." The D-coach faced his guys. "Go do some
damage."

The backs got in position. Mike saw Turk shake his
head. True, Mike hadn't sent in the tackles to block
Marcus, but the veteran player didn't need to be taken
down a peg like Turk did. Again, Mike blew the whistle, this time to resume play.

Cornerbacks set up. The snap. The catch. The long
pass. Turk ran. The backs butted each other. One got
through, and tackled Turk. Hard.

After that, the rookie got to the end zone a couple
times, but in three consecutive plays, he was taken
down. Mike called him off the field. "Gotta get around
'em, kid," he said smugly.

"Yeah, well, I need protection."

"You got near to as much protection as you're likely
to get in a game, hotshot." He threw a glance to the side.
"Marc, go show him how it's done."

Turk hustled back to the bench. From the corner of

his eye, Mike saw the kid mouthing off. He let it go, watched Marcus and a few more receivers, but when he looked again, Turk was still going at it, huddled in a group this time.

Mike called for the players to take a break and stalked over to the rookie, coming up behind Turk.

"He oughta try it with those ghouls out there. Bet he never had to face three-hundred-pounders."

"Don't bet on it."

Turk turned, and mutinous eyes raked him. "Yeah, whatever you say, Coach."

Mike shook his head. Some guys just never learned the easy way. He eyed Stormy; they were about the same size. Mike tossed the clipboard on the ground, and faced Marcus. "Strip, buddy. I want your pads, shirt and helmet." He turned to a gofer. "Get me a mouth guard."

Tim Mason jogged over. "What's going on?"

Mike shot a quick glance to the rookie. "Nothin' I can't handle." In minutes he was suited up. He shot another look at his son and Jacey, who was now holding Ty on her lap, and hoped he wasn't grandstanding for them. Too late now, anyway. In a few more minutes, he was on the field. A raucous cheer erupted from the fans at his appearance, and they began yelling, "King me!" It felt good to be in position. Good to be on the line.

"Don't go easy on me, guys," he said to the backs. "Otherwise I won't be able to teach that candy-ass a lesson."

Mike focused on the snap, the throw, and started to run. He caught the first pass easily and glided into the end zone.

"Again," he called out, not even breathing hard. Thank God he'd stayed in shape.

He wasn't tackled in three more tries.

Then a hell of a bruiser caught him in the ribs just as he picked a bad throw out of the air. He went down hard, felt his head jar, his back crunch, and his shoulder bounce off the ground.

God, it felt good.

"OH, LORD, I can't watch." Jacelyn buried her face in Tyler's shoulders as the gorillas headed right for Mike.

"Ouch." Eric, next to her, groaned the word.

She chanced a glance over Tyler's head. There were men in a pile on top of Mike. "Why's he doing this?" she whispered to Eric, so Tyler—who was cheering loudly with Kyle—wouldn't catch on to her worry.

"Don't have a clue." Eric stuck his head around her. "Kyle, why do you think Coach took the field?"

"Number eighty-two was mouthing off to him."

"Uh-oh. Nobody oughta mouth off to my daddy."

Jacelyn hugged Tyler tight.

"I think you're right, buddy." Kyle slugged Ty playfully on the shoulder. "He sure showed that guy."

Jacelyn shook her head. "Men!"

Practice ended a half hour later. Several players, by a prearranged schedule, headed to the designated area to sign autographs. Fans mobbed the booths. Jacelyn couldn't believe the throng of people who'd come today and now lined up to see the players.

As Mike jogged toward the section roped-off for family, Jacelyn was astounded by her visceral response. His shoulders looked huge in his navy coach's shirt that he'd changed back into. "Hey, buddy," he said, lifting Tyler from her lap and tossing him in the air. "What'd you think?"

"Awesome, Daddy. Did it hurt when those guys tackled you?"

Jacelyn noticed that he winced when he picked up Tyler.

"Yeah, son, it hurt. I'm not twenty-five anymore." He rolled his eyes. "Shouldn't be actin' it."

"You looked great out there," Eric told him. Just today, Jacelyn had found out that Mike and Eric had gone for a beer Sunday night.

"Thanks." Mike faced Jacelyn. "So, what'd you think of your first day at camp, Dr. Ross?"

"It's a bit more violent this close up," she said, shielding her eyes from the sun.

He cocked his head, then took off his cap and settled it on her. "Here, you're getting burned."

She smiled up at him.

"You guys wanna come to the locker room with me?" he asked as he put Tyler down. "I'd invite you, Dr. Ross…"

Kyle and Eric began to laugh. "Mom, in a locker room? That'll be the day."

Jacelyn cleared her throat. "I've had enough excitement for one morning." She grabbed her bag from the bleachers. "I'm picking out paint with Millie in a half hour, anyway."

"Paint? I thought your office was all done." This from Eric.

"It's for the Outreach Center. Millie and I are going to do it ourselves."

"Now?" Mike asked.

"No, Wednesday."

"Can I go with Dr. Ross?" Tyler asked.

"To pick out paint?" Jacelyn ruffled his hair. "Don't you wanna see the players, honey?"

He peered up at her. "Nope. I wanna be with you."

"Okay by me," Jacelyn told Mike.

Kyle shrugged. "I'll come get him when we're done, Mom. Will you be at the Center?"

"Yes." She held out her hand. "Come on, young man. We've got some decorating decisions to make."

Tyler placed his hand in hers. She grasped it and a wave of maternal longing swept through her.

Mike reached over and tugged on the bill of his cap. "Thanks, Jacey."

"What? For spending some time with one of my favorite guys?"

"He's a lucky boy, I'd say." Mike's look reminded her of Saturday night, and the intimacy of lying on the bed.

Any man in his right mind would want to lap you up like this morning's cream.

Jacelyn had to struggle to keep her voice even. "See you later."

Mike, Kyle and her brother went to the field house. She and Tyler headed in the opposite direction toward Basil Hall. As they walked in the bright sunlight, with the rich smells of summer surrounding them, they played I Spy. When they arrived at the Outreach Center, she found Millie inside the office with Gage Garrison. Millie smiled at Tyler. "Who's this?"

"Tyler Kingston, meet my friend Dr. Smith."

"Hey," Tyler said, turning his face into Jacelyn's side.

She mouthed, "He's shy."

Crossing to them, Gage squatted down. "You remember me, don't you, Champ?"

"Hey, Gage."

"What you doin' here?" Gage asked.

"I'm helping Dr. Ross."

Jacelyn smiled. Millie gave her a look that said, *What's going on?*

After having firmly decided not to pursue a relationship with Mike, Jacelyn didn't want to answer that question.

MIKE WAS HAVING TROUBLE concentrating on the TV screen before him. He'd planned to go with Tyler and Kyle to a movie—a 3-D production at the Imax theater. But something had happened to the film and the show had been canceled. Instead, they'd rented a cartoon, and Kyle had suggested they watch it at his house on the large-screen TV in the family room.

He'd also said they wouldn't be disturbing his mother because she was out on a date with Professor Hal.

Son of a bitch! Slouched on the couch, his feet up on an ottoman, with Ty nestled into him and Kyle on the floor, Mike couldn't focus on the DVD. Instead, he kept thinking about Jacelyn's skin and wondering if the jerk she was with was touching its creamy smoothness. He kept remembering the feel of her silky hair, picturing Harrison smelling it, sliding strands between his fingers. When Mike's mind strayed to X-rated territory, he swore silently, but viciously.

"What's the matter, Daddy?"

"Nothin', son." He sighed and sank deeper into the pillows of Jacelyn's overstuffed couch. It didn't help that he was sore from his little exhibition on the field today. What the hell had he been thinking, putting himself on the line like that? His lids grew heavy. As he drifted in that dimension between sleep and waking, he thought of Jacelyn again and how she was real easy on the eyes in her cute pajamas just a few nights ago...

"Mike?"

He stirred. A hand clasped his shoulder. The scent of lilacs surrounded him. That's what Jacey smelled like...some flowery lotion...

A shake, harder. *"Mike."*

His lids lifted. She was sitting on the couch. He reached for her, his hand brushing her hair, coming to rest on her shoulder. "Jacey. Mmm."

"Jacelyn!"

What the hell was that rude interruption? Mike closed his eyes again and willed it away.

"Mike, please. You're asleep on my couch." Now a really hard shake. Enough to rouse him.

"What?" His eyes opened and cleared.

It was Jacelyn all right, perched on the edge of the couch next to him. But Professor Hal hovered over her like a protective daddy.

"Hey, hi." Mike shifted. Oh, hell. Thankfully a throw pillow was on his lap. Dreaming about the woman before him had a downright obvious effect on his body.

"Mike, what are you doing here?"

"Huh?"

"Is that your car in the driveway?"

"Oh, yeah, it is. The SUV I told you about. I drove it to take us to the movies."

"What the hell are you doing camped out on Dr. Ross's couch?"

Jacelyn's head snapped around. "Hal, please. You're being rude."

"He's got his hands all over you and you expect me to be polite about it?"

"He was asleep."

"Oh, for God's sake."

Fully awake, Mike watched the professor. He looked loaded for bear, Mike thought, smiling.

"Mike." Jacelyn's voice was strained. "Please explain what you're doing on my couch."

"The Imax movie was canceled so we came back here to watch a movie instead. Not 3-D but it was fun." He looked around. "Where're the kids?"

"Upstairs, in Kyle's room playing his Nintendo, I think. I haven't gone up yet, but I can hear them."

"I must have fallen asleep."

Professor Hal's face was red. "Jacelyn, this is ridiculous."

Mike's gut clenched. Not just at Hal's rudeness, but by how he yanked Jacelyn to her feet. Mike came up on his elbows. "I wouldn't manhandle her if I were you, Harrison."

"Who the hell do you think you are?"

"A Southern gentleman who knows how to treat a lady."

Jacelyn pulled away from Harrison. "Stop this, both of you." She faced Hal. "You'd better go."

"*Me?* He should go."

"He will, as soon as Tyler and Kyle finish upstairs."

"You're kidding, right?"

Her hair swirled around her shoulders as she shook her head. For the first time, Mike noticed she was wearing a pretty peach one-piece thing that clung in all the right places. He clutched the pillow tighter to his front.

"Go, Hal. We'll talk tomorrow."

Eyes wide with shock, Harrison glared at Mike, then pivoted and stalked out. Like some hotheaded rookie, he slammed the door.

When Jacelyn turned back to him, she was obviously upset.

"I'm sorry, Jacelyn."

"It's not your fault. He was behaving badly."

"I mean, I'm sorry that you're upset because of me."

She sighed and sank down next to him.

He dropped his feet from the ottoman and straightened. "Arrgh…"

"What's wrong?"

"I wrenched my shoulder today at practice."

"Now there's a surprise."

Ducking his head sheepishly, Mike shrugged. "I shoulda known better. I was showin' off for the rookie." Rotating his shoulder, he winced.

"Hurt a lot?"

"'Fraid so. I went into the whirlpool at the field house, but Gage was too busy to give me a massage, which usually takes care of this right away. So it stiffened up on me." He patted the arm of the couch. "And sleeping on this thing didn't help."

She smiled shyly. And shocked the hell out of him by saying, "I could rub it."

Oh, man. "Now darlin', that's the best offer I've had in a long time."

"I highly doubt that. I know women hang around players."

"It's a true statement, cross my heart and hope to die."

"Take your shirt off, Coach," she said dryly, "then turn over."

He managed to shed the T-shirt and get facedown without dropping the pillow. On his stomach, his cheek buried in the couch, he groaned again, not because of the pain in his shoulder but because of the pain lower down.

When Jacelyn's hands slid onto his skin, it was nirvana. He closed his eyes to savor the sensation.

Fingers gentle on his neck…

"Did you have fun on your date?"

"No, we came home early."

Pressure on his deltoid…

"Why?"

"I was bored. I made excuses."

Fingertips digging into his shoulder…

"Ahhh…"

"Feel good?"

"Sweetheart, this is seven steps above heaven."

She found the strained muscle, dug into it…

"Oh, God, Jacey, you're killin' me."

A chuckle.

Long, deep strokes…now down his spine…

"Why do you date him if he bores you?"

"I've been asking myself the same question."

The heels of both hands at his waist…

"Ah, jeez, oh, God…" More moans.

After a while, she said, "I'm going to break it off with him. I don't want to see him anymore after…"

When she hesitated; he waited, then said, "After what a jerk he was just now?"

A very long pause. "I was going to say," she whispered softly, "after meeting you."

"That's it." His hurting shoulder forgotten, he flipped over. In one swift motion, he tumbled her down so she was half on top of him. Right where she belonged.

"Mike, don't."

He brushed her hair back and left his hands in it. "After what you just said, you expect me not to react?"

Jacelyn arched the lower part of her body. And giggled. "Well, you reacted all right. But I didn't mean to…" The woman actually blushed.

"Mean to what? Make me hard?"

She buried her face in his chest. "Mike…"

"Jacey, baby." One hand cupped her neck, one traveled down her back and rested intimately on her hip.

Coming up on her elbows, she stared at him intently. "What I said the other night still stands. I'm sorry if my remark was suggestive."

"Honey, you're suggestive just breathin'."

"Oh, God, nobody sees me that way."

"What, are they blind?"

She giggled again. He chuckled.

"Okay, okay. I'll let you up. After."

"After what?"

"A kiss."

"I can't kiss you here. The boys are right upstairs."

"Well, if that's all that's stopping you…" Mike set

her back, rolled to his feet, and in lithe, wide-receiver mode, maneuvered around her to stand. He grabbed her hand and pulled her up.

"What are you doing?"

He said nothing, just led her toward the kitchen. He surveyed the homey space, noting the hallway off it.

"What's down there?"

"A powder room first, then a laundry room at the end."

His eyes narrowed. "That'll do right fine." He dragged her down the long corridor. The laundry room had a washer and dryer, and not much else but a window facing the back; moonlight streamed in through the slatted blinds. Closing the door, he left the light off and backed her up against the wall. "Now, nobody'll catch us."

"Mike, that doesn't alter—" He took her mouth before she could finish the protest.

Jacelyn held back—for all of about twenty seconds. Then she sank into him. His hands banded around her waist and he slid one up to her neck, locking her to him. She sidled in close, rubbing against him like a kitten needing stroking.

He stroked. His hands slipped down to her fanny, clenched on it. She was supple and so feminine it made his breath catch in his throat.

It also made him harder than granite. "Jacey, darlin'," he murmured into the crook between her neck and shoulder. Man, she smelled good.

"Mmm." She burrowed into his bare chest. Inhaled him. Even licked him once. Then she tried to get closer. Like she wanted to be inside his skin.

Like she wanted *him* to be inside *her*.

Voluntarily she lifted her mouth again to his; the kiss went on a long time.

A voice came from far away—the front of the house maybe. "Mom?"

Shit.

"Mom, where are you?"

"Oh, no." Jacelyn eased her mouth away, letting go of her death grip on his neck.

"Son of a bitch."

She cuddled into his chest, ran her hand through the mat of hair there. "It's probably for the best."

"How can you say that?" he asked gruffly, his lips on her forehead.

Still holding on, she whispered, "This is wonderful, Mike. But nothing's changed since we discussed 'us' the other night."

"I want you."

"Mom?" The voice was closer.

She managed some distance between them. Not a good idea. In the shaft of moonlight, he could see her mouth was swollen, her hair a mess. He reckoned he'd never in his life see a prettier sight. One of the buttons on the peach thing was undone, giving him a glimpse of creamy skin. Reaching out—not because he wanted to—he did it up.

She straightened her shoulders. "We have to go."

"Mom…" Kyle's voice came from the kitchen.

He glanced around. "Yeah? Well, how do you suggest we get out of here together?"

"Oh, damn." She started to laugh.

And, despite the fact that his body was about to combust, so did Mike.

CHAPTER SEVEN

AT FOUR on Thursday, Jacelyn, wearing old shorts and an even older T-shirt, entered Basil Hall and headed toward the elevators to paint the Outreach Center. Though she was not looking forward to it— she hated all that preparation and the painting itself— she was humming softly. The tune was a sixties song she'd heard on the radio on the way in today, about stealing kisses in your mama's kitchen. The words rocketed her back to last night, to when Mike had kissed her senseless in the laundry room. What had she been thinking? And they'd almost gotten caught....

Jacelyn's mind had been muddled, but Mike had reacted fast. Before she knew it, he'd actually climbed out of the window, squeezing through the small rectangle. As he made his getaway, she'd teased him about quick escapes from fathers or jealous husbands. When he was out of sight, she'd left the laundry room, and found her son in the kitchen.

"Mom, you okay?"

"Of course."

"What were you doing down there?" He'd pointed to the corridor.

"Um, I spilled something on my outfit and was searching for some stain remover in the laundry room."

Kyle hadn't look totally convinced. *"Did you have a nice time tonight?"*

"Yes." Not with Hal, she remembered thinking, but those few moments with Mike had been ecstasy.

"Hey." Mike had appeared at the sliding doors. Thankfully, Jacelyn noted, the glass was pulled back to expose the screens.

"Coach? What were you doing outside?" Kyle's eyes had narrowed. *"And where's your shirt?"*

"I got hot and took it off. I went outside to get some air."

"You were asleep on the couch when we went upstairs."

Mike intentionally took charge. *"Speaking of that, where's Ty?"*

"Asleep in my room...."

And so they'd dodged that bullet.

Jacelyn rode the elevator to the bottom floor while she reminisced about Mike. When the doors opened, she heard commotion down the hall. Only classrooms not being used this summer were on the lower level, along with the Outreach Center, so the sounds had to be coming from her office. She checked her watch. Four o'clock. She was meeting Millie here, but who...?

Quickly she walked down the corridor. As she got closer, she heard some awful rap music coming from the Center. At the door, she went slack-jawed.

All the furniture had been moved to the middle of the room and covered with tarp. The newly replaced windows were open, letting in a warm July breeze. And at every wall were the biggest guys she'd ever seen—each one with a roller or paintbrush in hand and wearing old clothes, some of which were speckled with the deep peach she'd chosen for the walls. The men were laughing, joking—and painting her office.

She spotted Mike at the top of a ladder. He wore a black T-shirt that revealed a road map of muscles, and baggy denim shorts, both sporting globs of paint. "Can't we get some real music on that thing, Stormy? My ears are startin' to ring."

"Hey, Coach. We're doin' you a big favor at the end of a tough day."

"Didn't know I was gonna lose my hearing in the process," he grumbled.

Jacelyn came farther into the room. "What's going on here?"

Mike looked over his shoulder, as did the other guys. "Hey, Dr. Ross."

The rest of the team greeted her.

"Mike, what are you doing?"

He winked at her, turning her stomach upside down. "Not cooking a full-course meal, now, are we?"

"I mean, why are you painting our office?"

Setting his brush in the tray, he climbed off the ladder and came toward her. Thinking of last night, her heart beat escalated. Oh, this was not good.

He gave her a killer smile. "Well, bein' that we stole your other quarters, we thought we'd help make this place more livable."

"How did you know we were doing this today?"

"You told me at practice the other morning. And Gage got the details from Millie." He nodded to the corner, where the trainer was rolling paint on the east wall.

"Did Millie know you were going to do this?"

"No," came a voice from behind. "She didn't."

Turning, Jacelyn saw her friend in the doorway. "We've got helpers," Jacelyn said.

Millie scanned the area. "Angels, you mean. It's almost *done*."

"Needs another coat." This from Gage. Millie's face lit like the sun when she spotted him. Immediately she crossed to where he stood. There were soft murmurings and he moved in closer and straightened the collar of her shirt. Then he grazed her cheek with his knuckles.

"Looks like romance is blossomin' all over the place," Mike said softly to Jacelyn. "I wondered why he was so hot to do this."

She turned back to Mike. "It was his idea?"

"Like hell," Marcus Stormweather, who'd walked by them, put in. "Coach here blackmailed us into it."

Mike had a speck of paint on his cheek. Jacelyn smoothed it off with her fingertips, then swiped them over his shirt. "Blackmail?"

Grasping her hand before she could take it away, he squeezed it tightly…and leaned in almost imperceptibly. "I told 'em we'd have a double practice today unless they consented to do a good deed instead."

"What's a double practice?"

"Hell on earth, pardon my language, ma'am." This from another huge man on the north wall.

"Don't listen to Titus. He's the team wuss. In my day, double practices were routine. Tim Mason just gave 'em up a year ago." He raised his voice. "'Course, players were tougher then."

There were appropriately sarcastic comments from

the guys. Jacelyn scanned the area; she didn't know what to say. She couldn't remember the last time anyone did something so sweet for her.

Millie and Gage crossed to them. "How much longer, do you think, Coach?" Millie asked Mike. She was smiling idiotically.

"About a half hour. Maybe a mite longer."

"Just enough time. Let's go, Jacelyn."

"Where?"

"Grocery shopping. We're gonna make these guys a home-cooked meal."

Gage's eyes danced. "Bless you, honeybunch."

"Hallelujah." This from Marcus.

Another player chimed in. "Right on, Dr. Smith."

Titus gave her the thumbs-up sign.

Looking fierce, Mike thrust his hands on his hips. "We got a team meeting at six, guys."

"Aw, Coach."

"Come on, man, a home-cooked meal?"

Mike shook his head. "You only been here a week, so that don't hold no water."

Gage leaned into Millie and said in a stage whisper, "Meeting's only an hour, Millicent."

She grinned. "We can make spaghetti sauce in that time."

Raucous cheers all around. Jacelyn felt caught in a trap. A nice, cushy, feel-good trap.

"What do you think, Dr. Ross?" Mike grasped a strand of hair that had come loose from her braid and tucked it behind her ear. "I'm free after the meeting. Tyler and Kyle have a special campfire thing tonight with his day camp, then Ty's staying overnight at your house since I've got that early radio interview." His brow furrowed. "Unless you're busy." This time he leaned in obviously close. "You got another date with Professor Hal?"

"No dates with him anymore, Coach."

"Hmm. That's good to hear."

"So, what do you say, Jacelyn?" Millie asked.

"I say yes—" she glanced over at her friend "—*Millicent.*"

When they reached the door, she heard Mike call out, "We'll stop and get the dessert."

"THIS IS so good, it makes me want to cry." Mike twirled his fork in the cheesy fettuccine sauce which even smelled downright sinful. "Where'd you learn how to cook like this, darlin'?"

"From Eric's wife. She's Italian."

One of the receivers, Nick Santini, lifted his wineglass. Mike knew the players drank some, as he had in his pro days, but mostly they stayed away from the booze during training camp and the season. "*Salut,* Dr. Ross, Dr. Smith."

Millie lifted her glass and Gage clinked it. Those two had been peas in a pod tonight. They'd all carpooled over here after the team meeting, and Mike had ridden with Garrison, who'd said he was sweet on Millie and that they were *dating.* Mike wished like hell Jacey would—was able to—date him. He understood her reasoning, but he didn't have to like it. Though for two people who *weren't* dating, they were sure spending a lot of time together. Like tonight.

And like last night, which he couldn't think about too

much or he'd go nuts. Still, he noticed how sexy she looked even in old white shorts and the pink sleeveless top.

After Marcus made some comment about never having had pepperoni in marinara sauce the way Millie had cooked it, Jacey said, "Pass me the bowl, I haven't had any."

Mike stuck his fork into a spicy piece that was on his plate. "Here, I've had too much already. They'll have to roll me out onto the field." He extended the fork, but instead of putting the meat onto her plate, he held it to her mouth. Watching her sink even white teeth into the juicy pepperoni made his whole body tighten. He hoped the meal didn't end any time soon.

It didn't. Everybody was in a good mood and lingered—joking, complimenting the cooks, trading insults. When the conversation died down, Millie stood. "Why don't you fellas go sit out back while we clean up. You can take the dessert you brought to the picnic table on the patio."

"No way," Mike said. "My mama would skin me alive if I let the cooks clean up. Us guys are fixin' to do it."

Jacey stood and reached for his plate. "You don't have to."

"Let us," Gage told Millie. "*You* two go have coffee on the patio."

With only weak protests, the women got mugs of coffee and headed outside.

Like a well-oiled machine, the six men attacked the kitchen, though Mike's gaze kept straying to the patio.

Jacey and Millie were both stretched out on chaises, chatting amiably. He wondered what they were talking about.

MILLIE SIPPED her coffee and nodded to the house. "Those guys are really something, aren't they? I can't believe they painted the Center and now they're cleaning up."

"They're something all right." Jacelyn stared out into the pretty tree-lined backyard. The summer night was warm, and a sultry breeze wafted around them. "It wouldn't have occurred to Hal and Craig to help out, let alone take the initiative to paint the Outreach office."

Millie watched her. "What's going on with you and Mike, Jacelyn?"

"We've gotten to be friends. I'm glad, since Kyle and Tyler spend so much time together." Still Millie watched her. "What?"

"Well, for one thing, at the office I saw you wipe a smudge of paint off his face like a woman does to a man she's…involved with. And he tucked your hair behind your ear. Then at dinner he fed you the pepperoni the same way, without even thinking about how intimate that seemed."

"The joys of having a psychologist for a best friend." When Millie continued to stare at her, she shrugged. "I've only known him two weeks." But Jacelyn thought back to other things. Like the very sensual back rub… "I guess we've gotten close."

"There's something else. I overheard Hal telling Craig that Mike was at your house Monday night. Hal wasn't happy about it."

"I told Hal yesterday I didn't want to see him anymore socially."

"I'll bet that went over well."

It hadn't, of course.

You're kidding, right...? I hope this doesn't have anything to do with Mike Kingston.... You're a little old to be turning into a groupie....

She sipped her coffee. "Who cares if Hal's happy or not? He was mean and insulting."

"I guess you don't care. Not about Hal, anyway."

"What do you mean?"

"It's obvious you care about Mike."

"Did I hear my name mentioned?" He stood in the doorway, looking great in clean khaki shorts and a Bulls T-shirt, wearing a team cap.

Gage was behind him, similarly dressed. "We got the goods." He held up huge brown sacks.

The men crossed to the picnic table and set out the dessert.

"What is it?" Millie asked Gage. As he approached her, she scooted her legs over so he could sit on the edge of her chaise.

Gage sat. And touched her knee. "Cannolis, cream puffs and half-moon cookies."

Holding a bag, Mike stood by the table. "Want something, Jacelyn? You'd better get it now before those baboons come out and devour everything."

"A cannoli." Mike brought her one and dropped down on the end of her chaise, chowing down on a cheesy confection himself. Jacelyn watched his teeth close over it, watched him swallow and refrained from wiping a bit of sugar from his full, sensuous lips. Instead, she bit into her own dessert. "What are the guys doing in there?"

"Checking out Millie's CDs." Jacelyn cocked her head. Mike elaborated. "They saw the stereo in the living room and…" Suddenly, a sixties song came blasting out. "Do You Wanna Dance?" filled the air. "Oh, Lord, now it'll start." He pointed to the doorway. "Watch."

Out came Marcus, Nick, and the two other receivers moving and gyrating to the beat of the music. They were doing a combination of steps, and a couple of them were pretending to hold a mike and sing along, though they didn't know all the words.

Gage sprang to his feet. "This is my era, babe. Let's dance."

Suddenly the big stone patio became a dance floor. The guys moved the umbrella table and chairs out of the way as if they were weightless. Gage and Millie began to swing dance.

Millie, like Jacelyn, was good at the moves. So was Gage. So, apparently, was Marcus. In seconds, he had Jacelyn out of the chaise and on the floor. She fell easily into step with the big guy, who knew as many moves on the dance floor as she presumed he did on the football field. As a matter of fact, all the guys were good. Jacelyn remembered Eric saying that football players were known to take dance lessons to improve their agility.

All of them danced, except for Mike, who'd sat back on the chaise and watched the show. When a song ended, another guy took Jacey by the hand. After several dances, she begged off. The music still played, but the guys headed for the desserts. Millie and Gage announced they were going for a stroll around the property—two acres of wooded lot that Millie's husband had loved and she couldn't bear to sell after his death. Jacelyn crossed to Mike.

He was smiling. "Who would have thought the illustrious Dr. Ross could cut a rug like that?"

She flopped in a chair. "It was fun." She eyed him. "How come you weren't out there with us?"

"Can't dance," Mike said ducking his head.

"Come on."

"Nope, he can't." Marcus came up with four cannolis on his plate. He sat down in a chair and Jacelyn watched openmouthed as he wolfed them down. "We mock the hell out of him about it all the time. Sportscasters called him a gazelle on the field, but he can't keep time worth sh—beans."

Pointedly, Mike glanced at his watch. "Don't you have a curfew to keep, Stormweather?"

Marcus laughed. So did the other guys, who joined in razzing him. Still, Jacelyn noticed they finished their desserts and got ready to go. They thanked her for the food and the dances—Marcus made her promise to meet him on the floor of a local club sometime. Then they went around the side, looking for Millie to say goodbye.

Jacelyn stared after them. "They're nice guys."

"Yeah, *they* are. Some of the new guys are a pain in the butt."

"Like the rookie you wrenched your back for."

"Hey, that sore back got me some TLC from a pretty lady I know." His eyes shone with the suppressed sexuality that had been full-blown last night.

She smiled. "So are you, Mike. A nice guy."

"Me? I'm an SOB. Any one of my players'll attest to that."

"Maybe on the field. It was your idea to paint the office."

He sipped his coffee. "Seemed like the least we could do."

"It was classy and thoughtful. Thank you."

"You're welcome." His grin was lazy. "I can think of a way you can repay me."

"I'll just bet you can."

Reaching over, he picked up her hand. His was rough, callused and felt incredibly safe and strong. "Still intent on stayin' away, Dr. Ross? Even after last night?"

"Yeah, Coach. I am." She gave him a meaningful look. "I'm meeting with my department tomorrow to discuss you teaching as an adjunct in the Sports Studies program."

"Ah, I see. Well, I'd sure like that."

"I know you would."

"I'd also like *you,* in my—"

"Hey, there." Gage called out to them as he and Millie came back around the side of the house, arm in arm.

Immediately Jacelyn pulled her hand from Mike's. He asked, "Did you see the guys?"

"Yeah, they said goodbye."

Jacelyn slid off the chair. "I need to go, too. I have some things to finish up tonight for my meeting tomorrow."

Mike also rose. "Yeah, we should head out. Ready, Garrison?"

Millie and Gage exchanged a surprised look. Finally Gage said, "I guess I could run you home."

"What do you mean?" Mike asked.

Millie grasped Gage's hand and faced Jacelyn. "Jacelyn, would you mind dropping Mike off? The boys are sleeping overnight with friends." She smiled at Gage. "And Gage is staying here."

JACELYN SWUNG her practical Camry into Mike's driveway. "I didn't know you lived on the canal." His house was an A-frame, with wooden siding and trees bordering it. The night was calm with stars twinkling overhead and a light breeze floating into the window.

"Yeah, it's small, but it's great being on the water. Ducks come by every day for Tyler to feed."

"He must love it." Jacelyn stared straight ahead and left the engine running, the gear in Drive. Ready to bolt, Mike guessed.

Reaching over, he shifted the car into Park, and turned the key to Off.

She startled. "What are you doing?"

"I want to talk a minute and you're gonna beat it out of here like a jackrabbit out of a foxhole."

"That would be wise."

He took her hand off the steering wheel and cradled it in his own. God, he loved the feel of her. She pivoted a bit to the side, but didn't say anything. He began to trace her fingers. He wanted real bad to touch her skin. To taste it. He hadn't felt this edgy need for sex in a long time. Now it was happening almost every day.

"I'm surprised about Millie and Gage," she finally said, breaking the sensual spell. Intentionally, he was sure.

"Are you?"

"Yes, she hasn't known him that long."

"Doesn't take very long to know what you want, Jacey."

"I thought men *always* wanted sex."

Well, that was a quick left jab, meant to push him away, he reckoned. He leaned over and kissed her knuckles, then dropped her hand. "Come on, we're going for a walk."

"A walk?"

"Along the canal."

"I have to get home."

"It's not that late."

"I have a department meeting tomorrow." She watched him. "Or have you forgotten?"

"I haven't forgotten anything, sweetheart."

Especially what he'd heard Millie say earlier.

It's obvious you care about Mike.

But he didn't bring it up. He didn't want to spook her. Instead, he got out of the car and rounded it; she stayed where she was, so he opened the door, tugged her out.

"Come on, we won't even go inside. We'll just walk a piece."

"All right."

They headed around the back of the house and crossed the twenty yards down to the canal. Moonlight glistened off the water, and a chorus of crickets filled the air. The breeze off the water was cooler here. "It's so different here from Georgia. So much more luscious and picturesque."

"*Picturesque* is quite a word for a jock."

"Yeah, well, if I study the dictionary real hard, I can manage to add a few new ones to my vocabulary."

"I'm sorry, that wasn't a dig. I was teasing…." Jacelyn rubbed her arms up and down. "I'm nervous."

"Nervous? Why?"

"You make me nervous."

He noticed her shiver. "And you're cold." Whipping off the long-sleeved shirt he'd brought along, he said, "Raise your arms."

"Mike, I—"

"Hush, you're cold."

"I can dress myself."

He chuckled. "It's the undressing I'm thinkin' about most of the time."

"That's what makes me nervous."

He froze. "You think I'd do something against your will?"

"No, of course not." She lifted her arms and he slid the shirt over her head. It fell over her full breasts and hit her mid-thigh. When he tugged her hair out of the collar, and came close enough to smell her lemony shampoo, she leaned into him. "I'm worried about my own willpower, I guess."

He met her forehead with his. "Jacey, honey, if you feel that way…"

"Nothing's changed from what we talked about before. If anything, things are worse."

Mike kissed her hair. "Worse, how?"

"We're spending too much time together. I'm feeling more attracted to you every day."

"Is that so?"

"A lot."

"When's the bad news comin'?"

"And I like you."

He drew back and looked down at her. "I like you too, Jacey."

"I'm recommending you to teach in my department tomorrow, Mike. What will it look like to them, and to Lew Cavanaugh, if they find out we're sleeping together after that?"

Stiffening, he pulled away. "This has overtones of bein' ashamed to share a jock's bed."

She grabbed him this time, by the shirt. "No, it doesn't have anything to do with that. It has everything to do with my professional integrity, my professional image. I've spent years building just those things."

"Sorry." He sighed. "That's a hot button with me."

"Why, Mike? You've alluded to it before, but what's behind all this?"

Drawing in a deep breath, he stared out at the canal. "All my life I had to face that stereotype. With teachers. Other kids. Girls...it drove me nuts. And hurt, especially when I cared a lot about the people who acted that way. There was a special woman once, a real smart one, who treated me like her dirty little secret."

"Oh, Mike. I'm sorry. *I* don't think that." She hesitated. "In any case, besides the professional stuff, you'll be gone in a couple of weeks."

She looked so damn cute in his shirt. He wished she was wearing it under other circumstances, that she had nothing on underneath it and they were someplace private and he'd could just... "Yeah, but what a two weeks it would be."

She smiled, which was what he'd hoped for. "Okay, come on. Let's take that walk. After you can go home."

He grasped her hand. She stared up at him, then down when he laced their fingers. "Aw, Jacey, darlin', give me some crumbs."

She grinned. "All right, just so we're straight on the full-course meal."

Leaning over, he whispered, "I'll go to bed thinking about what the dessert could be."

"Stop, or I'm leaving right now."

He did stop the teasing. But he didn't let go of her hand.

CHAPTER EIGHT

KYLE LISTENED idly to Tyler's chatter after he picked up the boy from camp and drove him to Mike's house. Kyle's hands ached from practicing all morning. His heart ached for other reasons.

"Then Kay helped me make this in arts and crafts."

Kyle glanced in the rearview mirror at the football pillow Ty held up. "Yeah, buddy, you told me."

"I like Kay."

So did Kyle. But today even the thought of her didn't cheer him up. "Here we are, Ty."

When he saw his father come out onto the porch, Tyler loosened his seat belt and bounded out of the car, carrying the pillow. Kyle followed him.

Leaning down, Coach caught Ty as he dived for him, and lifted him up in the air. Watching the contact only made Kyle feel worse. His own father had never shown such affection for him.

After Coach fussed over the pillow, he smiled at Kyle. "Hey, kid. How you doin'?"

Just peachy. "Great."

"Thanks for keepin' Ty overnight."

"Thanks for giving me the rest of the day to myself."

"Well, the team's off." Coach held Ty close and kissed his head. "You got a big night to prepare for."

Kyle's chest tightened. "Not so big."

"Your mama said there'll be an auditorium full there tonight."

Minus one. "I guess."

Coach studied him. "Want to sit a spell?"

"I should get back."

"Got to practice?"

"No, I did that all morning. I have to give my hands a rest."

"Then come out back. We'll feed the ducks."

Kyle followed them around the side of the house, watched Ty grab some bread off the back porch, and they all headed down to the canal. He and Coach sank onto a bench, and Tyler crossed to the water.

"Careful, buddy, not too close."

"'Kay, Daddy."

Coach faced him. "What's going on, Kyle?"

He drew in a breath. "Nothing. Of importance, anyway." He stared out at the water. A rowboat passed them by, and across the way there was a lunchtime buzz of activity at a restaurant's outdoor eating area. "You ever been to Aladdin's?"

"No."

"You should go. My mom and I love it."

"I will." Reaching out, he patted Kyle's arm. "Spit it out, you'll feel better."

He was afraid he might cry if he talked about it. But the clamp in his chest just kept getting tighter. And he didn't want to dump this on his mom, who'd said she'd be home after her department meeting.

Coach waited.

Still watching the canal—it was easier if he didn't

look at him—Kyle said, "My dad's not coming to my concert tonight."

"No?"

"At least I think he's not. I haven't heard from him in a while."

"A while?"

"Since that day you brought Ty over to meet us."

"Your daddy hasn't called you in ten days?" Coach sounded shocked.

"It's not the first time. But usually, he jumps at the chance to see me play. Bet he's not coming this time, though."

"Maybe he'll show up."

"God, I hate worrying about this. It breaks my concentration up there. And he's a freakin' music professor. He knows that."

Coach swore.

Shaking his head, Kyle watched Ty this time. "He's mad about what I said to him."

"You could call and apologize."

Kyle's head snapped to the side. "I'm not sorry for what I said."

"No?"

"It's true. He's a lousy father."

"But the only one you got."

"I'm not taking back what I said."

"All right then. Maybe you could just make peace. Say you miss him. Ask him if he's coming tonight."

"I hate begging."

"Yeah, me, too. Sometimes you gotta set your pride aside for what you want, though."

"Maybe." Could it be that easy?

Coach reached in his pocket, got his cell phone and held it out. His smile was so encouraging, so assuring, Kyle took the phone and dialed his father's cell, which he was only supposed to call in case of emergency. His heart beat triple-time in his chest. *Please let him answer.*

He did. "Worthington." Though he sounded irritated.

"Hi, Dad. It's Kyle."

A long pause. "Kyle."

"How are you?"

"Very busy, at the moment."

Translated, *Too busy to talk to you.* The implication made Kyle's throat close up. "Oh, I won't hold you up, then."

He glanced at Mike who was watching him. Mike nodded.

"I was, um, wondering if you were coming tonight to my concert."

"I wasn't under the impression you wanted me there."

Swallowing hard, Kyle glanced again at Coach, who reached over and squeezed his shoulder. Left his hand there. Kyle said, "I want you there, Dad. I mean it."

Another long pause. "Well, I'm afraid it's too late. I've made other plans."

Now he felt as though his father had slapped him. "Other plans? You knew about the date all summer."

"Yes, I did. As I said, it didn't appear as if you wanted me there. So Stephanie and I are busy elsewhere."

Stephanie, the current young girlfriend. Kyle couldn't talk around the lump in his throat.

After a moment, his father said, "Kyle? Did you hear me?"

"Yeah, Dad, I heard you loud and clear. I guess I'll see you around." He clicked off.

He couldn't look at Coach. And he didn't have to say anything, because Coach swore again as he took the phone.

Feeling his eyes sting, Kyle bolted off the bench and crossed to the water. Oh, God. He felt the tears spill over. He swiped at his face but they wouldn't stop.

Then he felt a hand on his shoulder again. "I'm sorry, Kyle."

He couldn't say anything.

"Adults, sometimes they're stupid with kids. There are all sorts of power plays, and some parents think they can behave any way they want with their children."

"He…" Kyle hiccupped. "He just doesn't care about me."

"He cares," Coach said, clasping Kyle's other shoulder, too. It felt good. "As much as he can. Some people have limits on their affection. It's no reflection on you, or your mama."

"That's what Mom says." He choked out the words.

"It's true. He's a fool to distance himself from a terrific kid like you."

That did it. The sobs came, deep from his belly. It just hurt too much to keep inside.

He felt Coach tug on his arm. He tried to resist, but Coach was strong enough to turn him around and drag Kyle to his chest.

Kyle hung on like a little boy. And cried like a girl. He couldn't stop himself. It didn't last long, thank God. He became aware of Coach rubbing his back, murmuring something. Finally he could pull back. He swallowed hard and looked up at Mike. "This is so lame. I'm embarrassed."

"For cryin' when somebody rips your heart out?"

Kyle felt a tug on his shorts. He looked down to see Ty there, staring at him wide-eyed. "Daddy says it's okay to cry. His *players* do."

That made Kyle smile. "I guess it's okay, if his players do it."

Coach grinned. "I'm sorry, Kyle. There's no way to make this better. It sucks like a bucket of ticks."

Kyle stared at Coach. "There's something you could do that would help," he said without letting himself think about what he was going to ask.

"You want me to go beat him up?"

Kyle felt a grin tug at his lips. "No, I want you and Ty to come to my concert."

A huge smile spread across Coach's face. "Why, we'd be honored." He ruffled Kyle's hair. "Someday, we're gonna be able to say we knew you when."

Kyle swallowed hard. "Thanks."

"I can come, too?" Ty asked.

Kyle reached down and put his hand on the boy's shoulder. Coach reached out and put his on Kyle's. And suddenly, the day seemed a little brighter.

JACELYN BEGAN the meeting. "We'll start by confirming our schedules and time frames. As you know, the course selections are all in for next semester, except for any drops or adds after the term begins. I know Lew has met with those of you whose workload has been affected by the lower enrollment numbers." She scanned the room. "Mainly you, Craig, and you, Sara."

Sara Minton smiled. "I don't mind not teaching the Business Law course this semester. It needs to be revamped, anyway, as it's become too general for our needs. But…" She shrugged. "I wish there was some other class for me. Money will be tight."

"I'm sorry."

"Combined with the loss of summer-school pay," Craig put in. "It's a problem for me, too."

"I don't know what to say, Craig."

"We've all been through this," a teacher in Business Education put in. "Things have an ebb and flow."

"That's right. You were short a course two years in a row, weren't you, Pat?"

"Yep. Now we have an overflow." He smiled. "Go figure."

Jacelyn turned to Jake Lansing, who'd sat back and watched the proceedings. "Jake, would you like to make your proposal now?"

"Yeah, sure." He smiled as he faced the department. "We have a course next semester that's going to be taught by outside personnel. It's called Sports Stakeholders. It will examine the interaction of athlete, coach, owner, business and media."

Jacelyn listened as he described the curriculum. Some of the staff seemed interested, a few rolled their eyes. "And I'd like to propose Mike Kingston teach it."

Craig leaned forward. "I object to some dumb jock teaching in our department."

Lansing's face hardened. "I resent that term."

"I resent your ridiculous program taking away my income."

"That's enough, both of you." Jacelyn purposely kept

her voice calm. "Craig, Lew Cavanaugh wants the Bulls in this program. We don't have much choice."

"Just Lew Cavanaugh?"

"What's that supposed to mean?"

"You want them, too. Particularly Kingston."

"I think Coach Kingston will be an asset to our staff. His expertise will go a long way with the kids."

"His charm doesn't hurt."

"Excuse me, I don't understand that remark."

"Never mind, Jacelyn. We all got the message. The jocks are taking our income, as well as making their own millions."

Lansing leaned forward. "Last I heard, this college supported the Sports Studies program and agreed to have the Bulls' summer camp here. I was told the administration wanted the Bulls as guest lecturers and adjuncts."

"You're right, Jake." Sara Minton spoke up. "Most of us supported you and the team." She threw a disgusted look at Craig. "Others didn't. As Lew Cavanaugh said, this is all good for the college." She smiled at Jacelyn. "I think your idea to hire Kingston is a good one."

All but two others agreed. Finally, the tense meeting was over.

And Jacelyn was furious. "I'd like you to stay, Craig," she said gritting her teeth.

He faced her squarely. "Sure."

When everyone left, she pivoted her chair to the right. "Exactly what were you implying during the meeting?"

"I think it was obvious."

"You meant it to be obvious to everybody. But just in case I misunderstood, spell it out for me."

"It's no secret you're hot for the Coach."

"What?"

"You're not really protesting, are you?"

"I don't have to protest."

"You were seen being carried across campus by him."

She hated defending herself. "I hurt my foot and couldn't walk."

"Hal found him asleep on your couch."

"Is Hal behind this gossip?"

Craig reddened. He knew better than to imply that. "No, of course not. He talked to me right after you gave him the boot."

"What *is* this, junior high?"

"Don't look at me. I'm not the one mooning over some football player."

She counted to ten. "I'll say this once. My decision to ask Coach Kingston to be an adjunct is based on professional reasons only."

"I don't hear a denial about the personal stuff."

"I don't owe you a confirmation or a denial, Craig."

He stood then, his face flushed. "Maybe not me. But you sure as hell are accountable to Lew Cavanaugh." His look was sly. "Of course, if you'd appoint me to teach one of those Sports Studies classes, I might not feel the need to go to Lew. I could do the Stats one. Then one of the other Sports Studies guys could pick up the Stakeholders thing and we wouldn't need Kingston."

"Are you blackmailing me?"

"Is the course mine?"

"No."

"Fine." He turned and stalked out, calling over his shoulder, "This isn't over."

Jacelyn was stunned. Had he actually threatened her? She couldn't believe it. Standing, she went back to her desk and started to input numbers into her computer. It was slow going as her mind kept reverting to Craig's comments. She wondered if everybody in the school was talking about her. Should she go to Lew herself? No, that would give Craig's remarks credence.

An hour later there was a knock on her door. She glanced up to find Lew in the doorway. "Well," she said, "that didn't take long."

"YOU LOOK real spiffy there, young man." Mike smiled at his son's outfit as they left the car and headed toward Hochstein's music hall.

"We match, Daddy," Tyler said taking his hand. Mike's heart melted when the boy did things like that. He loved being a father.

His thoughts catapulted to Kyle, and Kyle's dad. What the hell was wrong with the guy? Sure, Mike had been an absent father to Tyler for a lot of years, but that was because Trudy had wanted it that way. And because they'd never been married. Still, he'd had the boy regularly during the off-season and on vacations when Trudy would let him.

Tyler was chattering on, cute as a button in his dark slacks, white T-shirt and the navy blazer Mike had just bought him today. Mike's shirt was silk, but otherwise they were twins. All dressed up for Kyle's concert.

There's something you could do that would help... come to my concert.

"You know, sport, you gotta be real quiet tonight here."

"Okay."

"You ever been to a music performance, Ty?"

"Nope, you?"

"Can't say I have."

Jeez, he was culturally deficient. Jacelyn probably spent most of her life in concert halls. They were so different, he was constantly amazed that he wanted her so bad.

Inside the building, he realized they were early. Thinking about whether to look for her, try to sit with her—probably not a good idea—Mike ushered Ty into the auditorium. It was a good size, with graded seating of about sixty rows up and as many seats wide. He didn't spot Jacelyn, so he decided that was a sign. "Come on, Ty, let's sit in that—"

"There's Dr. Ross." The kid took off like a bullet. So much for good sense.

Mike followed him, and reached Jacelyn's row in time to see Ty launch himself at her. And in time to see her hug his son tightly. "Hey, little guy. What are you doing here?"

"Came to see Kyle play."

"Oh!" Her look was full of pleasure. Suddenly he wanted—real bad—to keep that expression on her face. "It's so sweet of you to come."

"Can't miss the grand performance." Mike smiled at Eric who sat next to Jacelyn. "How you doin', buddy?"

"Terrific. Nice of you to come."

He said hello to Kay, and nodded to the seats on the other side of Jacelyn. "These taken?"

"Not now. I was saving them for Millie, and…" Her voice trailed off. "Never mind. Millie called my cell to say one of her boys is sick. So the seats are free. Sit down."

They sat, with Ty between them.

Jacelyn tousled Ty's hair. "You look pretty handsome tonight, young man," she said smiling. But Mike noted lines of strain around her face. Had something happened, or was it just because jerk-head Worthington hadn't shown? He couldn't say anything though. He'd promised Kyle he wouldn't.

Um, Coach, don't tell Mom about this. It'll just upset her, and Dad already does that enough.

They made small talk until the concert began. There were three featured artists playing with the Philharmonic—on the violin, the trumpet and the piano. Kyle was last. Mike settled in.

He tried to concentrate on the music, and not think about Jacelyn. The program was halfway through when Ty started to squirm. "Maybe I should take him out," he whispered to Jacelyn in between solos.

"No! Wanna sit on Dr. Ross's lap."

"You'll get her pretty dress all wrinkled, Champ." And it *was* pretty—pink sleeveless silk that melded to her form.

"No, he won't." Jacelyn reached out and took Tyler onto her lap. He cuddled into her.

Just before Kyle's performance, Tyler fell asleep in Jacelyn's lap. Mike tried to take him so she could enjoy her son's time on stage, but she shook her head. She seemed to like having his boy there. Mike watched as she brushed his head with her lips.

Hell of a thing to be jealous of your own kid!

Mike was distracted from Jacelyn when Kyle began

to play. The music took possession of the air, filled it, dominated every inch of the auditorium. He couldn't tear his eyes away from Kyle, who was a regular maestro on stage.

The audience was impressed, too. When Kyle's performance ended, everybody stood. Mike took Tyler from Jacelyn, and she stood, too. It was then he saw that she was crying.

Ty woke up, of course. He hugged his father sleepily. When the applause died down, he asked, "How come Dr. Ross's crying?"

"Because I'm happy, sweetie."

"Is that why Kyle was crying this morning, Daddy?"

THEY ALWAYS went to Phillip's European Restaurant for dessert after a concert. Kyle invited his uncle and the Kingstons to join them; Eric begged off but Tyler wanted to go, so there was little Jacelyn could do about spending more time with Mike. In any case, she wanted to know what Tyler's comment had referred to.

All in all, she was feeling pretty raw. She was still reeling from her talk with Craig, then Lew. And, of course, there was the fact that she felt like a hypocrite—she *was* hot for the coach. On top of everything, Neil hadn't come to the concert. When she'd asked Kyle, as casually as she could, if he'd talked to his father, he'd said yes, and Neil wouldn't be attending. He'd also said he didn't want to discuss it.

When the kids went to check out the dessert case, she said to Mike, "I need to talk to you."

"I reckon you do."

"Kyle's got his car."

"Best you drop by my house after dessert. I'll put Ty to bed and we can talk then."

She hesitated about being alone with him, but this couldn't wait. "Fine."

Dessert was fun and Kyle was lighthearted the entire time. She was grateful to Mike and Tyler who were obviously making up for Neil's absence. Usually when his father pulled a stunt like this, Kyle couldn't get over his hurt feelings. Neil had ruined many evenings for them.

When Kyle left to drive Kay home and the Kingstons took off, Jacelyn waited about ten minutes in her car, then drove to Mike's house. He was on the front porch, on the old wooden swing that seated two.

"Is Ty asleep?" she asked, coming onto the porch.

"Conked out on the way home and never woke up." He motioned to the swing. "Sit."

She did, next to him. And was assaulted by his presence. He'd removed his sports coat, and the white shirt stretched tautly across his chest. He smelled all male. Because of his size, he stretched his legs out and rested his arm across the back of the swing, but didn't touch her. "What's goin' on?" he asked.

"A lot of things. First, why was Kyle crying this morning?"

"I, um, I can't tell you, Jacey."

"Why?"

"He brought Ty back around noon and I could tell he was upset. After he, um, told me some stuff, he asked me not to share it with you."

That hurt. "I'm his mother!"

Mike kicked the swing back and forth. "Now don't

get all hot and bothered, darlin'. Sometimes a guy's gotta vent, and he doesn't wanna do it on somebody that'll hurt as much as he's hurting, if you get my drift."

Her chest unclenched. "I get your drift. It was because Neil didn't come to the concert tonight."

"Well, now, if I could betray a confidence, I'd probably confirm that."

"That's why you and Ty came tonight."

"Hell, no. We came to hear the next Liberace."

Jacelyn smiled.

He tipped her chin. "That's good to see."

"What?"

"That smile."

"There hasn't been much to smile about today. I'm so mad at Neil."

"I'm none too happy with him myself. He's a first-class jerk, Jacey. I'm sorry."

"Me, too, for Kyle."

"That boy's a gem." When she didn't say more, Mike asked, "What else happened today?"

"Well, first the good news. I need to meet with you tomorrow formally. To offer you an adjunct position in the Sports Studies program."

"So it went okay? With the department?"

"Partly."

"What does that mean?"

She explained her encounter with Craig Anderson.

Mike swore. "I'm sorry. I keep causing you trouble."

"He went to Lew Cavanaugh."

"What?"

"Made the same complaints."

"To the president of your college. God, this was just what you wanted to avoid."

"Lew was a perfect gentleman, though."

Jacelyn, I want you to know about the complaint lodged against you. I also want you to tell me you're not involved with Mike Kingston.

"What did you say to Cavanaugh?"

"I lied."

"What?"

"I told him I wasn't hot for the wide receiver coach of the Bulls."

"You told the president *that?*"

"Actually, those were Craig's words. In milder terms, I assured Lew there was nothing unprofessional going on between you and me."

"Well, except for a couple of slipups, there isn't."

"Nor will there be, Mike."

"Yeah, I'm beginning to get that. What did Cavanaugh say?"

"He said he'd hate to see me ruin my reputation at Beckett for a summer fling."

"Ouch."

"I'm sorry. I did make it clear to Lew I wouldn't have anyone dictate to me who I was friends with. That you and Ty were a part of Kyle's life and nobody had the right to tell me I couldn't see both of you."

"Good."

"Good?"

"Well, not really good." Mike ran a hand through his hair. "I want you in my bed, Jacey."

"Oh, God." Hearing it so bluntly put, she froze for a minute, then started to get up. "I have to go."

"Wait!" He held her arm. "What I meant was, I want you there, but I won't pressure you. I won't flirt anymore, tease you anymore." He ducked his head. "Steal any more kisses."

She swallowed hard. She was going to miss that. "I appreciate that. Can you come see me tomorrow at school, to formalize the offer?"

"Sure."

"Then would you do me a favor?"

"Anything."

"Stay away from me for a few days."

"So nobody talks?"

"No." Jacelyn stood, needing to put some distance between them. "So I can get my equilibrium back."

"Sure thing, darlin'."

She stared at him for a minute, then circled around and descended the porch steps. Halfway down the walk, she looked back. He'd come to the railing and was gripping the post, watching her. "This isn't what I want, you know," she said starkly.

"Me neither. But we don't have much choice."

"Good night. And thanks for what you did for Kyle. I'll never forget it."

CHAPTER NINE

As HE WATCHED Johnny Turk hotdog it on the Ohio field in the scrimmage against Cleveland, Mike gripped the clipboard until his knuckles turned white. "What the hell does he think he's doin' out there?" Though his tone was curt, his words were quietly uttered.

"His girlfriend's in the stands." This from Marcus, who stood next to Mike, also assessing the play.

The July sun beamed down on them, a pleasant counterpoint to the blood boiling inside Mike.

"What's eating at you, Coach?"

He shot a quick glance to Marc. "Nothin'. Why?"

"You've been—what do women call it—*remote* and *distant* all week."

Tim Mason sent in another play and Mike watched Turk try to sidestep some cornerbacks. One circled behind him, waiting to tackle him if he caught the ball, or catch the pass if it was overthrown. Mike yelled, "Behind you, Turk."

It didn't matter anyway. Turk missed the throw, tipping it out of bounds.

He swore to himself. "Get ready to go in, Marc."

"I'm ready." When Mike didn't pick up the conversation, Marcus did. "The guys are calling you by your old nickname."

The Cool King. Even in his playing days, Mike rarely lost his temper; instead he turned inward and froze everybody out when he was mad or frustrated. His teammates and coaches used to respect that. It had worried the hell out of the players once he'd turned coach himself. When he was in one of those moods, everybody gave him a wide berth.

All week, except when he was with Ty and Kyle, he'd kept to himself. He was steely. Unfriendly. And mad as hell at the world. Because, true to his promise, he hadn't spent any time with Jacey. She'd asked him to stay away and he had. He'd changed the game plan, and come up with an alternative strategy. Just get the hell through the rest of this summer camp and then skip town.

It was hard, though, since they'd met up a few times....

First for the formal offer to be an adjunct next semester.

Congratulations, Mike. I know this is what you want. I thought it was.

Then one afternoon, he'd picked Tyler up at the pool in the subdivision where Kyle lived. He didn't know Jacey had gone with them and, from the expression on her face, she obviously hadn't realized he'd be coming for his son. He could have gone his whole life without seeing her in a bathing suit, thank you very much. Though it was a simple one-piece red thing, with little cutouts at the top, it rode high on her legs and shot his blood pressure to kingdom come.

He'd also bumped into her at school twice. Both times they'd been polite and phony with each other.

The pencil he held in one hand broke in two.

"Something wrong, Coach?"

He glanced over to see Gage standing next to him. Gage who was hot and heavy with Millie these days. She was coming to the scrimmage with her boys.

After he sent Marc in, he looked over at his friend. "I'm pissed at the new kid, is all." Even to his own ears, his excuse sounded lame. "Seriously considering cutting him."

"Uh-huh."

Silence. Bring on the Cool King.

Gage watched the play, wincing when the quarterback got sacked hard. "He'll need work," Gage said dryly.

"Yeah. Hope it doesn't cut into your love life."

Instead of getting mad, Gage laughed. "You got it bad, buddy."

"Don't know what you're talkin' about."

"You're jealous as hell of Millie and me."

Mike glanced at Gage. No sense in lying to a good friend. "Yeah, I reckon I am."

"She's here."

"You said she was coming."

"I don't mean Millie."

"Huh?"

Gage handed Mike binoculars and pointed to the area of the bleachers where coaches' and players' families sat. "Look over there."

Through the lenses, Mike scanned the section. He saw Marcus's wife, who was watching Tyler, since he'd flown down with Mike. Millie and her boys.

And Kyle? How'd he get here? He looked to the kid's right. "Holy hell. Jacey's here."

Gage snorted. "Like I said, you got it bad."

Mike just stared at the bleachers.

JACEY COULD SWEAR Mike was watching her from across the field. For the hundredth time she wondered what she was doing in Cleveland, Ohio, at a preseason Bulls scrimmage. She'd asked Mike to stay away, and he'd honored her wishes. She'd tried to stay away from him, too. But when Kyle had badgered her to take him to the game, and Millie had coaxed her to come along, she'd weakened and agreed to attend the out-of-town competition because she'd been utterly miserable all week.

"I think he's seen you," Millie said from next to her.

"Oh, well…" She kept staring.

Gage waved, but Mike turned away.

She wasn't surprised. He'd been cold and distant every time she'd run into him this week.

Ty's coming on the plane with me Saturday. It'd be right nice if Kyle could come, too.

When?

The night before.

He can't. He has a recital.

Are you tryin' to keep him away from me, Jacey?

No, I'd never do that. He cares about you and Tyler.

She'd had to bite her tongue to keep from saying, *I do, too.*

Every day, like some silly schoolgirl, she'd watched him—from where she couldn't be seen—take his run around the track after camp was over or before it started. She'd also watched him coaching and demonstrating techniques for the guys. He was a good leader. Players listened to him. He didn't lose his temper, throw things or scream.

And every night, she slipped into his Bulls shirt for bed. She'd worn it home after they'd walked by the canal and hadn't returned it. No wonder she couldn't stop thinking about him.

Talk had died down about his teaching in the program. Craig had apologized to her for flying off the handle. Lew Cavanaugh never brought it up again. For all purposes, her life was back to normal—except for time she spent with Tyler, which she treasured.

During her musings, the Bulls won the scrimmage.

"Hey, Mom, wasn't that great?" Kyle had Ty by the hand.

She smiled. "Yes, I enjoyed it."

He raised his brows. "Who are you and what have you done with my mother?"

"Stop! I had fun. I just wish Eric could have come." Her brother had had to take care of his daughters this weekend while his wife was away on business.

"I'm real glad they looked good out there. Coach has been weirding out all week. I think he was worried."

Tyler let go of Kyle's hand and went to stand by Jacelyn. He leaned into her and wrapped an arm around her waist. "My daddy's a good coach."

Jacey hugged him to her. "Yes, Tyler, he is. He's a good man."

The boy looked up at her with his owl eyes. "You coming to dinner with us?"

"Me? No, honey, I'm going with Kyle and my friends."

Kyle straightened. "Listen, Mom, we got a plan. The Smiths are going to the Rainforest Café. They want you and me to come. And since Ty's never seen it, we're gonna ask Coach if they could go with us."

"And we're gonna have a sleepover." This from Tyler.

"A what?"

Kyle faced her. "It was Ty's idea, Mom. Remember how me and Ron and Timmy used to have sleepovers? We were tellin' Ty about it and he said he wished we could have one tonight. The Smiths thought it would be fun to do again—just like old times. So we all want to stay in Millie's room, and she could bunk with you. That way it'd be just us guys chillin'."

Jacelyn sought out Millie's gaze, and her friend nodded. "Fine by me."

"Oh, okay. But I think I'll pass on dinner. I'll go to the hotel and get room service there."

Just then Mike and Gage jogged across the field and came up to where Jacelyn and the boys stood at the bottom of the bleachers. Mike looked so good up close, his hair windblown, his color high. Both men wore khaki slacks and the team's blue-collared polo shirts.

Gage went to Millie's youngest and headlocked him. "What'd you think, Tiger?"

"It was awesome, Gage."

Leaning over, Mike squeezed Tyler's shoulder. "Hey, guys." He smiled warmly at Kyle. "I thought you couldn't come."

"Mom drove me up."

"Your recital go good?"

"Yeah, great."

Mike finally looked at Jacelyn. "This is a surprise."

"I gave in to Kyle's pleading."

His gaze turned cool. "Oh, I see."

"I wanted to catch the game, too, Coach." She tried for a smile. "You were pretty good out there."

"Thanks." He asked Ty, "So, what d'you wanna do tonight, buddy?"

"Can we go to the Rainforest Café, Daddy, with Millie and the guys?"

Mike looked at Millie for confirmation.

She shrugged. "They have it all worked out."

"Sure, if it's fine with y'all."

"Now we just gotta convince Mom to go with us."

"Really, I…"

"Please, Mommy." Kyle swung an arm around her shoulder, and played the wheedling little boy.

It sounded silly to protest, since she really had no excuse. And in her heart, she wanted to go with them. "All right, I'll come."

Mike held her gaze a moment then said, "Great. Just great."

"COME SEE the Talking Tree, Jacey." Once in the restaurant Tyler reached out to take her hand, but Mike held him back.

"Hey, little guy. It's *Dr. Ross*."

Jacelyn smiled weakly. "I said he could call me that. Or at least *what his daddy calls me*. He asked last week. We seem to all be past the formality stage."

They sure as hell were past formalities. Especially since Mike couldn't stop thinking about the way she'd felt leaning into him at the canal, sitting next to him in the swing, the kiss in the laundry room…

Damn, he had to stop this.

"If it's okay with you."

Jacey nodded, stood and followed the boys to the huge tree in the center of the dining room that talked to patrons about saving the planet. She wore simple beige cotton slacks and a button-down navy shirt with a matching sweater thrown over her shoulders.

Mike wondered what she had on underneath. Something as sexy as the garter belt, he'd bet.

"Hey, Coach, where are you?" Garrison asked.

Thinking about things I shouldn't. "Nowhere." He sipped his beer. "The guys were lookin' pretty good today. How's Watson's ankle?"

"Healing," Gage said. "He'll be ready to train next week."

They discussed more of the players and their conditioning. Finally Mike realized the tangent they'd gone off on. "Sorry, Millie, this is probably boring as hell to you."

"No, not at all. Every day I pick up tidbits for my Psychology of Sports course."

"You just using me for that class, babe?" Gage grinned.

"And other things."

"How's it going with the faculty these days?" Mike asked.

"Pretty quiet." She glanced to where Jacelyn stood by the tree with Tyler. Kyle was taking a picture of them. "Talk's died down, if that's what you mean."

He ducked his head. He hated discussing this with someone other than Jacey. "It is. I'm glad."

Mike watched the boys wander around while they waited for their food. Water dripped from numerous fountains, and in several tanks around the room, fish darted and cruised. He caught sight of Jacelyn approaching the table.

"That tree is so cool. Kyle took pictures." She sat down. "They're having a good time."

"So I see." Mike frowned. "What's all this about the boys spending the night together?"

"It was Ty's idea," Millie said. "After Kyle told him the three of them used to have sleepovers when they were younger." At Mike's hesitation, she added, "They're all great kids, Coach. They'll watch over him."

"It's not that. He has nightmares since his mother died. Though there have been a lot fewer, lately."

"Kyle knows how to handle those, Mike," Jacey put in. "Ty's more than ready to do this."

"Okay, sure."

She smiled.

Millie asked, "What time are you driving back tomorrow, Jace?"

"Early. I'd like to run some preliminary numbers on the Outreach allotment at home."

"When are you meeting with Ed Dickinson to finalize the amount?"

"Next week. It's just a formality, though."

"What are we talking about?" Gage wanted to know.

"The Alumni Association provides half of the Outreach funds for scholarships."

Gage asked about the Outreach Center, and how she and Jacelyn had come to be in charge. Mike was interested to listen to a little bit of her past. He learned she'd gone to Beckett on a scholarship and Millie had paid for school by working and with grants and school aid.

"Did I see you and Lansing with an alumni guy this week?" Gage asked Mike.

"Yeah, as team liaison, I wanted to talk about some internships. Alumni are always a big asset to a Sports Studies program, especially getting placements for the kids."

"Which you're a part of, I hear," Millie said. "Congratulations, by the way."

"Thanks." Though, right now, it was a hollow victory. He felt a little like the time he'd run in the winning touchdown for a game, but his best friend on the team had gotten hurt on a tackle and never played football again.

Staring over at Jacelyn, he could see she felt the same.

MILLIE CAME OUT of the bathroom, fully dressed. In her hand, she held a duffel bag. "I'm not sleeping here tonight."

Jacelyn looked up from one of the two double beds, where she sat leafing through a hotel magazine. "No?"

"I'm staying with Gage."

"Ah, I see."

Watching Jacelyn, Millie cocked her head. "You don't approve."

Jacelyn sighed. "It's not that. Never. Besides, the only thing I'd worry about is your boys…"

"Finding out I'm shacking up with a jock?"

"Was that a slam at me?"

"Sort of." Millie came to the bed and dropped down on the edge. "I worry that you gave Mike up for the wrong reason."

"It's so complicated, Millie. And murky now."

"I suppose it is." She nodded to the door. "As far as the boys finding out where I slept, they're on a different floor, and I told them to call my cell if there was a problem. It's a risk I'm willing to take." When Jacelyn didn't respond—jealousy was clogging her throat—Millie took her hand. "You know, Jace, when Tom died, I regretted so much of what I didn't do with him. That's what happens when you lose someone you love. You regret the things you didn't do, not the things you did."

"I understand." She squeezed her friend's hand, sensing Millie needed to talk. "What do you regret not doing?"

Her grin was girlish. "When we were dating, Tom wanted to have sex about six months before I said yes. I was crazy about him, but afraid of it. Then when we were first married, there was this obgyn convention in Cancun. He wanted me to go, but Ronny was little and I was afraid to leave him with my parents." Her look was sad. "And sometimes, I wish I'd had another baby."

Jacelyn remembered the conversation she'd had with Mike, on her bed, about the very same thing.

"I vowed after Tom's death that I wouldn't waste any time if I fell in love again."

"Are you in love with Gage?"

"No. I've only known him a few weeks. But I like him. He's smart and funny and handsome as all get out. His wife died five years ago, so we have a lot in common." She stood then, and faced Jacelyn. "And he's great in bed."

Jacelyn laughed. "Well, there you go."

Millie grinned again. "You have choices about Mike, you know."

"Yes, I know, and I made them."

"Sometimes choices are wrong and we need to regroup."

Jacelyn swallowed hard. "I've been miserable."

"Gage says Mike has been, too."

"I know, I can tell."

"Well, think about it." Millie wiggled her brows. "While I'm off having hot sex." She rolled her eyes.

"Who would have thought at forty-five I'd feel like a teenager again."

"It's nice. Now go. Don't keep your beau waiting."

"I'll be in room 435."

"All right."

At the door, Millie turned to look out over her shoulder. "It's right next to Mike's room—437, in case you're interested."

"Go, Millicent."

After Millie left, Jacelyn wandered around the room. It was ten at night and she was restless. She tried watching TV but the male lead on a movie reminded her too much of Mike. She tried reading, but had only brought a romance novel. What had she been thinking? Finally, she ran bath water, pinned up her hair and climbed in. The heat was soothing. The water stroked her skin. Closing her eyes, she imagined Mike's hands on her. Imagined *him* stroking her, touching her, making love with her.

She'd bet her PhD *he* was great in bed, too.

MIKE WAS like a caged tiger, prowling the room. He forced himself to calm down; flopping onto the mattress, he sipped a beer and turned on the TV. Blindly, he flipped through the channels with the remote. He settled on a showing of *Shane.*

But he couldn't get Jacelyn out of his mind. It wouldn't be so bad if he wasn't alone. If he didn't know she was by herself right down the hall. If she hadn't looked so good after the game with her hair all windblown and her cheeks ruddy. If she hadn't stared at him at dinner as if she wanted him for dessert. Settling back into a mound of pillows, he told himself her welfare came first. He was leaving town in less than two weeks. His life was in Buckland, and he traveled a lot. How could he ask her to have that summer fling Cavanaugh talked about, then go on his merry way, leaving her to do damage control back in Rockford?

Then again, could he let her go completely? Could he bear to see her next spring when he came up to teach his course? She'd probably be dating someone else. Making love with a Beckett guy.

This was a no-win situation.

There was a knock on the door. Mike frowned and put the beer down. The kids had said they'd call if something was wrong, but still... He bounded off the bed, crossed to the door and whipped it open.

And there she stood wearing a light raincoat. From the top peeked some peachy-colored satin. Oh, God. He looked into her face. It was glowing with anticipation. Still, he had to think of her first. "Jacey, you don't want to do this."

"Oh, yes, Mike, I do."

All his good intentions flew out the proverbial window. He dragged her inside and slammed the door shut. A hot tide of passion rose up within him, making his whole body vibrate. He pressed her into the wall and took her mouth. It was as demanding as his. He devoured her; she consumed him.

Mike fumbled with the buttons on her coat. When it fell to the floor, his hands closed over her breasts and she gave a long, low, lusty moan. He kneaded her, plumped her, reveled in her. His hands slid over the watery-silk feel of whatever the hell she had on and found the supple flesh of her bottom; it was covered in the same satiny material. He dragged her close, her middle meeting his. She arched into him, short-circuiting his senses. His lips left hers and went to her neck. She mirrored his actions, and took a bite out of his shoulder. A jolt of lust shot through him.

"Jacey, oh, darlin'."

"I want this so much," she murmured. "I want you."

"Not nearly as much as I want you." He slid the straps off her shoulders. "You're sure?" he asked, kissing the bare flesh there.

"Absolutely."

He drew back. "What will…"

Her fingers came up to his mouth. "Shh, no questions. No *talk*. Let's just do this."

He chuckled. "You got a real romantic streak, sweetheart."

She practically climbed up him. He gripped her bottom and lifted her; she circled her legs around him. "Please, Mike. I want this."

"Then let me at you." He stumbled to the bed. Because she was kissing his chest, grinding against him, he dropped her a little too fast onto the mattress. Hungry desire coursed through him as she stretched out. The peach thing slipped, revealing the creamy swell of her breasts. Her hair was a wild tangle from his hands. He wanted her with a primitive intensity.

Mike bent one knee on the bed and closed a hand over her throat—trailed it down to the top she wore. "This is real pretty, love, but I wanna see you. Lift up."

She raised her arms and he slid the camisole off. The sight that greeted him made his stomach clench. He cupped her breasts, then bent over and took a nipple in his mouth. Still kneeling on the bed, he slid his hands beneath her and drew off the satiny matching pants. Then he straightened.

"You are by far the most beautiful thing I ever laid eyes on. I got a notion just to stare at you all night."

"Mike." She reached for his shorts. He moved in close so she had better access. The navy briefs he wore were tight, hitting him at the thigh. Jacelyn tugged. Harder. When the waistband reached his erection, she freed him. He was heavy with need, and kicked off the boxers the rest of the way. She drew in her breath when she saw him, then clasped him in a strong, sensuous grip.

His breath left him then. "Honey, don't. I been wantin' this so long, I'm gonna go off like a shotgun."

Still she stroked him till he forced her hand away. Turning, he hurried to the bathroom for one of the condoms he carried in his shaving kit. Back at the bed, he tried to put it on, but his hands were clumsy. She giggled.

"Like what you do to me, woman?"

"Oh, yeah."

He couldn't remember ever being this needy. Finally, he sheathed himself, stretched out on the bed, covered her—and showed her what she did to him.

She took his mouth. He took hers.

And then things spun out of control.

"WHAT MADE you come here?" Mike asked.

She was in his arms, naked, sated and so pliable she wanted to weep. "Not one thing exactly." She kissed his chest. It was rock-hard, sprinkled with hair and slick with sweat. "I've been so sad all week."

"Me, too. Not being with you tore me up but good." He drew lazy circles on her back. "I was shocked as hell to see you at the game. You said Kyle talked you into it."

"He didn't have to talk very hard."

He kissed her head. "We gonna discuss where we go from here?"

"I have no idea where we go from here." She came up on her elbows, draping herself over him. "But let's not talk about it now. I just want to enjoy being with you." Reaching down, she let her hand float over his ribs, flirt with his stomach, go lower and brush his groin. He was half aroused already.

He kissed her nose. His face was relaxed, his shoulders, too. But there was something in his eyes. "So, it's just sex?" He meant his tone to be teasing, but Jacelyn heard the underlying anxiety in it.

"Making love with you was wonderful, Mike. Special. Different." She smiled sweetly. "It wasn't just sex."

Meeting her forehead with his, he swallowed hard. "I'm real glad."

"Me, too."

CHAPTER TEN

JACELYN AND Mike had been back from Cleveland for three days but hadn't seen each other, though they'd spoken on the phone every night. She had, however, spent time with his son. They always had fun together, like now.

"Okay, sweetie, let's try it again." Jacelyn reset the CD and turned to Tyler. His deep-brown eyes reminded her of warm hot chocolate. "You're doing great, buddy."

"Wait till my daddy sees." He grinned and placed his little hand in hers. "Rock Around the Clock" blasted from the stereo. That song was the easiest to swing dance to, so she'd put it on for Ty when he'd shyly asked her to teach him how to do that dance like Kyle and she did it.

"Your daddy will be proud, all right."

They began to jitterbug. Tyler had a sense of grace and innate rhythm, like his father. Unlike Mike, though, he picked up the dance moves easily. Enjoying herself, she taught him to step lightly, sway in to one side, then the next. She showed him how to turn, do a twirl over his head, slide her arm along his back. When he got the gist of it, he giggled like the seven-year-old he was.

"Okay, Champ, time to stop fooling around and get

down to some serious business." Kyle had come to the door, smiling at the two of them. "These days Mom's spending more time with you than I am."

Tyler laughed. "You guys are fun."

"Yeah, well we gotta get going. Kay's waiting in the car."

Jacelyn looked down at the boy. "You sure you want to do this, Ty?"

"Yes, ma'am. We get to sleep in a tent, build a camp-fire, and cook marshmallows." Tyler looked thoughtful. "It's okay my daddy couldn't come."

The camp Kyle attended in the mornings was hav-ing an overnight for kids and parents; Mike couldn't go with Ty because he had practice early the next day and a strategy session late this afternoon.

Leave the night for me, darlin', he'd said sexily when he'd told Jacelyn he wouldn't be going on the trip but would finally have an evening free. The summer train-ing camp lasted only one more week and the players and coaches had a full schedule. She knew he was running on caffeine and junk food.

What would she do when the camp was over? By tacit agreement, they hadn't talked about that. They also hadn't discussed keeping their relationship a secret, though neither had told the kids. The issue of being seen together hadn't come up since there had been no op-portunities to go out. They were having dinner with Millie and Gage Friday night, but no one had talked about where they were going.

After Kyle and Tyler left, Jacelyn checked messages on her cell phone. One was from Ed Dickinson; the alumni president asked for a meeting tomorrow. She called him back and set up the time with his secretary for afternoon.

The second call was from the registrar at school. Denise was a friend, and Jacelyn greeted her warmly when she called back.

"Hi, Jacelyn. I've been trying to reach Kyle about the changes he made in his schedule and can't get him by cell."

"I didn't know he'd changed his schedule."

"Well, he did. But we have no idea to what, because of a computer glitch. It's probably just a time switch, or maybe a different teacher. Have him call me."

Jacelyn made a notation on the pad by her phone for Kyle to call the registrar. Ripping off the paper, she went upstairs to put it on the desk in his room, but stopped in the doorway. It was a young man's room, now. She remembered when his private space had been decorated with action figures—He-Man, Ninja Turtles and X-Men. For years, the big yellow Wolverine had stared down at her every time she'd read Kyle a story.

Now, different posters graced the walls. There was a beautiful Monet landscape he'd gotten at the Louvre when he'd gone to Paris with the school's French club. A montage of various composers hung over his bed. She scanned the other side of the room. Hmm, when had he put those up? Quotes from famous people. She crossed to the sayings, scripted in calligraphy of varying colors. *You miss one hundred percent of the shots you don't take. If you think you can't, you can't. You've only failed when you don't try again.* Nice sentiments, Jacelyn thought. They were good rules to live by. Interestingly, they were all sports quotes by famous coaches or athletes. She noted a few more new things—all of them athletics-oriented. Looked like Mike and the Bulls were having some effect on Kyle. Well, that was okay with her. Mike was a good man and a good father.

She set the note down on Kyle's chunky wooden desk, by his phone and notepad. Her eyes strayed to the pad. Kyle made lists. It was an endearing habit, if a bit compulsive.

> Call Kay about camp.
> Buy new book.
> Ask Dad?
> Schedule—do it now!
> Get condoms.

Jacelyn's gaze skidded to a halt on the last directive. Oh, my. This was something she didn't know about. Oh, she realized he was nineteen, but still, the proof that he was having sex stopped her. Of course, she'd talked to Kyle about sex, but he didn't share much with her—not uncommon with teenage boys and their moms, Millie assured her. She'd promised herself, when the time came that he was sexually active, she'd be sensible about it, but now that it was here, her heart was in her mouth.

IN HIS dorm room, Marcus Stormweather rolled his eyes. "Jeez, Coach. How can you be such a klutz?"

"Who you callin' a klutz, Stormweather?"

Marcus glanced at the clock. "We've been at this an hour."

"But I got it pretty damn good, don't I?"

"You do passable swing." Marc scanned Mike's white shirt, paisley tie and his Italian suit pants.

His suit coat was in his car. He was taking Jacey out to dinner. And by some fluke, the kids were gone, too. For the second time in a week, he had a whole night with her. "Let's do it one more time."

As Marc went through the motions with Mike again, his mind drifted to the night ahead with Jacelyn.

Enjoy it now, buddy. After next week, who knows what'll happen. It wasn't that they couldn't work out a schedule when camp was over. He'd be tied up with the team for five months of the year, but after that, he'd be free. Besides, he wasn't sure he even wanted to stay in football, and was investigating his options—teaching or perhaps going back to school. Meanwhile, Tyler needed stability, so they were making a permanent home in Buckland. Just a hop, skip and a jump from Rockford. No, it wasn't time or distance keeping them apart. It was commitment. They'd both avoided talking about a future together. It was like players not discussing a winning streak.

"Hell, Coach, concentrate."

He did. Step, step. Twist. Turn. Damn it, he tripped over his feet. Suddenly he heard chuckles and felt the heat of a light. He turned to see a video camera taping all of his pitiful attempts to jitterbug.

"I hope that ain't got no film in it," he said to Nick Santini and the other receivers with him. "I might just have to kill you."

Santini laughed. "She must be something, Coach, for you to be embarrassing yourself so bad."

He couldn't help but grin. She *was* something. She was worth this and a hell of a lot more.

When Jacelyn opened the door to him an hour later,

that thought came back even stronger. It was a warm night, and she had dressed for it. She wore some kind of overlapping-in-the-front gauzy material in deep swirly shades of blue and pink, reminding him of cotton candy. It had tiny little straps and one of those plunging necklines that revealed just the right amount of skin, cupped her breasts, nipped in at the waist and ended midcalf. On her feet were high-heeled sandals. Her toenails were painted a deep red.

"Well now, darlin', if you aren't the prettiest thing."

"You clean up good yourself, Coach."

Mike kissed her on the cheek. "Hi."

"Hi."

"Got your bag ready?"

"Yes." She picked up a flowered case on the floor next to her. "But where are we going?"

"Not too far. I have to be back for practice by nine tomorrow morning." He took the small suitcase as she locked up. "There's a great Italian restaurant this side of Buckland. It's private and out of the way and the owners there know how to cover for famous people." He leaned in closer. "It's got a small inn attached, about ten rooms. We got a nice one for the night."

"They cover for famous people? Like you?"

"Well, I get hounded some in Buckland. Anyway, they also got a band and a dance floor."

"I thought you couldn't dance."

"I can find my way around a waltz. And that means I get to hold you in that dress." They'd reached the Ferrari. From behind, he whispered in her ear, "'Cause as soon as we get to our cozy little room on the third floor, I'm gonna have it off you, sweetheart."

"Hmm, I can't wait." She leaned back into him. "It's been too long."

"Way too long."

THE LITTLE INN nestled on the Niagara River had a picturesque view from the table by the window where Jacelyn and Mike sat. The smoky gray sky was twinkling with stars and reminded her of Mike's eyes. Jacelyn stared over at him; he was dressed in a meticulous suit and snowy-white shirt that set off the tan he'd gotten at camp. He was one of the most masculine men that she'd ever known. And for a while, he was hers. A sinking sensation in her stomach told her that the *for a while* was beginning to be a problem.

"What's wrong, Jacey?"

"Wrong?"

Reaching over, he smoothed the frown from her forehead. "I hate seeing those furrows here. Are you worried about something?"

"Who could be worried in a gorgeous place like this?" She nodded to the front of the dining room. "And he's great."

The saxophone filled the air with songs so sweet they brought tears to Jacey's eyes. With a piano and guitar backup, the little Italian musician played continuously throughout their drinks. Right now, he was doing some mean jazz. "Makes me want to dance."

"Hmm." He looked up. "Here's our meal."

"Signore Kingston, gnocchi for you. Signora, you will like Pino's scampi."

"I'm sure I will, Mrs. Sapori."

"Call me Concetta." The older woman grinned at Mike. "You make my Michael happy."

"Yes, Concetta, she does."

After the wine was served, they dug in. Mike offered her some gnocchi from his own fork and sneaked some of her succulent shrimp. They clinked glasses and toasted, taking every opportunity to touch.

Before ordering coffee and dessert, Mike pushed back his chair. The sax player had taken a break and the band was playing some neat swing music. "All right, let's get this over with."

"Over with?"

"Yeah, come on." He led her to the dance floor. Took her in his arms. "You're gonna have to help me out here."

"Mike, you don't know how to swing."

"Yeah, I do. Sort of."

She was laughing as he did a pretty passable jitterbug. He tripped over his feet a couple of times, then over hers, but he did it.

As a slow song began, he pulled her into his arms. "Now this is more my style." Mike held her close. She could hear the steady thump of his heart and feel his muscles through his suit and smell his aftershave.

"Where did you…how did you learn that?" Jacelyn asked.

"The guys taught me."

"The guys, as in football players?"

"Uh-huh. It was quite a sight, I'll tell you."

"I'd have loved to see it."

"They took videos. Gonna use them for blackmail would be my guess."

"I can't believe you did that for me."

He tugged her closer. Buried his face in her hair. "Believe it."

Over espresso, they were holding hands across the white linen when the saxophone player approached them. "For the *signora*," he said. Then he proceeded to belt out a smooth version of "Misty." Jacelyn had always thought the Johnny Mathis classic was one of the most romantic songs ever written.

When it was over, Mike nodded to the sax player. *"Bene, bene, Giuseppe."*

"Grazie."

After he left, Jacelyn watched Mike. "You had him play that for me, didn't you?"

"Yeah, darlin', I did." He kissed her hand, rubbed his cheek against it. "You make me feel what that song says."

And right then, with the moon shining on them, his hand clasping hers, and the soft clatter of diners in the background, Jacelyn lost her heart to the man seated across from her.

"Thank you, Mike."

He winked at her. "Want dessert?"

"Yes, I want dessert. Get the check. Quick."

"THERE?"

"Yes, there, Mike, there."

She lowered her hand. Grasped him fully.

"Oh, Jacey."

His mouth was everywhere.

"Mike."

A bit later…

"Come for me. First." His thrusts were hard.

"No, togeth—" The world exploded then, and she

had to close her eyes. Sensation, feeling, heat encompassed her.

When consciousness returned, she realized he'd held back.

"Your turn."

She pushed at his chest and he followed her lead, lying into the pillows. She straddled him, was impaled by him—his back bowed off the bed.

"Jacelyn, darlin', you feel so…oh…oh, move, just like that."

She moved. But so slowly he couldn't stand it.

His head buzzed, his mouth went dry. "Don't. Can't. Damn it to hell. Jacelyn, please!!"

She quickened the pace.

But not enough.

He withstood it as long as he could, then he gripped her hips hard and took control. He plunged, plundered and finally felt his body implode.

When he could think again, with her resting on top of him, he realized that never in his life had he experienced such searing, mind-numbing pleasure. But there was more to it. As he stroked her hair, he stared up at the ceiling.

Mike was afraid he'd fallen in love.

"YOU KNOW, I love watching you on the field."

"Yeah, how come?"

She was giving him a back rub as he'd hurt his shoulder again demonstrating moves in practice. "I don't know. It's so primitive."

"Jocks are like cavemen."

"You know I don't think that way anymore."

She kneaded his upper deltoids, then trailed her hands down, loving the play of muscles along his spine. When she reached his lower back, he moaned.

Jacelyn kissed his shoulder. "I've been studying up on football."

"Yeah?"

"Uh-huh." As he was on his side, she was able to slide her hands around to his chest. Brush his abs. Trail lower.

"Unless you're ready for the second half, baby, I'd watch straying into foul territory like that."

His phrasing gave her an idea. "Help me with the football jargon, though. I still don't know what a lot of the terms mean."

"You gotta be kidding. With what you're doin' to me?"

She laughed and continued to flirt with his body. "Come on, you can handle it."

Mike chuckled. "Well, right now, you're doin' some pretty good clipping."

"Clipping?"

"Uh-huh. It's an illegal hit from behind below the waist."

She ran her hands down his flank, around to his thigh.

"That's called encroachment, baby."

Leaning forward, she breathed into his ear. "I'm making a pretty good pass, don't you think?"

"Star quality." As she teased him, he said, "Your aim could be a little better, though."

"Well, practice makes perfect." Insinuating her hand between his legs, she bypassed his penis. Instead, she nudged her knee between his legs from behind.

"You're killin' me, that's what you're doing." He was fully aroused. He grabbed for a condom from the nightstand.

Her hand shot out, grasped his wrist and took the latex from him. "This is an interception, in case you don't recognize it." Still from behind, she tore the packet open and rolled it on him. Then proceeded to take him fully into her hand. "Is this what they call holding?" she asked sexily.

"Jace…"

She massaged him. Loved the feel of him. Loved that sex could be fun and not serious all the time.

"I can't…"

Still she squeezed, played, manipulated. He growled, "That's it," and flipped over. "This," he said through gritted teeth, "is a man in motion." He pressed her into the mattress. "*This* is called going for it." He lifted her hips and thrust into her. Her playfulness had made her ready again, too. He filled her fully, wonderfully.

"W-what's this called, Coach?" she asked breathlessly.

His eyes glittered like hot smoke when he said simply, "Possession."

THEY WERE driving back the next morning, feeling sated, happy and something else Mike was afraid to name in broad daylight. He shook his head.

"What?" Jacelyn asked.

He reached out and grasped her knee. She wore a pink skirt with a white top. Her legs were bare. "I'm feeling pretty damn sappy."

"Me, too."

His grin matched hers. "Thanks, darlin', for a wonderful night."

"My pleasure."

"Mmm. Mine, too." After a few moments of contented silence, he said, "What time are the guys getting back?"

"Noon. I need to talk to Kyle before my meeting with Ed Dickinson."

"The alumni guy?"

"Yes."

"They love having the Bulls at Beckett."

"I'm a little partial to having them on campus, too, now."

He chuckled. "What do you need to talk to Kyle about?"

"Well, first his schedule." She told him about the call from the registrar. "There's another thing, too." She sighed.

"What?"

"When I went to leave the message on his desk, I found something."

He waited.

"A list I'm not sure I was supposed to see." She gave him a sideways glance. "It had *get condoms* on it."

"Ah." He shrugged. "He's almost twenty, sweetheart."

"I know. And he's serious about Kay. It's just that—I don't know—I've tried on numerous occasions to get him to talk about sex with me. He listens, answers a few questions politely, but never shares anything."

Mike felt laughter rumble out of him. "If my mother ever did that when I was young, my ears would still be red."

"I get that, but I bet you talked to your father about it."

"Yes, ma'am. And Logan."

"Your older brother."

"Yeah. Didn't Worthington ever talk to Kyle?"

"Kyle was eleven when Neil left. Plenty of time before that to do the basics. But he didn't, of course." She sighed. "Then when Kyle started dating, Neil wasn't around much."

Mike put his hand over hers. "Want me to say something to him? Even though he's practicing safe sex, that doesn't mean he shouldn't have an adult to kick it around with."

She didn't answer; her eyes were misty blue when he looked over at her. "What?" he asked.

"That is so sweet of you to volunteer."

"I like Kyle."

"I know you do. He knows it, too."

"We might be close enough to talk about this. He's spent a lot of time with me. Shared some things."

"About his father, about the concert." She was silent a moment. "No, but thanks for the offer. He's my son, and even if he's a boy and I'm a woman, I'm going to bring it up, one more time at least."

"Well, if he doesn't talk to you, think about mentioning me."

"I will." She was quiet for a moment, then smiled at him. "You're a really nice guy, Mike Kingston."

He didn't know why he said it. It just slipped out. "Nice enough to be seen in public with?"

There was a very long pause. "Is that what you want?"

"I'm not sure. I guess I'd need to know a few things, first."

"Like what?"

Catching sight of a rest area off the highway, Mike pulled into it. He put the car in Park and faced her. Slowly, he ran a hand down her hair. "Are we gonna see each other after next week? After camp ends?"

She sucked in a breath, as if she didn't expect his question. Finally, she asked, "I don't know, are we?"

"Do you want to?"

Her chin raised and she met his gaze unflinchingly. "Yes, I do. Do you?"

"Ah, darlin', you bet I do." He rubbed his knuckles up and down her cheek. "This—us…" he swallowed hard "…this means something to me."

Her smile was angel-bright. "To me, too."

His heart bumped in his chest. He hadn't realized how much he wanted to hear her say that.

"We'll tell the kids first," she said matter-of-factly.

"Okay."

"And I'll need to talk to Lew again." Her brow furrowed. "I'll, um, tell him it's not just a summer fling." She bit her lip. "Is that all right?"

He knew what she was asking. Sliding his hand to her neck, he pulled her as close as he could get, given the gear shift. "It's not a fling, darlin'. It's a whole lot more."

And so ironic, he thought after he kissed her soundly and pulled back out on the road. Women had sought after him all his life. He'd enjoyed them, cared about them, but he'd never found one he wanted to really pursue. Who would have thought he'd fall for a PhD? And who would have thought she might just return his feelings?

CHAPTER ELEVEN

ED DICKINSON had big shoulders, a brawny chest and a glib smile. He'd been quarterback for the Beckett football team fifteen years ago, and had been involved in the Alumni Association since he'd graduated. In some ways, he'd always intimidated Jacelyn; today, though, he didn't. She guessed it was because Mike made her comfortable around athletes.

"Sorry to keep you waiting." Ed ran a firm which supplied paychecks to area businesses. "Never a dull moment."

"No problem." She sat in his plush office, in his plush chair, sipping coffee.

He dropped down at his desk and adjusted the sleeves of his suit coat. "There's no easy way to tell you this Jacelyn, so I'm just going to spit it out."

Her heart speeded up. Damn it. She was feeling wonderful today after her night with Mike. Whatever Ed was going to tell her was apparently going to spoil her mood.

"For the next school year, the Alumni Association is only going to provide half the amount of funds for the Outreach Program that it gave this year."

Oh my God. She and Millie had been hoping for an

increase. She drew in a heavy breath. "This is unexpected. Why?"

"First, let me say it wasn't my decision. I tried to talk the board out of the cuts. There was strong sentiment on the other side."

"Do they realize what we do with the money? Help kids afford to go to Beckett?"

"Yeah. They want to give the other half of the money to Beckett students, but for a different purpose."

"To other students? Where?"

"In the Sports Studies program."

"Excuse me?"

"Your new program appealed to us for funds for internships."

"Sports Studies is completely financed by the school."

"They want to increase the summer internships not provided for in the budget. I met with Jake Lansing and Mike Kingston about it. And I'm meeting again with the King as soon as I can corral him."

She swallowed hard. "Mike knows about this?"

"Sure. We all got together a few weeks ago. He's team liaison and we brainstormed possibilities for summer internships. They cost money, though, and he asked us to shoulder some of that."

Mike had done this behind her back? "I can't believe this."

"Alumni associations come in all shapes and sizes. Ours happens to favor athletics. I'm sorry, Jacelyn."

"Is this permanent?"

His brow furrowed. "What do you mean?"

"Is your donation being cut just this year, or every year from now on?"

"I don't know for sure. But I wouldn't count on us for more than half."

"Right." She stood.

"I know you're disappointed."

That didn't begin to cover what Jacelyn felt. Stunned, she said her goodbyes and left Ed's downtown office. The bright sunshine didn't feel so warm or comforting this time, as she drove directly to school.

Mike had known about this and not told her? That was impossible. Mike had gone after her alumni funds and deceived her? No, that couldn't be. She wouldn't believe it. Not after what had happened between them this morning, not after what she'd learned about him the last few weeks.

She'd find him and get to the bottom of this.

"HEY, COACH."

Mike looked up from his desk in the Sports Studies office to see Kyle standing in the open doorway. He was dressed in the camp T-shirt and denim shorts, holding a Bulls cap. "Hey, Kyle." He looked behind the boy. "Where's Ty?"

"Kay's at your house with him. Ty's taking a nap."

"I'll bet he's tuckered out." He nodded to Jacey's son. "Come on in." Kyle crossed into the room. "Did you have a good time?"

"The best."

"You don't look like you did." Mike frowned; alarm drove up his spine. "Is everything all right? Is Ty okay?"

"Oh, yeah, sure. I, um, I need to talk to you about something personal."

Mike glanced at his watch. He had an hour before an afternoon session with the team. "Want to grab something to eat?"

"I'm not very hungry."

Remembering Jacelyn's comments about the condoms, Mike pointed to a chair. "Well, sit then." He stood and crossed the room to close the door. When he came back, he dropped down beside Kyle. "What's botherin' you, son?"

"I…" Kyle glanced out the window. Fiddled with the brim of the baseball cap. "Hell." He faced Mike squarely. "I gotta tell Mom something today, before she finds out any other way. And I'm afraid."

Uh-oh. Jeez, Mike hoped Kay wasn't pregnant. "What are you afraid of?"

"Upsetting my mother."

"What would upset her?"

The kid drew in a heavy breath and his eyes grew even more troubled. "I'm changing my major."

Mike had been expecting such a different thing, it didn't compute for a minute. "Oh, well, that doesn't sound like the end of the world."

"It's bad."

Still, Mike didn't get it.

"I'm going into the Sports Studies program."

"Ah, I see." Leaning forward, Mike linked his hands between his knees. "You've got a lot of musical talent, Kyle. Not that I'm any judge. But everybody agrees you're near about a genius."

"I know I'm good."

"And I understood you were gonna go train at Julliard after college. They're the pros of music."

"I know." Mike waited. "I just don't wanna do it anymore, Coach."

"You don't want to play the piano anymore?"

"No, I want to play. I'll always play. And I'd keep up some lessons still. But it's been my life for so long, and it's…not what I want anymore." He shook his head. "Maybe it never was. Maybe it was just a way to please my father."

"Whew! This is mighty big."

"Don't I know it. Mom's going be upset."

"Well, maybe. But I'll bet she'll understand. She loves you to pieces, Kyle."

"Yeah."

"You want me to come with you when you tell her?"

He shook his head, stared down at his hands. "No. I guess I just had to say it out loud before I told her. And maybe get some moral support."

This was sticky. It was obvious Kyle was after Mike's approval. Man, what right did he have to give it? Whose side was he on? Were there sides?

"There's another part of this. My dad's gonna freak. He'll probably disown me. And he'll take it out on Mom like he always does."

Mike thought about defending the boy's father but in his gut, he knew Kyle was right. "Well, let's cross one bridge at a time. First things first. You need to tell your mama."

"Yeah, okay."

"She's—" There was a knock on the door.

Kyle stood. He was scowling, but seemed determined. "Go ahead and get that. I'm going to find Mom and do this."

"You sure?"

"Uh-huh."

Mike rose and they both crossed to the door. When he opened it, he found Jacelyn on the other side. "Mike, I…" Her gaze landed on her son. "Hi, honey. What are you doing here?"

The kid just blurted out, "I need to talk to you, Mom."

She glanced at Mike, then back to Kyle. "Is something wrong?"

"Um…"

Stepping forward, Mike grasped the edge of the door. "Look, why don't I leave you two alone in here? I've got some—"

"No, don't go, Coach. I changed my mind. I want you here when I talk to Mom."

STARING INTO his mother's eyes, Kyle felt his stomach pitch. Suddenly, he knew he couldn't do this alone. He glanced at Coach, who'd been, in part, responsible for this whole thing happening, at least right now.

Coach said, "I think maybe your first instinct was right on, buddy."

"What are you talking about?" His mom's tone was worried, big-time. He'd heard it before when something went wrong for him. She did love him, a lot. That gave him courage.

"I need to tell you something." He grasped her arm. "Could we all sit down?"

Coach stayed where he was. "Kyle, really, I don't think I should—"

"Please."

Coach nodded.

They sat in the chairs around a table in the corner. Drawing in a deep breath, Kyle studied his mother. She seemed upset already. Still he had to let her know what he'd done. "I've got something to tell you, Mom."

"So I gathered."

"You won't like it."

"For God's sake, honey, just tell me. You're scaring me."

"I'm changing my major here at school. Actually, I've already done it at the registrar's office."

"Changing it?"

"I don't want to major in music performance anymore."

"Did you decide on teaching music instead?"

They'd talked about that. His mom seemed okay with it, though his dad would hate even that switch.

"No." He glanced at Coach who nodded to him.

He was tense, too, though he lazed back with an ankle crossed over his knee.

Kyle faced his mother like a man. "I'm going into Sports Studies, Mom."

"What?"

"I enrolled in the Sports Studies program."

Her face was blank, as if it didn't register. "I don't understand this. You're a musician."

"I am, Mom. And I always will be. But I don't want to do it for a living."

"Why not?"

"I'm tired of music. I've done it all my life." He knew how to get to her on this, but it would hurt. "It doesn't make me happy anymore."

She swallowed hard. "Music doesn't make you happy?"

"Practicing, focusing my whole life on a keyboard."

"How long has music not made you happy?"

"A long time. I want to work with people. I just wasn't sure how until lately."

"I see." Now she clasped her hands together on the table. Her knuckles turned white. "What made you choose Sports Studies? There are a lot of ways to work with people."

"I love sports, you know that. When Beckett put in the new program, I read up on it and thought maybe it could be for me. Then after…" he looked to Coach "…after seeing what sports is like up close, I decided to go for it."

"What would you do exactly?"

"I'm not sure. Jake Lansing says there are all sorts of jobs. I figure the internships they offer will help me decide."

Something he didn't understand flickered across her face. She was quiet, though, as if she was trying to get control. "Well, this is a lot to take in." She seemed to notice Coach, then. He hadn't said anything, but he was watching her. "Did you know about this, Mike?"

"Yeah. I—"

"Did you encourage him?"

"I don't know what you mean by that."

"Never mind, it doesn't matter."

"Mom, I've thought a lot about this since the spring. It's what I want to do."

"I can see you think it is. But I'm not sure you understand what it means in the long term."

"How?"

"Honey, sports are games. Do you really want to just *play* the rest of your life? Spend all your time on fields or in gyms?"

From the corner of his eye, he saw Coach shift in his seat, his hand gripping his ankle. "That's simplifying it a mite, isn't it, Jacelyn?"

Her gaze swung to him. "Is it?"

"Mom, I could say the same for music. It's just *playing,* only in another kind of arena. Instead of a field or gym, I'd be spending my life in a concert hall. What's the difference?"

"One's meaningful, significant, cultural. The other's…" She stopped herself, glancing at Coach again.

"The other's what, Jacelyn?" he asked tightly.

"Nothing, I'm not thinking straight. This is just my shock talking. I shouldn't say any more."

"I'm sorry, Mom."

"Oh, honey, don't apologize to me for this. I'm just worried you're making a mistake."

"I'm not."

"I wish I could believe that."

Kyle stood. "I gotta go. I told Kay I'd be back by one so she can go to her practice."

"All right, honey. We'll talk more later."

Coach's gaze narrowed on her. "Can you stay here a minute, Jacelyn?"

She didn't say anything but didn't get up, either. Kyle circled around the table and kissed her cheek. She held on to him a minute, but said no more. Coach rose and followed him to the door. After he opened it, he put his hand on Kyle's shoulder. "It'll be all right, kid."

Kyle looked back at his mother. Her head was bowed, her posture slumped. And he'd done that to her. Feeling like crap, he said, "I'm sorry I'm not the person you want me to be, Mom."

Like lightning, his mother threw back her chair, stood and strode across the room. Forcefully, she took his arm and drew him around to face her. "Don't you *ever* say something like that again. You are a kind, sensitive, wonderful person, Kyle Worthington. I'm so proud of the young man you've become. And I love you for it."

He couldn't help it. He threw himself into her arms and hugged her tightly. She grasped on to him, too. Over her shoulder he saw Coach back away and turn around. "Thanks, Mom."

She held on like she used to when he was little and had done something wrong. "It's okay, buddy. This'll work out."

"Thanks for saying that." Finally he was able to draw back. She smoothed a hand down his hair. "Now go or Kay will be late for her practice. We'll talk more later."

"Okay." He turned to the door. "Thanks, Coach."

"Sure thing."

Shakily, Kyle walked out, leaving his mom behind to deal with the fallout of the bomb he'd just dropped.

MIKE LEANED AGAINST the desk and crossed his arms over his chest. Jacelyn had her back to him, as if she was trying to compose herself. He knew she was all torn up about this thing with Kyle but he didn't go to her. She'd said some things that had put a distance between them. Still, this was hard for her and he didn't want to make it worse. So he said, "It's a shock, I know."

She pivoted. She wasn't crying, though her face was full of emotion. "How long have you known about this?"

"He just told me today. A few minutes ago."

"Then you didn't encourage him to change majors?"

"What?"

"Answer the question, Coach. He said he'd just been thinking about it since Beckett accepted the program, and after he spent time with you, he made his decision. I want to know if you encouraged my son to give up his music?"

"How can you ask me that?"

As if just realizing what she'd said, Jacelyn bit her lip and closed her eyes. "I don't know. I'm sorry. I hardly know what I'm saying. This is all such a surprise, and he was here with you, and you were talking to him. Then there was that thing with the Alumni Association."

Waiting a minute, trying to get a grip on his temper, Mike crossed to the table and yanked out a chair. "Come sit over here."

When she did, he got some bottled water from the fridge and joined her at the table. "Drink this."

She sipped the water. "I can't believe it."

"I know this isn't goin' down very smooth."

"Oh, Mike, he's so talented. He'll be wasting it on God knows what."

Don't take it personally, he told himself. "People have a lot of different gifts, Jacey. Maybe Kyle's got some you don't know about yet."

"It sounds like you support this…this switch?"

"Truthfully, I don't know if I do or not. He's a great pianist. But if it doesn't make him happy…"

"How could I not *know* all this about him?"

"He kept it from you on purpose. He said he was afraid to tell you. That you'd be disappointed."

"Why did he come to you?"

"A lot of reasons, I think. I told you when we were talking this morning about sex that he and I had gotten kinda close. Maybe he just wanted to run it by me for practice."

"Maybe he thought you'd agree with him."

Again, Mike folded his arms across his chest. He felt sweaty beneath the blue T-shirt. "Maybe I do."

She shook her head. "The thought of it. Damn, was it my fault for encouraging his interest in sports, taking him to games? Neil warned me." She covered her mouth with her hand. "Oh, God, Neil will flip. He'll never be able to deal with this."

"All the more reason for you to, honey."

"What do you mean?"

"Kyle's gonna need you to stand up to Neil on this."

"I'll always be there for Kyle. I'd do anything for my son."

The little hard ball forming in his stomach softened just a touch. "For what it's worth, you were terrific with him just now. You put his welfare above your own. I've never seen anything as unselfish as what you just did."

"Well, I feel terrible."

"Which makes what you did even more special." He frowned. "What happened with the alumni?"

She threw her head back. "Oh, Lord. They're cutting their Outreach support by half."

"Why the hell would they do that?"

"They're giving it to the Sports Studies program for

internships." Jacelyn watched him. "Ed said you asked for it."

"I didn't ask for *your* money."

"No?"

"'Course not. Lansing and I talked to Dickinson about financing internships, but I didn't know it would come from scholarship money."

She shook her head and scrubbed her hands over her face. "Ironic, isn't it. Kyle could get some of that money now."

"I'm sorry. That's another blow."

"I feel like I'm losing everything to you guys."

"We aren't the enemy. I thought you and I got past that."

She swallowed hard. "Maybe getting past it was a mistake."

"What do you mean by that?" He asked the question but he was afraid he already knew the answer.

"Kyle said spending time with you helped him make this decision. My approving of all this camp stuff was as bad as taking him to games, letting him do these athletic things. I should never have allowed him to take the summer job."

She was hitting below the belt here. "It's not like he's chosen a life of crime, Jacelyn." He couldn't keep the coldness from his tone.

"Yes, well, his father's going to see it as such."

"That's his father's problem, not ours."

"Ours? You just said you don't disagree with his decision. That you support it."

"Don't go on the offense, baby, just because you're upset."

She rose abruptly. "I need to go."

"Jace, stay. We should…" He was distracted by a movement at the door.

Tim Mason stood in the entryway. "Ready, Mike?"

Mike stared at him. "Huh?"

"We got a session in five minutes." He nodded to Jacelyn. "Sorry to interrupt, but I wanted to run something by you on the way over."

"It's okay," she said. "I was just leaving." With a quick goodbye, she hurried out of the room. Mike stared after her.

"What was that all about?"

"I'm afraid to say."

"Meaning?"

"Nothin'. Come on, let's go. I need some distraction right about now."

ITHACA, NEW YORK, was a postcard-pretty little town about a hundred miles from Rockford, and home to prestigious Cornell University. It also housed Ithaca College, where Neil Worthington headed the music program. Jacelyn drove through the tree-lined streets as Kyle navigated. "Turn left up here, Mom."

His voice was hoarse, anxious. She'd been through this so many times, running interference for Kyle and Neil. Maternal instinct made her say, "It'll work out, honey. One way or another."

"More like another. Though Coach thinks it'll be okay."

She kept her eyes on the cobblestone road of the street where Neil lived. "Coach?"

"Yeah, I talked a long time with him last night before I called Dad. He, um, volunteered to come with us today."

Oh, that'd go over big. Jacelyn was already expecting World War Three. If Mike, a symbol of everything Neil held in contempt and the person who seemed at least partially responsible for Kyle's decision, had come along, it would be the icing on the cake. "You said no?"

"I said no. You shouldn't even have come. I could do this alone."

"Not in a million years."

When Kyle had called Neil and asked to talk to him in person, Neil had said he was too busy to drive to Rockford. He was finalizing the arrangements for the Labor Day Music Festival and he couldn't get away.

Kyle voiced his thoughts: "Damn it, Mom, he can't even make time for me when my life is in crisis."

Catching sight of number 336, Jacelyn swerved into an empty space at the curb. Slowly, she put the car in Park and faced her son. "Your life isn't in crisis, honey. This is just a change of plans. Crisis is when somebody dies. When somebody gets cancer. When there's a war and you're drafted."

Kyle stared over at her. "Coach is right. You're something else."

"What do you mean?"

"Aw, Mom, I know you don't want me to switch majors. This whole thing has got you in knots. But you're helping me anyway. Coach says that unconditional love is the most precious thing there is."

"I'd do anything for you, Kyle."

"But you wish I wasn't changing majors."

"Yes, honey, I do. I'm sorry, I have to be honest

about this. And I can't help what I feel. But it doesn't matter right now. If you're not happy, I want you to take steps that you think will make you happy." She'd deal with her own misgivings, her own doubts, her own confusion, by herself.

Especially over Mike. She was surprised he'd praised her to Kyle. He wasn't happy with her reaction to this turn of events.

Nor with the fact that she'd canceled their date tomorrow night to have dinner with Millie and Gage in public at a restaurant.

Does this have any hidden meaning, Professor?

What do you mean?

You backtracking on me?

Mike, cut me some slack. I'm dealing with a lot now.

His eyes had flared hotly. *You got all the slack you want, sweetheart.*

"Mom, we going inside?"

"What? Oh, of course."

They exited the car. Mid-August in upstate New York was hot, and Jacelyn felt the sweat pool between her breasts as they walked up the flight of steps to Neil's front door. She knew he'd bought the old Victorian a few years ago, but had never been here. Kyle had either driven down alone to see him, or Neil had come to Rockford.

Her son reached out and rang the doorbell.

She looked at him quizzically.

He ducked his head. "I don't have a key."

"Oh, honey."

He shrugged just as the door opened. A young woman not too much older than Kyle stood in the archway. "Hi, Kyle." She turned a highly made-up face, despite the fact that she was in workout gear, to Jacelyn. "Hello, Jacelyn."

"Stephanie."

"Come on in. I'm just on my way out. Neil's in his study." She rolled her eyes. "I'll be glad when this festival's over."

Jacelyn made an innocuous reply, then stepped into her ex-husband's house. Stephanie skittered away on sneakered feet.

"What's that line, Mom? About bearding the lion in his den?"

Smiling weakly, she ruffled Kyle's hair. "Well, at least you haven't lost your sense of humor."

The house was beautifully laid out, with tasteful furnishings and artwork. She remembered that Stephanie was an interior designer. They walked back to Neil's den. From the doorway, she saw he was seated in a big leather chair, facing a wide window that overlooked a small fenced-in yard. Into the phone, he spoke harshly. "I don't care how much fancy footwork you have to do, Louis. I want the hall ready next week or you'll have to deal with the consequences."

Neil slammed the phone down into its cradle, swirled his chair around and caught sight of them. "Kyle. Jacelyn." He glanced back at the phone. "I can't stand dealing with incompetents. This show is three weeks away and the hall isn't even ready."

He looked at Kyle, then pulled out a drawer, and from it drew an envelope. "Here's your tickets, Kyle. You wanted one for you and that girl, right?"

Numbly, Kyle accepted the tickets. He kept them in

his hand, didn't stuff them into his pocket. Neil nodded to a leather couch. "Sit, and tell me what all this is about."

They took seats on the couch.

"What was so important that you and your mother had to drive down here to tell me?" His eyes narrowed. "You haven't gone and gotten that girl pregnant, have you?"

"No, Dad." Kyle glanced at Jacelyn.

Jacelyn had volunteered to break the news to Neil alone, or to tell Neil with Kyle along, but Kyle had said it was his responsibility. "Go ahead, honey." She sat close to him. Her heart was thumping in her chest and her hands were clammy. She hated the fact that Neil could affect them both like this.

"Dad, I've changed my major at Beckett."

"Oh, Kyle. I've told you, music education isn't all it's cracked up to be. Few people are as successful as I am." He shook his head. "No, it won't do. You have incredible talent, much more than I. You can't waste it in a classroom. Performance is a must for you."

Kyle straightened his shoulders. "I'm not changing to education."

Brow furrowed, Neil ran his hand through his hair, and for the first time, Jacelyn noticed it had thinned considerably. "I don't understand."

"I'm going into the Sports Studies program."

"Is this some kind of joke?"

"No, Dad."

"Well, I certainly won't allow that."

Her son straightened his shoulders. "It's a done deal."

"Nothing's a done deal." Neil picked up the phone.

"I'm calling your advisor. Paul Hadley will fix this. We won't talk about it again."

"Paul Hadley's not my advisor anymore. Jake Lansing is."

"The jock?" He rolled his eyes. "God save education today. Kyle, this simply isn't going to happen."

"I'm sorry, Dad, it is." Kyle didn't look away. He held his father's gaze unflinchingly. "I'm not changing back to music."

Faced with his son's obstinacy, which he rarely saw, Neil leveled an angry gaze on Jacelyn. "This is your fault."

"Dad—"

"No, Kyle. It's my turn now." Jacelyn straightened her shoulders, too. "This is no one's *fault,* Neil. Your son has made his own decision."

"Because you've allowed him to dabble in this athletic nonsense. Because you've let him hang out with that Kingston person and his child. Because you've *never* known how to discipline him."

Since her thoughts still ran along the same lines, she didn't contradict Neil. "Can we forsake the blame and pull together to do what's best for our son?" From the corner of her eye, she saw Kyle gripping the tickets for Neil's show. His posture was impossibly tense.

"Please, Dad," he said.

"Please what? Sit back and let you make the biggest mistake of your life? Give my *approval* for you to ruin your future?"

"I'm not ruining my future. Don't you even want to know why I did this? What I think about my future? About my life in general?"

For a brief moment, something flickered across Neil's face. Something paternal. But then he shook it off. "No. It's not relevant."

"It is, Neil. He's not happy with his music."

"That's ridiculous." He steepled his hands. "And even if it's true, it doesn't matter."

Both Jacelyn and Kyle stared at him mutely.

Folding his hands on his desk, Neil arched a brow. "So, you've made your decision. Well, here's mine. I will not finance any Sports Studies major."

Her son's face hardened. "It doesn't matter. The tuition's free at Mom's school because she works there."

"She won't sign for it."

Kyle's gaze whipped to her. "Would you do that, Mom?"

The fear in her son's voice, in his eyes, pummeled her. "Of course I wouldn't, honey." She looked at Neil. "You're wrong, Neil. I'd never do that to my own child."

"So you do support this decision. Well, I don't." He faced Kyle. "I won't be paying for your room and board, or handing out spending money. I won't finance any more of those private music lessons you so like while you make this ludicrous choice."

Kyle stood. "Fine, I'll be a Resident Advisor. My room will be paid for. Or I'll live at home. And I'll find a way to pay for my music studies."

Neil came out of his chair. Next to Kyle, broad-shouldered and tall, Neil seemed small and unmanly. "How dare you defy me like this?"

Kyle lifted his chin. "I'm doing what's best for me."

"You don't have a clue what's best for you."

"No, Dad, *you* don't have a clue." He looked at Jacelyn. "Let's go, Mom."

Jacelyn rose, and Kyle headed for the door without her. "Neil, please…"

His glare was so brutal she shrank back. "You're a bad mother, Jacelyn. And irresponsible. You've ruined your son's life." Then he turned toward the door. "Kyle?"

Her son pivoted and the flicker of hope on his face made Jacelyn catch her breath. "Yeah?"

Neil strode across the room and stopped in front of his son. Slowly, he reached out—and yanked the tickets from Kyle's hand. "Looks like you won't be needing these."

"Dad…"

Staring at his son, Neil lifted the envelope and ripped it in half.

CHAPTER TWELVE

IN THE DIMNESS of the den, Jacelyn sat at the beautiful oak piano they'd bought Kyle when he'd turned ten and picked at the ebony and ivory keys. The too-high tinkling sound vaguely resembled Beethoven's "Ode to Joy." A song Kyle loved to play.

You're a bad mother. You've ruined your son's life....

Putting her head down onto the cool wood, she wondered...worried...that Neil's accusation was true. Was she a bad mother for letting Kyle follow his interest in sports? For letting him work for Mike this summer? Had that caused him to choose athletics over music?

More pathetic notes.

Superimposed over the keys, she saw Neil's contemptuous look as he'd ripped up Kyle's tickets—and tromped on his heart. Her son had blanched. *"Please, Dad, don't do that."*

For a split second, Neil had looked horrified by what he'd done. Then his face blanked. *"Why not? You're rejecting music, aren't you?"*

"Didn't you hear anything I said?"

"I heard you want to be some macho jock who contributes nothing to society. Well, go ahead. You won't be in my world, then."

Jacelyn had hurried Kyle out of Neil's house. She knew he was ready to break down—which he did once he was inside the car. He sobbed like a child in her arms. Holding him tightly, soothing his hair, she'd cried, too.

How could a father do that to his son?

Had she inadvertently helped bring them all to this point by getting close to the Kingstons herself? Mike was so charismatic, so appealing.

"Oh, God."

At the very least, Jacelyn's change in attitude toward the sports program, toward the team's training camp being housed at Beckett, could have signaled Kyle that it was all right to switch his major.

No, no. He said he'd been thinking about it since last spring.

He'd said that, but he'd never done anything to indicate it.

The doorbell rang. *Please don't let it be Mike.* She'd told him she'd call him to let him know how things went with Neil today. But she hadn't because she was so confused about what Neil had said and Mike's role in Kyle's decision.

Again, the bell pealed. Rising, she straightened the navy top she wore with tan capris and left the den. She whipped open the front door. And there he stood.

Looking so good, so handsome in a dressy sport shirt of gray and white, black shorts, sandals on his feet. His hair was a little windblown. She felt the sting of tears and didn't know why.

"Jacelyn."

"Mike." She bit her lip. "I'm sorry I didn't call you. I—"

He held up a hand. His wrist was circled by an Ace bandage. "Don't. I'm not here to see you. I'm here for Kyle."

"Really?"

"He called me about five. Asked to see me. Alone, without Ty."

"Where's Ty?"

"At Millie's. With Timmy."

"I would have watched him."

"Not a good idea right now." He glanced at the stairs. "Kyle's here, isn't he?"

"Yes, I looked in on him an hour ago—he's asleep." She cleared her throat. "He had a rough day."

"I reckoned things didn't go right for y'all when Kyle called. He sounded pretty tore up."

Stepping back, she said, "Come on in." Jacelyn led him to the family room. "Can we talk a minute?"

He jammed his hands in his shorts pockets. "Didn't imagine you'd be wantin' to talk to me."

"I didn't phone you because I wasn't sure I did."

He straightened. The gray shirt made his eyes the color of thunderclouds. "Fine, call your son."

"No, don't take that wrong."

Mike's laugh wasn't pleasant. "There aren't too many different ways to take a statement like that, dar-lin'."

"I'm upset. I'm not thinking clearly. I know I said some things yesterday that offended you—"

"You got that right."

"And I didn't want to do it again."

"It's why you backed out on our date." He glared at her. "You're ashamed to be seen with me, all over again."

"I'm not ashamed to be seen with you." She nodded. "Please, sit down. Now that you're here, I can't let you go like this."

Dropping into a chair, he crossed his leg over his knee. His foot bobbed up and down but he said nothing.

"I'm confused, Mike."

"About your feelings for me?"

"No. Yes."

"Well, that's clear as a bell."

"Listen, Neil said some things."

"Like what?"

"Like I'm a bad mother for allowing Kyle to give up his music."

"It's not your fault. If there's a fault to be had, which I'm not sure there is." He watched her. "What else did he say?"

"That I encouraged Kyle's decision to go into Sports Studies by taking him to games, letting him pursue his interest in athletics after Neil left."

"That's just normal behavior, Jacelyn. Kids like sports." He raised his chin. "It's good for them."

"He said some things about you."

A dark scowl. "What?"

"That your influence on Kyle was negative and I shouldn't have allowed him to spend so much time with you and Ty."

Mike sneered. "Where's he *getting* all this? He doesn't know me from Adam. Hell, he doesn't even know his own son."

She swallowed hard.

"Jacey, you don't believe that bullshit, do you?"

"Kyle said being around the team, with you, helped him along this path."

"That doesn't mean I've been a bad influence on him. Or even that I'm responsible for this switch."

"I think you're responsible. To a degree at least. Mike, he never said anything about taking Sports Studies before you came into his life."

"I don't—"

"No, let me finish. There's something else. You're a good father. You represent sports to him. Neil's a crummy father and he represents music. Maybe he chose you over Neil, sports over music."

"That has gotta be the craziest thinkin' I ever heard."

"No, it's not." Kyle's voice came from the doorway. Jacelyn looked up to see her sleep-rumpled son standing there.

"What did you say, honey?"

"Dad was right, Mom."

Jacelyn's eyes widened.

"I'd rather be like Coach than him."

Her heart in her throat, she asked, "Was Mike the reason you changed your major?"

"No, not completely. I've wanted to switch from music for a long time. Coach gave me the courage, made me feel good enough about myself and about athletics to do it. He made it seem okay to choose a career in sports."

CUTTING THE TEAM to its fifty-three-man roster was the least favorite part of a coach's job. As Mike sat in the meeting to determine the first downsize, the tension was as thick as honey right out of the comb. Every night after practice, the staff had gotten together to determine the relative merits of each player; the exhibition game last week had given them even more input, as would the next one coming up Saturday in Tennessee. Even though a cut player could be kept for the practice squad, the blow to his athletic career was monumental.

"Okay, here's the list." Tim Mason was grim-faced. "Two quarterbacks, three wide receivers, four running backs, two tight ends, four offensive linemen, three defensive linemen, two line backers, four defensive backs, two safeties."

Mike stared at the wide receiver number. He knew one for sure that was gonna go. He should cut two today. Man, this was hard. His shoulders ached and his eyes felt gritty. All the problems with Jacey on top of no sleep, and he was ready to bend steel with his teeth.

The meeting, begun at eleven o'clock right after the morning practice, lasted until one. Finally, they had the first round of cuts determined. After a lunch break, they'd notify the players and deal with the repercussions. Most of the guys would tough it out. A few would be furious. Mike expected grief from Johnny Turk right away. And the mood he was in today, he wasn't sure how he'd handle the rookie.

He left the meeting and headed for the track. He'd worn his running shoes, and two shirts so he could chase the demons away with some good old-fashioned sweat. If he had time, he planned to hit the weight room after.

Forcing himself to focus on football, he spent the first three laps going over the team roster in his head to make sure he'd gotten it right on his end. On the fourth lap, his mind beelined to Kyle. The boy had been so low last night it had nearly broken Mike's heart....

He'd taken the kid for fast food because guys had an easier time talking to each other if they were doing something. Mike had pretended interest in the French fries and burger in front of him but Kyle didn't even touch his meal. After he'd told Mike the whole sorry story, he'd confessed, *"I cried in front of Mom."*

"What'd she do?"

"She cried, too."

The thought of Neil Worthington having the power to set Jacey off like that made his blood pressure sky-rocket. He ran faster, thinking about the boy some more...

"Your father might cool off, Kyle."

"My father is always cool, Coach. Cutting me out of his life didn't seem to faze him a bit."

"I reckon you're not seein' things clearly, son."

Kyle had looked at him with an expression Jacelyn often assumed. *"You weren't there."*

Realizing that defending Worthington wasn't what Kyle needed, Mike asked, *"What can I do to make this better?"*

"Talking about it to you helps."

"I'm glad."

"And you could do something for Mom. I know you two have kinda gotten to be friends. I feel bad I dumped all this on her."

Mike had rolled his eyes at the irony. Little had Kyle known Mike himself was part of the problem. That was even clearer when he'd brought the kid home. Jacelyn had been waiting for them, sitting on the couch watching TV. She'd stood and wrapped her arms around her waist. "Hi, buddy. Are you all right?"

Kyle had smiled, genuinely. "I'm okay, Mom." He turned to Mike. "Thanks, Coach. I feel...better."

After Kyle had gone up to call Kay, Jacelyn had watched Mike. There were questions in her eyes.

He'd immediately gone on the defensive. "I didn't encourage him about the sports thing, Jacelyn. He just vented."

"I'm glad you could make him feel better."

He'd sat then, because he'd promised to help Kyle. "He's worried about you."

"About me? Why?"

"He knows his changing majors is a blow. But he doesn't know the half of it."

"What do you mean?"

"He doesn't know about us." Mike's tone had been bitter. "Then again, nobody does, do they?"

"It all happened pretty quickly between us. Hardly enough time to tell the kids."

"Or the president of the college."

"I can't deal with all that now, Mike."

He'd been angry at that, so he'd bolted up off the chair. "Fine. Let me know when you can make room in your life for us." He'd stalked to the door, but looked over his shoulder after he opened it. "If there is an *us*..."

The memory made Mike run harder. That on top of cutting the team this morning meant he needed the physical outlet. The early-afternoon sun felt good beating down on his head; sweat poured into his eyes. He'd lost count of the number of times he'd rounded the track. As he neared the field house, he saw a flash of yellow and green—Jacey in pretty summer clothes. He slowed down and approached her. Consciously, he forced his breathing to even out.

She looked tired, her face taut, her eyes strained. When he stopped, she held out a bottle of water to him.

"What's this?"

"A peace offering?" She bit off her lipstick. "I saw you when I drove in."

"Mmm." He took the water and drank thirstily.

"You shouldn't be running in this heat."

Wiping the sweat from his brow with the end of his shirt, he stared out at the track. "I had to."

"Why?"

"It was either that or break something."

"You had the first cuts today."

He cocked his head. "How'd you know?"

"You mentioned it before. I'm sorry it fell during all this."

Mike couldn't help himself. He reached out and traced a circle under her eye. "You didn't sleep."

"Not much."

"Kyle okay?"

"Actually, he was whistling this morning when he left to get Ty."

"And that didn't help, did it?"

"What do you mean?"

"My time with him cheered him up, therefore I'm somehow responsible for this."

She took a step back and he cursed his tongue. "I have to go. I have a meeting with the Outreach staff to decide what we're going to do about the loss of income to our program."

"Adding insult to injury."

"I guess."

Leaning over, he braced his foot on the bleacher. "Are we gonna get past this, Jacey?"

"I want to."

"Do you?"

Slowly, she lifted her hand. He was sweating, but she cradled his cheek in her palm. "Yes. Do you have any free time today?"

"We meet with the team at two to drop the bomb. I'll be free from about four to five, then we have another session with the rest of the guys."

She checked her watch. "I'll make sure I'm done with the Outreach thing by four." Jacelyn studied him. "Have you eaten today?"

"Didn't think I could stomach anything."

"Let's meet in the Cyber Café in Basil Hall. That way you can get some food before your next round."

He smiled at her concern for him. "All right." He looked at her. She stared at him. The gulf between them seemed wider than a lake down home. How had they gone from such intimacy just days ago, to this? "See you then."

She glanced at the track. "You done here?"

"I hope not, Jacelyn."

The words hung heavily in the air.

"I CAN'T WRAP my brain around this." Jacelyn threw the folder on the table. She was stretched out on the couch, while Millie sat on the chair in their now-sunny Outreach office. She thought of the day the players had painted it; the memory battered her already bruised heart.

Sighing heavily, Millie shook her head. "It's awful. We'll be able to do so little for the next school year."

"The choices are impossible," Jacelyn said. "We lose the National Merit Scholarship finalist or the kid with twelve brothers and sisters."

Millie held up a folder. "The Hispanic girl who's worked her way to college despite the fact that she had a baby." In her other hand she held a second folder. "Or the Nigerian boy who made us cry in the interview."

Jacelyn bit back the emotion. "Damn it. We thought we were going to be able to give money to all of them. Do it for early decision in December."

Millie propped her feet up on the table. "It's so hard not to resent them." She smiled, though.

"Why the grin?"

"Gage said last night I shouldn't hide my feelings. It's human to be mad at the Sports Studies program and the Bulls for getting our money."

"*He* sounds more like the psychologist."

"He said when Mike met with Dickinson, he didn't know the funds would come from us."

"Sure, it's not their fault."

Millie raked a hand through her dark hair. "I'm angry, too. But not at Gage."

When Jacelyn couldn't talk around the lump in her throat, Millie cocked her head. "You look terrible. It isn't just because of this cut in money, is it?"

"No. Though this is hard for me."

"Somebody's hurt your baby. It's okay to be upset."

"Somebody hurt my other baby, too."

"Meaning?"

"Kyle. Oh, Millie, he's changed his major to Sports Studies."

"What?"

"I just found out two days ago."

"He's giving up music?"

"He says he's not. He plans to continue his lessons. He just doesn't want to do it for a living."

"Oh, my lord. What a blow." Millie glanced to the table where the application folders lay. "Wow. Talk about adding insult to injury."

"That's exactly what Mike said."

Her friend studied her for a minute. "Is this why you backed out of dinner with us?"

"Yes." She sighed. "Neil says Kyle's change of heart is my and Mike's fault."

"Nasty Neil strikes again." When Jacelyn stared at her Millie said, "Tell me you don't believe him."

"I supported Kyle's interest in sports after Neil left and when I found out he loved them so much. I let him take the summer job with Mike. I encouraged him to get close to the Kingstons."

"Which has been nothing but healthy for both of you."

"Neil says Mike's a bad influence on Kyle."

"*Neil* is a bad influence on Kyle."

Weary, Jacelyn laid her head back and closed her eyes. "I'm confused."

"About Mike?"

"I guess. After our trip to Buckland, I was going to talk to Lew and tell him this wasn't a summer fling and I was pursuing a relationship with Mike."

"Sound good to me."

"I've changed my mind."

"Why?"

"I can't deal with all this at once. Kyle's change in major and Neil's complete rejection of him come first. I have to figure that out before doing anything else."

"I don't think there's anything to figure out."

"Of course there is."

"Jace, what if you *are* partly responsible for Kyle's change of majors? Does it make any difference?"

She bit her lip. "It might. If I was responsible, maybe I can do something to change it back."

"You're not thinking straight now. Don't do anything rash."

"You're probably right." She glanced at her watch. "I'm meeting Mike at four. To talk."

"What are you going to say?"

"I'm not sure. I just need to smooth things over with him. When I first found out about what Kyle had done, I said some things I know hurt him." She rubbed her neck. "Hell, this is a mess."

"Just don't make it worse by not thinking it through."

"I won't." Jacelyn stood. "Thanks, Millie."

"You're welcome."

Jacelyn hurried out of the Outreach office and took the stairs up to the Cyber Café. She found Mike at a computer in the corner. He'd showered, and his hair was wet and slicked back. He wore a navy collared shirt and jeans. When she reached him, he smelled like heaven. "Hi."

He looked up at her, his eyes wary. "Hey."

"How'd it go?"

"Pretty bad. I thought Turk was gonna take a swing at me."

"Oh, Mike, I'm sorry." She nodded to the food counter. "Are you going to eat?"

"No, not now." She caught a glimpse of some financial Web site before he closed the program. "Let's just sit over there and talk." He nodded to a group of couches.

"All right." They crossed to a sofa in the corner. It wasn't in the center of things, so no one would probably notice them. She chided herself for having the thought. It would hurt Mike if he knew she didn't want to be seen in public with him.

They sat. His knee bumped hers and his arm rested across the top of the couch behind her. An intimate position. She forced herself not to move away.

"How'd it go with Outreach?"

"Horrible. We're going to disappoint so many kids."

"Can you get money from other sources?"

"Probably not. By now, they're pretty much assigned. No matter what we do, the next school year's most likely going to be a bust."

"Maybe I can help."

Jacelyn shook her head. "I don't want to talk about this with you."

He stiffened and sat back, drawing his arm away from her. His gray eyes were hurt. "What's safe ground here, then?"

"I don't know."

"What did you want to meet about?"

"I just wanted to be with you, I guess."

"Well, that's something at least."

She felt emotion, hard and heavy, swell in her chest. "After the other night, I hate this distance between us."

"Me, too."

"I'm so confused. It feels as if everything's shifted. Like standing on sand in Mexico when the tide comes in. Suddenly the ground gives out under you."

He reached over and laced their fingers, resting their joined hands on the couch. It felt so good to have him touch her again. Just that small contact.

She held on. "I'm so worried about Kyle."

"He's almost a grown man. He has to make his own decisions."

"I know. I just feel so—" she looked around "—responsible."

"Thanks to good old Neil."

"Millie calls him Nasty Neil."

Mike grinned. She did, too.

"That's good to see."

"I'm sorry I haven't been better about this."

"Jacey, darlin', I—"

"Oh, well, this is just perfect." The voice accompanied a shadow that blocked the sun from the windows. Jacelyn looked up to see Neil standing over them. "I was right, wasn't I?"

Her whole body stiffened. She felt Mike tighten his grasp on her hand. For support? Or was he staking his territory? "Neil, what are you doing here?"

He stared at their clasped hands. "I can't believe it. I knew you'd let this jock into your lives. I didn't realize you were screwing him, too."

"Now just a minute." Mike let go of her hand and stood. "You're crossin' the line, pal."

Jacelyn stood, too. "You misunderstand, Neil."

"Yes, well, given this—" he indicated the couch "—and what I just heard from Hal Harrington, it appears my assumption about Kyle's sudden change of heart is accurate."

"Neil, listen—"

"Really, Jacelyn, I thought you were above this... groupie mentality."

Mike stepped close to Neil. "Apologize to the lady, right now, or I'm gonna knock you on your ass, Worthington."

Oh my God. A brawl in the café was just what they needed. She stepped in between the two men. "Mike, stop it. Neil, what are you doing here? Did you come to see Kyle?"

"I came to see Paul Hadley to discuss what damage control we could do here."

"Would you talk to Kyle while you're here? He was devastated last night."

She thought she saw a flicker of emotion—longing, maybe—in his face. "Yes, well, I'm none too happy about it myself."

Mike stepped around Jacelyn. "This is your son, man. He cried last night when he was tellin' me what happened."

Neil arched a brow, all traces of vulnerability gone. "Playing surrogate father already, Kingston?"

"Apparently, somebody has to."

Neil focused on Jacelyn. "I can't believe you've gotten yourself into this mess and dragged my son into it with you."

"It's not like that, Neil."

"No?"

"No. Please, can we just talk about Kyle for a few minutes?"

"Sure you can tear yourself away from lover boy?"

"He's not…we're not…" She cut herself off and turned to Mike. "Do you mind, Mike? I'd like to talk with Neil alone."

Stiffening, Mike took a step back. He leveled a blistering glare on her. "Go ahead and consult with your ex, babe. I'm outta here."

She watched him stride away. Her stomach sank, and she knew, deep in her heart, she'd just done something which, more than likely, she wasn't going to be able to fix. Their words on the field today came back to her.

You done here?

I hope not, Jacelyn.

FOR THE FIRST TIME since they'd split up, Neil looked really old, and something else…unhappy. A chink in his armor? Maybe she could capitalize on it. Seated across from him in the Cyber Café, Jacelyn purposely blocked out all thoughts of Mike. She ignored the little voice inside her that warned that Neil often tilted her life out of focus and she didn't see things clearly when she was with him.

Her ex-husband sipped his tea. "I'm not happy about all this, Jacelyn." His tone wasn't accusing, though.

"Neither is Kyle. I wish you'd talk to him."

Staring across the small area, Neil waited a moment before he answered. "That's what Stephanie said."

"She did?"

He cleared his throat. "She said I'm going to regret alienating him. She and her father don't talk, and I've seen how it has affected her." Drawing a breath, he said, "I feel bad about this."

A concession from Neil was a miracle. "Oh, Lord, Neil, listen to Stephanie, please. Listen to your heart. Kyle needs you in his life."

His hands gripped the cup, and he studied the tea as if it could give him answers. Finally, he looked at her. His eyes were troubled. "I can't possibly give my approval for this change in direction. It's such a waste."

"I didn't give my approval either, Neil."

"There's approval, and there's approval." He glanced over at the couch. "Silent acceptance of all this jock stuff indicates to your son that you approve. Fraternizing with them makes it even worse."

"If I've made mistakes, I'll take responsibility. But that doesn't alter the fact that Kyle needs you in his life, without conditions."

Coach says unconditional love is the most precious thing in the world.

She pushed away the reminder.

"I was upset on Wednesday, when I said that about the music festival."

The vise around Jacelyn's heart loosened a little. Maybe this was going to be all right.

"I came here to see Paul, but I was hoping to bump into Kyle, or you, I think." Neil shook his head. "I just didn't expect to find you holding hands like some teenager with Kingston."

"I won't talk about Mike with you. Except to say he's a good man."

Instead of yelling at her, Neil leaned over and braced his elbows on the table. "Can you honestly tell me that your involvement with him, that Kyle's attachment to him and his kid hasn't influenced his decision to change majors?"

She thought about Kyle's comments. *He's a great dad, Mom.* She remembered seeing them together, playing football in the backyard, on the field. Still, she hedged. "Kyle says he's been thinking about changing majors since last spring."

"He may have been considering it. But why didn't he tell us then? Mike Kingston sealed the deal."

Jacelyn leaned back and closed her eyes. "I'm afraid that might be true, too."

"I'm glad we agree that Kingston's a bad influence."

Her eyes flew open. "I didn't say I thought that."

"But you're willing to admit it's a possibility."

Jacelyn just stared at him.

"When are they leaving?" Neil asked.

"What?"

"When are the Kingstons leaving?"

Her throat felt tight. "Next week."

"Thank God. You'll have to make sure Kyle doesn't have any contact with them after they're gone. He shouldn't go to the games. He shouldn't do e-mail. Be vigilant about all that, Jacelyn. I'm having Paul set up some lessons here, and we'll continue the ones at Hochstein." He ducked his head. "I'll pay. Meanwhile, I'll try to spend some time doing music things with him. Maybe we can avoid this train wreck."

"Wait a minute." She sat up straight. "I'm not sure I want to cut him off from the Kingstons."

Neil looked surprised. "You're not planning to see that man after next week, are you?" When she didn't respond, he said, "Oh, God, Jacelyn, you don't think of this thing between you as long-term? So, you had a fling. Put it behind you. He's an athlete. He travels. He has young, nubile females throwing themselves at him all the time. You don't want to be caught up in all that."

She'd already been caught up in that once. And the reminder dented her self-confidence. "You'd know about young nubile females throwing themselves at men, wouldn't you?"

"Yes, well, attractive male teachers have their share of passes. Listen, cut your losses now. Get Kingston out of both your lives and I'll do my part to get Kyle on the straight and narrow."

"Mike's coming back second semester to teach in the Sports Studies program."

"Oh, hell, this just keeps getting worse—you hired your lover?"

You slept with one of your students. She had the thought but shook it out of her head. Recriminations wouldn't help. "Neil, this isn't where I want this conversation to go."

"I imagine it's not. In any case, you could probably undermine his teaching here."

"What?"

"Give him bad evaluations. Tell Lew you made a mistake and don't want him back the following semester. Find fault with his methods, with his relationships with the kids. There's any number of things that would get him out of the college, and your life in general." Neil shrugged. "Hopefully, by then, we'll have Kyle dropped from the sports program. We've got to play hardball here." He zeroed in on her. "You know, if you wouldn't sign for his tuition, this would be a moot point."

"I won't do that to Kyle."

"All right. At the most he'll lose one semester." Neil stood. "I've got to get back to Ithaca."

"See Kyle first."

He hesitated.

"Please, he's home right now."

"All right. I'll go see Kyle. On one condition."

"What's that?"

"You'll cooperate in what I just outlined."

"I have to think it through, Neil. I'm not committing to anything right now."

"Fair enough." He pulled out his cell phone. "I'll call Kyle."

CHAPTER THIRTEEN

TWO DAYS after Jacelyn and Mike had met Neil in the Cyber Café, Mike was barely hanging on to his temper. But he was forced to put on a happy front because he'd been coerced by the boys into a bike outing by the canal. Just like one big happy family. Seething, he watched as Jacelyn laughed out loud when Tyler's bike wobbled and he stopped it with his toes. They were about ten feet away, but he could hear her clearly. "I think the bike's a little too big for you, buddy."

The kid's dark eyes narrowed with determination. He was a Kingston at heart. "Nah, Daddy says I can do it."

"Come on, then. I'll walk along with you a bit." She glanced over at Mike and Kyle, who stood by a bench, their own bikes propped up on an iron rail next to hers. "You guys wait here while Tyler gets his bike legs."

"Yes, ma'am." Mike knew his tone was stony, but he was as mad as all get out at her.

Kyle sat on the bench and Mike noticed he and the boy had dressed alike, in sneakers, jeans and T-shirts. "I'm worried about Mom. She isn't sleeping much these days, even though things are better with Dad."

Mike dropped down next to Kyle. "Better?"

"He came to Rockford two days ago. Just to see me. We talked. I think things are going to work out, Coach."

Mike's gaze strayed to Jacey. *Not for everybody.* "Hope so, buddy."

"You haven't been around much lately."

"End of camp's always busy. Thanks for spending so much time with the little tyke. And for keeping him overnight."

"I wish we could go to Tennessee with you, but since we can't, it'll be fun having him stay with us. You know how he liked the sleepover in Cincinnati and camping. Mom's looking forward to having him at our house, too."

His son and Jacelyn came into his line of vision. Tyler was giggling, and so was she. It had occurred to Mike over the last few days that he might have blown it big-time. What if he and Jacey didn't work this out? What would happen to Ty, who Mike had willingly let get attached to her? With the recent loss of his mother, Tyler was especially vulnerable.

"What's wrong, Coach?"

"I'm thinking Ty's gonna miss y'all after this weekend."

"I'm going to miss him, too." Kyle scowled. "But we'll see each other, right?"

"You and Ty? Sure."

Kyle cleared his throat and stared out at the canal. The water lapped softly and a crewing canoe sped by. "How about you and me, Coach?"

If your mother lets me see you. Mike had a bad feeling about Jacelyn's talk with Neil. She hadn't called him since then and he hadn't contacted her either. "'Course we are, kid."

Jacelyn and Ty approached them. She looked cute today in yellow shorts, a white T-shirt and a wide-brimmed straw hat to protect her against the mid-August sun. "Well, I think he's ready." She glanced at her watch. "What time do you have to be at the airport?" she asked Mike.

"Four." The team was flying to Tennessee for the last exhibition game before the official season began. He stood and crossed to his ten-speed. "We'd better get goin' if we're gonna ride these things."

They rode along the canal like the freakin' Brady Bunch. Mike didn't say much, and neither did Jacelyn, but the kids chatted like…brothers. Watching them, Mike cursed again, wondering why he'd let this happen?

Because you thought she had faith in your relationship.

He couldn't have been more wrong.

If you can tear yourself away from lover boy.

He's not…we're not…

Mike had spent a lot of time thinking about what she'd been going to say. Had she honestly been going to outright deny him, deny their relationship? Because the thought pissed him off so much, he'd blocked it, blocked *her* for two days.

They pedaled away a good part of the morning, the water lapping, the trees rustling. His heart aching. Then they stopped for lunch at Aladdin's, the outdoor restaurant right across the canal from Mike's house. "Sure you can find something on the menu, Coach?" Kyle teased after they were seated under an awning at an outside table overlooking the water.

Mike rolled his eyes at the mostly Greek menu. "I'll manage."

Ty crawled onto Jacelyn's lap while she explained the selections. After they ordered, he squirmed to get down. Standing, Kyle took Ty's hand. "We'll go feed the ducks while we're waiting for our food."

The boys left. And Mike was alone with Jacelyn. She stared out at the canal, then finally peered over at him. "You're angry at me."

He felt his jaw muscles tense. "You got that right."

"It's why you haven't called me."

He arched a brow. "Far as I know, you got a phone that works both ways."

"I thought some time away from each other would be good."

"Well, you're gonna have all the time you need right soon. We're headin' out of town Monday morning."

She bit her lip. "I know. I feel bad that you're leaving."

This was bullshit. He never sat on the sidelines and let the game take its own course. He was a player, damn it. "So, I wanna know. Is this how it's gonna end between us?"

"I hope not."

"You told Neil we weren't involved."

Her eyes widened. "I did not."

"Two days ago in the Cyber Café."

"I never said that."

"Yeah, you did. Or you started to at least. So I reckon you're either lyin' to me, or kiddin' yourself."

She sighed. "Neil gets me confused. Whenever I'm with him, talking to him, he manipulates the conversation, and afterward, I can't exactly remember what I said."

"It's as clear as a bell to me." He ran his hand around the water glass, rolled the condensation between his fingertips. "How come he saw Kyle?"

"Because I begged him to."

"Doesn't it bother you to demean yourself like that?"

"I'd do anything for Kyle."

That's what Mike was afraid of. "And what did you do this time, Jacelyn? Besides deny your relationship with me to your ex-husband?"

A flush rose up from the pretty white scoop of her shirt. Her eyes lit with fire. "You know what? I'm sick of being pushed around by both of you. Badgered to do what *you* want me to."

"What does he want you to do?"

"Stop it!" She threw back her chair and stood abruptly. "I'm going to help the boys feed the ducks until we're served."

He grabbed her hand, not gently. "You go ahead and do that, Professor. But answer something first. Are you going to the farewell party the team's giving Sunday night?"

"Yes, of course. The whole Business Department's attending, at Lew's request."

"Are you gonna sit with me, or with the *whole Business Department*?"

"I said not to push me, Mike."

More forcefully, he held on to her. "I wanna know. Now."

"Stop it."

Dropping her hand, he shook his head. "Never mind, darlin'. I just got your answer. Consider yourself officially uninvited to sit at my table." He nodded to the water. "Go see the kids. I'll call you when the order comes."

With one brief look, she walked away.

His heart hurt that it seemed pretty damn easy for her to turn her back on him.

THE NIGHT of the ill-fated bike outing, Tyler stayed with Jacelyn and Kyle. As she held the boy against her side, she relished the feel of him. She was very afraid this was the last time she'd get to hold him like this. "And then, Zeus said, 'I am king of the world, Poseidon. In all things you must obey me.' And Poseidon replied, 'Never.'" She glanced over at the clock. "Time to go to bed, honey." She kissed his head. He didn't move. "Tyler?" She whispered the word. He didn't budge.

Lying back into the pillows she closed her eyes. The soft summer air drifted in from the window, but it didn't soothe her as it usually did. Emotion battled to get out when she thought about what had happened earlier...

Ty had climbed onto her bed with the book. She'd begun to read about Zeus and Poseidon. "They're brothers," she told the little boy.

"Wish Kyle was my brother," he'd said after a moment. She'd swallowed hard.

"Gonna miss him."

"He's going to miss you, too."

"Kyle says we'll do stuff still."

"You will. Kyle cares about you."

"You, too, Jacey?" he'd asked innocently.

She'd hugged him hard. "Oh, of course, I care about you, too. We'll see each other, I promise."

She was lying. Mike was so angry at her. With good reason. She'd been immobilized when Neil had made his suggestions—more like commands—the other day. Underlying his words was the ultimatum: if she didn't do what he said—cut Mike out of their lives—he wouldn't see Kyle. She smoothed Tyler's hair. In some ways, she felt as though she was being forced to choose Kyle over Tyler. If she did what Neil wanted, Kyle would survive all this with some sort of relationship with his father intact. If she pursued a relationship with Mike, Ty would be happy.

"Hey, Mom. Is the little guy asleep?"

"Yes." She smiled at Kyle, who seemed more cheerful than ever. Why not? That was a hell of a secret he'd been keeping.

Sinking down onto the bed, he stretched out at her feet. "I'm going to miss him."

"He's going to miss you, too."

"Yeah, well, we'll see him, and Coach."

"Hmm."

He raised his chin. Every day, he seemed bigger, older, more grown up. The faint growth of beard shadowing his jaw accented that impression. "Can I ask you something?"

"Sure."

"I've been so wrapped up in the decision about my major, I think I missed some things. At least that's what Kay says."

"Really, like what?"

"Is something going on with you and Coach?"

"Going on?"

"Uh-huh." His eyes twinkled. "Kay says you give

each other goofy looks all the time. She thinks you're interested in each other—that way."

"Speaking of *that way,* there's something I want to talk to you about, too—the reminder you left on your notepad to buy condoms. I saw it by accident. I wasn't snooping."

He didn't flinch, and looked over at her with adult eyes. "I'm almost twenty years old, Mom."

"I know, honey, and I'm not passing judgment. I'm bringing it up because I want you to know you can talk to me about sex if you need to. It's pretty murky waters when you're young, and an adult's perspective on it can help."

"I know. Sometimes I wanna talk about it." He shook his head. "Don't take this wrong, but not to you, Mom. You're a girl."

"Can you talk to your dad about it?"

"Hell, no." His brow furrowed. "I might talk to Coach, though."

Oh, Lord. "Fine." Their connection with the Kingstons kept getting stronger. "Just tell me this. You practice safe sex every time, right?"

"Right."

"And you care about Kay."

"Of course I do."

"She cares about you."

"Well, yeah."

"All right. I just wanted to say *out loud* that it's important to care about each other—a lot—when you have a sexual relationship with somebody."

"We do."

"Okay."

Kyle sighed and looked directly at her. "So, now, you answer my question. Is Kay right about you and Coach? Is something going on? Because it's all right with me if it is."

She took a deep breath. And watched the young man before her. She remembered him and Mike tossing a football to each other, and Mike hugging him after his concert. And then there was Tyler. *I'm gonna miss you...we'll still see each other.* What had they been thinking? If she admitted to a relationship with Mike now, both boys would get their hopes up. Was it time to cut the ties?

"No, Kyle, nothing's going on with me and Coach." The bald-faced lie stuck in her throat, but nonetheless, she finished, "We're friends, is all."

THE LINE of scrimmage had been clearly drawn at the Burgundy Basin Inn, a party house near the college. On one side of the huge room decorated in muted tones of mauve and gray were the Bulls, all dressed to the nines in fancy suits and designer aftershave. Among them, as reinforcements, were Lew Cavanaugh, Millie Smith and her boys, Kyle and Tyler, Jake Lansing and the three other teachers in the Sports Studies program.

Facing them on the offense was the lineup from the Business Department. And the beautiful, maddening head of the team huddled with them.

"She sure is a looker," Marcus Stormweather, seated at Mike's left, commented as he followed the direction of Mike's gaze. Ty and Kyle sat on his other side at the round table, having a spirited discussion with Gage.

"That she is." Mike's tone was bitter.

"Something wrong, Coach?"

"End-of-camp blues, is all."

"Blues 'cuz you're leaving her?"

"Nah. I'm not big on change. It takes me a while to come down from camp. Did when I was a player, too."

"Yeah, we heard how you used to raise hell right after it was over."

"Not any of my finer moments."

"Good game Friday, Coach." Mike glanced across the table to see Jake Lansing addressing him.

"Thanks, Jake."

"Did you get the information I sent you on your course?"

Mike nodded. He'd banished thinking about teaching at Beckett in the last week. Mainly because he didn't know how he'd manage to come back up here and see Jacey and not touch her, not hold her, not make her moan and beg for him. Damn her. Why was she doing this to them?

"Hey, Coach." Kyle leaned over Ty to talk to him. "How come Mom isn't sitting here with us? She never answered me when I asked."

"Protocol."

"What's that mean?" Ty asked. He was happily digging into some fancy cheesy salad with anchovies in it.

"What's expected of you."

"Why do people 'spect Jacey to sit with them? She belongs with us."

The innocent remark made Mike's gut clench. At one time, he'd thought she belonged with him, too. Now she seemed as unapproachable and unattainable as a goddess. She was dressed in a burnished gold dress that clung to every curve. The neckline was just a bit too plunging to be acceptable to the staid department. The men didn't seem to mind though. He gripped his wineglass and tore his gaze away from the sight of her.

Man, he had to get out of this town. He was having a hell of a time not thinking about her, not going to her house, not grabbing the phone and dialing her number. He needed to be back on his own turf. Dinner was finally served—more fancy shrimp stuff that Ty and Kyle raved over and Mike pushed around his plate. He watched the boys. Nowadays, they acted like brothers. His earlier concern, that he'd made a mistake there, too, came back to him. His kid was going to have withdrawal symptoms soon. Just like Mike. They were addicted to the mother/son duo all right.

After dinner, the program began. First, Tim Mason spoke. He told the crowd how much the Bulls had enjoyed their first summer training camp at Beckett and how they were hoping for a long association.

Damn.

Then Jake Lansing took the podium and pointed out all the benefits of the Sports Studies program and that they were looking forward to the Bulls' contribution to the courses. He cited the speaker series and the first real teacher, the King, in the curriculum. The team cheered and the Business Department clapped politely.

Finally, the program ended with a video with captions superimposed over the footage. Mike, the day he suited up to give Turk a lesson… "Oops, the rookie gets Kinged…" Mason bullying the new guys… "Mason massacres Martin…" Gage tending to a sprain… "Our own personal angel…" Then there was candid footage in the dorms. The guys having a pillow fight, studying plays, sparring in a computer game. It ended with Mike's "dance lesson" with Marcus. There were ear-splitting whistles and raucous applause as Marc tried to teach Mike to do the steps and he tripped over his feet. All for Jacelyn.

He shot a quick glance at the next table over. Her gaze flew to his.

You did this for me? her look said.

I'd do anything for you, his answered.

"Hey, Dad, how come you were learning how to dance?" Ty asked.

"Because I was outta my mind," he quipped, thinking he *was* crazy—to believe she cared enough to make this work...to believe a jock and a professor could make it...even to want somebody like her in his life.

Finally, the video, and the program, were over. Jacelyn approached them while everybody made to leave.

"Hey, Mom, have a good time?" her son asked.

"Sure. It was fun." She looked uncertain. "So what time are you leaving tomorrow?" she asked Mike. Her eyes shone with vulnerability and he wanted only to hold her and tell her things would be okay. But of course, they weren't.

"Early."

Kyle socked his arm. "Not too early. We're going to be up late, Coach."

At Tyler's request, the boys had arranged another sleepover at the Smiths'. Ty, Kyle, Timmy and Ron were spending the night on the living-room floor with Millie at home to chaperone.

"Hey, little guy," she asked Tyler, "will I see you again, before you leave?"

His boy's expression was almost panicky. "Will I, Daddy?"

Mike put his hand on his son's shoulder. "Yeah, sure." He looked at Jacelyn. "We'll come by your house on our way out, if that's okay."

Ty inched closer and grasped Jacey's legs. "Don't want to say goodbye," he whispered softly.

Jacelyn bent down and hugged him.

"I know, sweetie. I don't want to either."

Mike knew how both of them felt.

STILL WEARING the slinky, way-too-sexy dress she'd bought for the farewell party, Jacelyn pulled in to Mike's driveway behind his Ferrari. Compelled to see him, and without thinking about what she was doing, she got out of her Camry and approached his house; the breeze played peekaboo with the hem of her outfit. She stood at the front door for a minute, trying to calm her racing heart. What if he kicked her out? What if he was with someone? Oh, God.

Don't think. She rang the bell.

No answer.

She rang again.

After the third time, she felt tears spring to her eyes. Why wasn't he answering?

Then he did. Dressed in gray fleece shorts and nothing else, he pulled open the door. For a minute, he just studied her. Then he said in a cold, grave tone, "Are the kids all right?"

Raising her chin, she shook back her hair and tried to compose herself. "Yes."

He stared hard at her. His fists clenched at his sides,

as if he was trying to resist touching her. She didn't know what she'd do if he asked her to leave. A feeling of raw panic rose inside her. Finally, he stepped aside and allowed her into the house.

The foyer was dim and Jacelyn's heart pounded like a thousand drums. He remained stone-faced. Again, she felt emotion prickle the back of her throat, moisten her eyes.

He asked, "Why are you here?"

"I…" She swallowed hard. "I…don't know."

He shook his head as if he was disappointed—disgusted—with her. "Then maybe you shouldn't have come."

"Mike, please, don't send me away."

"What do you *want* from me, Jacey?"

"I need to be with you. I couldn't stay away." She glanced upstairs. "Please, I…please…"

This time, he turned his back on her. "I think you should leave."

"I don't want to leave." She sidled up close and touched his shoulder. "Make love to me."

He stiffened.

"Please."

He waited an interminable few moments, then turned around. His stony look had been replaced by one so intense, so poignant, she sucked in a breath. Cradling her face with his hands, he kissed her nose. "I want to. Always."

He bent over and scooped her into his arms; without saying anything more, he strode up the steps. In his room, he stood her by the bed. He didn't turn any lights on, though, leaving the space illuminated only by the moon coming in through the shutters. Gently, he unzipped her dress, easing it off her shoulders. He kissed her skin there—butterfly-soft brushes of his lips. Letting the dress drop to the floor, he knelt, removed her shoes and stripped off her stockings. Again the soft kisses—on her stomach, this time. He stood and unclasped her bra, cupped her breasts, his eyes flaring with heat and need. He picked her up again and set her on the bed. Her hair spread out on his pillow and he leaned over and inhaled its scent.

The tenderness of his ministrations made the tears flow. She couldn't believe she was losing all this.

Shedding his own clothes and lying down beside her, he brushed away the moisture on her cheeks. "Please, darlin', don't cry."

"I…" She choked on the emotion she was feeling.

He kissed her eyes, her nose, the underside of her jaw. With exquisite care, he kneaded her breasts, slid his hand over her rib cage, her stomach, then he touched her intimately. When she was ready, he cradled her into his chest and slipped inside her.

There was more tenderness and a poignancy so acute it only made her tears flow harder.

CHAPTER FOURTEEN

"I'LL PUT ON some coffee while you get dressed." Mike watched as she headed for the bathroom, naked as the day she was born. He could really get used to that view every morning.

"Do I have time for a shower?" Her voice was stronger this morning, which was a good thing. Her vulnerability last night had just about ripped him apart.

He checked the clock on the nightstand. "A quick one. Kyle said he'd bring Ty back by nine and we're cuttin' it close."

Stopping at the door, she threw him a flirty look. "Well, if you hadn't made love to me before I could open my eyes, we wouldn't be in this situation."

"Oh, yeah, baby, I really regret that." Glad for her sass, he matched it. "Scoot, or I'm gonna take you again, right against that wall."

She giggled like a schoolgirl, which he much preferred to the tears, and disappeared into the bathroom.

He called out to her, "I'll get your stuff from the car." She had clothes in the trunk, she'd said, to wear home. Trundling down the stairs, he stopped to make coffee, then headed to the door. When he yanked it open, he started.

"Kingston."

Mike just stared at Jacey's ex; finally he got his wits about him. "Worthington. What are you doin' here?"

Neil glanced at the driveway. "Well, I originally came to talk to you about Kyle. I got your address from the college." He shook his head. "That was before I saw my wife's car in your driveway. I don't suppose she just dropped by this morning."

My wife. "I wouldn't reckon that was any of your business, pal."

"It certainly is if it affects my son."

A son you pretty much ignored up until now. Still, if the guy was willing to strike up some relationship with Kyle, Mike would be damned if he let his own anger interfere. "What'd you want to say about Kyle?"

He looked past Mike. "May I come in?"

What the hell? They were all adults. And maybe this would drive home that Jacey was with Mike now and not him. Though they hadn't talked last night and were too rushed this morning, Mike knew in his heart he and Jacey had a future.

Neil entered the house and Mike led him to the living room. "Sit."

Stiffly, Neil took a chair. "Where is she?"

Mike hesitated. "Upstairs."

"I guess that means she didn't keep her part of the bargain. I was afraid of this."

His blood ran cold. "Bargain?"

Worthington jammed a hand through his hair. Mike hadn't seen him quite so agitated before. "I thought she wouldn't, so I came here to talk to you about it."

"About what?"

"Jacelyn not associating with you anymore. She said she wouldn't see you again and would keep Kyle away from you in hopes that he'd get over this godforsaken desire to change his major."

Mike felt as though he'd been tackled hard and gotten the wind knocked out of him. "Jacey agreed to that?"

There was a noise on the steps. In seconds, Jacelyn walked into the living room, looking like a fallen angel. Her hair was damp from the shower and her light complexion was rosy with heat. She wore only his bathrobe. It skirted the floor, and right now she was trying to tie it shut, but even the belt was too long. She was peering down, studying it. "Hey, did you decide to keep me naked…" She glanced up finally. "Oh, my God."

Neil stood and swore violently. Mike shot a glance at him. He seemed genuinely angry, and something else. Holy hell, was the guy still interested in Jacey? A quick and horrible thought sliced through Mike's brain. What if Worthington wanted Jacey and Kyle back? Would she choose her ex over him?

"Neil, what are you doing here?"

"I came to talk to Kingston. I feared you weren't going to do what you said you would."

Jacelyn seemed flustered. Guilty. Belting the robe as tightly as she could, she swallowed hard. "I…"

Mike closed his eyes. She'd really done this awful thing.

He felt a hand on his arm. "I didn't agree to anything," she said softly.

He looked at her. She was standing next to him, staring up at him. He remembered her just minutes ago, coming alive in his arms.

"You most certainly did."

Both their gazes flew to Neil.

"Did you or did you not agree to consider getting these Kingston people out of Kyle's and your lives in hopes that *his* absence would allow Kyle to see reason?"

She faced him again. "Mike, please—"

"Answer the question, Jacelyn," he said simply.

"All right, I agreed to *consider* it. I told you last night things were all confused, all murky. But I never agreed to *do* it."

Neil stood. "Damn it, Jacelyn. Put your son's welfare above your hormones. Can't you do that for Kyle?"

"I'd do anything for Kyle." She shook back her hair. "But I never agreed that getting him away from Mike is the right thing." She gripped Mike's arm. "I never said you were a bad influence on him."

"But you didn't say I wasn't."

She cocked her head.

He added, "If you'd even consider this obscene proposition, lady, you must have serious doubts about my place in his life."

Neil stepped forward. "Of course she does. The boy is obviously blinded by your stardom. Why else would he forsake music?"

Mike started to defend himself, but stopped. What would be best for Kyle? Could he help the boy he'd grown to love like a son? "Can't you just cut Kyle some slack here, and see that maybe your dreams for him don't make him happy?"

"Kyle is the best young pianist in the state, if not the country. I won't sit by and allow him to throw all that away."

Again, Mike bit back his temper. "Not even if it makes him unhappy?"

"He was happy until you came to Beckett."

"He says he wasn't."

"What does he know?" Neil shook his head. "He's not even twenty years old."

Jacelyn stepped forward. "You married me when I was twenty, Neil."

That stopped the guy for a minute.

She added, "He knows his own mind, at least for now."

Worthington flushed. "I can't in good conscience agree to this, Jacelyn. I just can't."

"Then don't," Mike suggested. They both looked at him. "Agree to disagree, but don't cut him out of your life. He loves you, man."

"I don't need directions from you on how to treat my own son, Kingston."

"Yeah, Neil, I think you do."

Worthington drew in a breath and straightened. "I'm leaving." He frowned at Jacelyn, scanned the bathrobe, and said in a voice full of emotion, "I certainly hope you intend to be dressed before my son arrives."

She checked the clock on the mantel. "Oh, God. He should be here any minute."

Neil glared at her. "Sometimes I wonder if you're the one who's the bad influence on him." With that he turned and walked out.

Jacelyn was shaking by the time the door slammed. Mike stood frozen like a statue. Finally she asked, "Would you get my clothes? I don't want to be in a bathrobe when the kids get here. Then we need to talk."

"Do we?"

"Of course. Neil made things sound terrible. I can explain."

"Sure you can. I'll get your stuff."

She dressed quickly in the downstairs bathroom, and came out to find Mike gone. Glancing through the kitchen window, she saw him down by the canal. She hurried out to him, afraid that Mike was so upset he'd end their relationship. No, she wouldn't let that happen. She wanted Mike in her life, in Kyle's.

He was seated on the bench, staring at a flock of ducks circling near the edge of the water. She knew Tyler loved to feed them, so they were probably waiting for bread. She placed her hand on his shoulder from behind. "Mike."

Instead of turning or answering, he kept his gaze focused on the canal.

"Listen, about what Neil said…"

"I have one question. I want a truthful answer to it."

"All right."

"Do you think I'm a bad influence on Kyle? Especially if I was part of the reason he changed his major, or even made changing majors look more desirable." He turned toward her now. "Because I been thinkin' about that. It's a very real possibility that I had a part in him deciding to do this, or at least gettin' the courage to broach it." He pierced her with a hurt, accusing stare. "So, if I *was* responsible, do you consider that my example was bad for Kyle?"

"Mike, that's a loaded question."

"No, it's not. It's pretty damn simple. Do you object so much to who I am—a jock—that you don't want your kid to become one?"

"I want what's best for my son."

"You didn't answer the question."

"I can't. Without hurting you."

"Then there's my answer."

"Mike, please, I care so much about you…"

He bolted off the bench and grabbed her arm. "Don't you dare say that to me. You don't care about somebody and then disapprove of the person he is. I'm an athlete. I always have been, and I'm not ashamed of it. If it's such a horrible thought that your son could be involved in athletics, too, then that says you object to me, you hold me and what I am in contempt. So don't say you care about me."

"But I do."

"Well, darlin', what you just admitted, if only by the absence of a denial, cuts to the bone. I don't cotton to a woman in my life who wants me in bed, but is ashamed of me out of it."

"I'm not ashamed of you."

"No, then why didn't you sit with me last night?"

She bit her lip.

"Oh, yeah, I forgot. You were confused. So did a night in the sack clear it all up for you? Because if it did, I must be a really good lay."

"Don't demean what happened between us. It's so special."

"Why not, Professor? You demean it every time you deny our relationship."

"I'll do it now."

"What?"

"Be seen in public with you."

"Sweetheart, that's too little too late. I reckon what

happened here today is pretty much irrevocable." His mouth twisted in a wry expression. "And, yeah, I know the meaning of the word. Victor explained it to Nikki on the soap opera. It means you did something that can't be changed, can't be taken back."

A car door slammed.

Both of them glanced toward the driveway. From where they stood, they could see Kyle's car. Jacelyn turned to Mike, panic welling inside her. "Mike, we need to talk more."

"No." He stared at the house. Soon Tyler appeared at the back door. "What we need to do is say goodbye. All of us."

KYLE WATCHED Tyler race down the grassy slope. His heart hurt at the thought of the kid and Coach going back to Buckland, but he had a good feeling about all this. As he followed Ty, he knew deep down he'd see them both. A lot.

Kay had told him last night she didn't believe that his mom and Coach *weren't* involved. God, he hoped that was true. But why would she lie to him?

Watching Ty throw himself at Kyle's mother, and seeing her hug the boy made Kyle even happier. Then Ty went to Coach who swung him up into his chest.

Kyle whistled until he reached them. "Hi, guys," he said happily.

"Hey." Coach's voice was raw. "How was the overnight?"

"Awesome, Daddy. We stayed up until four playing Xbox."

"You're gonna be one tired camper, then."

Kyle shrugged. "I figured he could sleep on the way home."

"Sure he can."

"Mom?" He got a good look at his mother's face. "You okay?"

"Yes, of course." She wrapped her arms around her waist.

Oh, Kyle got it. And *it* was good. Reaching out, he ruffled Ty's hair. "You're gonna miss this little guy, aren't you."

"I'm going to miss both Kingston men."

Yes! That was good news. Kyle smiled at Coach, who looked…sad or something. "Me, too, Coach."

Ty laid his head on his father's chest. "We're gonna see you. Soon. Kyle said so."

His mother swallowed hard. "Okay, if Kyle said so."

Kyle watched her. Something more than the Kingstons leaving was wrong. "Mom? What are you doing here? Coach and Ty were going to stop by our house on the way out of town."

Coach let Ty slide down to the ground. The boy immediately crossed to Kyle and stood by him.

His mother said, "I was up and out. I decided to meet you guys here."

Coach glanced at his watch. "Your mother has an appointment at nine, so she needs to say goodbye now." He stared at her hard.

She stared back. The vibes between them were really wacky. Without answering, she turned to Ty and knelt down in front of him. "Come here, buddy. Give me one last hug."

Ty threw himself into her arms, burying his face in

her shoulder. She clasped him to her. Over them, Kyle looked to Coach. His face was stony.

"I'm gonna miss you," Ty said.

"Aw, sweetie, I'm going to miss you, too."

"Love you, Jacey."

From where he stood, Kyle could see tears in his mom's eyes. "I love you, too, buddy."

Coach turned his back on them. Kyle watched his Mom give Ty one more hug then straighten. "Well, I'd better go."

Ty just stood there, his eyes bright. Tears tracked down his mom's cheeks. She asked Kyle, "Will I see you at home?"

"Yeah, I'm gonna help get them packed, and say goodbye then."

"All right. I'll be leaving."

"Aren't you going to say goodbye to Coach?"

She stilled, looking at Coach's back. "Mike?"

He turned around. "Goodbye, Jacelyn."

His mother swiped at the tears. She didn't say anything for a minute, then she crossed the few feet between them, and put her arms around Coach's neck.

At first, Coach didn't do anything. Then he gave her a bear hug that could crack ribs.

"Goodbye, Coach," his mother said weepily. Tearing herself out of his arms, she pivoted, stopped to kiss Tyler's head and practically ran up the hill.

"THAT'S ABOUT IT." Mike slammed the trunk to his rented SUV with more force than he'd intended. "I shipped the rest last week with the Ferrari."

From a few feet away, Kyle stood holding on to Ty's

hand. Mike had blocked the emotion he felt while saying goodbye to Jacelyn. He was, however, unable to put a lid on what he was feeling for the kid before him. How in hell had he gotten so attached in four short weeks?

"Guess this is it." Kyle's eyes were clear.

Of course, he didn't know they were saying goodbye to the family that, somewhere along the line, Mike had been hoping for.

Bending down, Kyle hugged Ty to his chest. The boy asked, "When we gonna see you?"

"Soon. I promise, buddy."

"Ty, Kyle starts classes next week, and your second grade begins pretty soon."

"Yeah, but he's coming to the games, aren't you, Kyle?"

"Oh, I almost forgot." Digging into the pocket of his jeans, Mike dragged out an envelope. "These are for you."

Kyle straightened—Ty holding on to his waist—and took the envelope. "What are they?"

"Passes for the season, to sit in the space reserved for friends and family."

Opening the flap, Kyle examined the tickets reverently. "There are four passes in here."

"For you, Kay, your uncle and your mother." Mike glanced away; he'd gotten them a while ago. "Don't know if she'll be wantin' to come, though."

"I bet she will."

Mike shook his head. "Anyway, it'll be nice to have you there. We're gonna have a great season." He ruffled Ty's hair. "Okay, Champ, one more hug and we gotta go."

Kyle knelt back down.

Tyler clung to Kyle's neck. "Gonna miss you."

"I'll miss you, too, buddy." Then Kyle whispered, "I love you, Ty."

"Love you, too."

That made Mike's eyes sting. In a blur, he got Ty situated in the car. He slammed the door and then had to face Kyle. The look of pure, unadulterated love on the boy's face made Mike weak in the knees.

"I don't want to say goodbye, Coach."

Mike didn't have to fake the emotion in his throat. "Me, either, kid." He nodded to the tickets. "But you'll be coming to Buckland, right?"

"All but the first game."

"Why?"

"That's Dad's music festival." Kyle's smile was sunbright. "He wants me there, now."

If Mike needed a reminder of his place, or lack of it, in this family, Kyle had just given it to him. "Oh, sure." Still, he loved the kid so he went through with what he'd planned. Taking a paper from his pocket, he handed it to Kyle. "This is my cell phone number. If you ever need anything, or want to talk about anything, call me." Then he gripped his shoulder. "Stay in touch, buddy."

Kyle threw himself into Mike's arms, and hugged him like Ty had hugged Jacey. "I will, I promise."

Mike held on tight. Hell, at least he could say what he felt to her kid. "I love you, Kyle."

"Love you, too, Coach."

And that, Mike thought, drawing away, was that!

CHAPTER FIFTEEN

"I'M GETTING married."

Distracted by what she'd been forced to buy this morning at the drugstore, Jacelyn stared at her best friend. Millie was beaming like a blushing bride. "What did you say?"

"Gage and I are getting married. Over Columbus Day weekend when school's off for four days. We'd like you and Mike to be attendants."

"You're kidding, right?"

Millie held out her hand where a sparkling ruby nestled in a bed of diamonds. "Nope."

Battling back her own misery, Jacelyn stood, hugged Millie and oohed and aahed with appropriate awe over the gem. "Congratulations." Tears stung her eyes. "Oh, Mil, I'm so happy for you."

"I never thought I'd find somebody to spend the rest of my life with. After Tom died, I figured I'd had my chance at happiness. Hell, some people don't even get *one* opportunity. But here it is again." She said meaningfully, "And I'm grabbing the ball and running for the goal."

Her analogy made Jacelyn think of Mike, whom she missed with an intensity she hadn't thought possible.

"Are you all right?" Millie asked. "You look like I just told you I had a terminal illness."

Jacelyn sniffled. "Of course I'm all right. I'm happy for you." She looked around the office. "What does that mean for your job, Mil?" If she was losing her best friend, too, Jacelyn figured she just might die.

"I'm not sure. Right now, I'm keeping the house. The boys love their school here. I work in Rockford. During the season, Gage is going to come up on his days off, and we can go to Buckland on weekends. Then when football's over, he's free most of the time. At least for now, I'm staying put. Who knows for the future?"

Jacelyn's smile was genuine. "He's a wonderful man."

"Hmm. Second chances don't come along very often, do they?"

Turning, Jacelyn busied herself with the letters they were writing to applicants for the next school year's Outreach Scholarship money. Letters of rejection. "No, I guess not."

"And you blew yours."

Jacelyn looked up sharply. "Yes, I did. I blew my relationship with Mike. I know that now."

"Without trying to fix it."

"I tried to fix it. I called him that first week after he left. But he wasn't interested in even talking to me. So other than the two times I saw Tyler, I haven't spoken to him."

The phone rang and Millie went to answer it. Jacelyn sat on the couch and thought about her time with Tyler....

Mike had phoned her late at night at the end of the first week they'd spent back in Buckland. She'd tried to reach him twice that week and at first thought he was returning her calls.

Look, I hate to ask for favors, but I need one. Ty misses you. He's cryin' at night again. Can he see you?

Of course. Anytime. Mike, did you get my messages?

Yep. I don't want to go down that road again, Jacelyn. Let's stick to your relationship with Ty.

They'd made arrangements for the boy to come up just before school started for him in September, and Jacelyn had eagerly awaited their arrival. She'd been devastated when Mike's father pulled his car into the driveway. He'd brought Ty, and he picked him up. Still, she and the boy had a wonderful two days together, bike-riding, cooking and playing games. She'd missed him terribly when he left.

"Sorry," Millie said. "That was the groom. He calls me twice a day at least."

Jacelyn felt a streak of jealousy so strong it embarrassed her. She forced a smile.

"So you saw Ty twice, but not Mike."

"Right. The second time Kyle brought him back after the game and Mike arranged for Eric to drive him home."

And mild-mannered Eric had been upset....

Jacey, what's wrong with you? You ditched Mike for what? A life that hasn't made you happy in a long time.

I didn't ditch Mike.

Well, you're both acting like you did. He's a rejected man if I ever saw one.

"So you're just giving up." Millie's comment brought her back to the present.

"What am I supposed to do? Stalk him?"

"Maybe. A few meager phone calls sounds like a half-hearted attempt to me. He probably thinks so, too."

Confused, Jacelyn just shook her head.

"Gage says he's miserable."

She tossed down the folder. "He can't be too miserable. For this week's game, Kyle went down a day early to baby-sit Ty Saturday night. Mike had a date. A pretty brunette, Kyle said."

Millie waved off the remark. "You could go to the games with all of us. You've missed three."

"No. I'm not groveling." She looked at the package by her purse. *At least not yet.*

"You know I'd accept that if you weren't looking like something out of *Dawn of the Dead* these days. Think you can tolerate being in my wedding?"

"Of course." Her smile this time was genuine. "I'm really happy for you." She glanced at the folders. "We needed good news after finalizing all this. It breaks my heart to see our program cut to shreds."

Thank goodness, Millie let Jacelyn change the subject; her friend shook her head at the stacks before them. One pile was almost a foot high. The other had five folders in it. "I feel bad, too. We gave money to four times as many kids last year."

"But there'll be internships for the jocks."

"Does it still hurt so much that Kyle's one of them?"

About to tell Millie that everything hurt these days, she was distracted by a knock on the door. Lew Cavanaugh stood in the open archway. His usually reserved face was bright with animation. "Hello, ladies." He held up a FedEx letter. "I have something for you."

Dropping down in her seat, Jacelyn felt the familiar

exhaustion overcome her. "Good news, Lew?" She didn't know how many more negative things she could handle right now.

"The best." He crossed to her and held out the letter. "Read what's inside."

Jacelyn slipped out a sheet of paper; a white envelope fell into her lap. The stationary told her the note was from the Buckland Bulls. It was addressed to Lew.

Again the strange animation in the president's voice. "Read it out loud to Millie."

"'Dear President Cavanaugh. It is with great pleasure that I inform you of the Bulls' campaign for contributions to your Outreach Scholarship Fund. Enclosed is a check made up of donations from players, staff and owners. Given the success of this drive, we plan to continue it throughout the year, and in years to come, as a token of our investment in the educational program at Beckett College.'" Jacelyn felt her heart turn over in her chest. She closed her eyes and tried to quell the emotion this news brought out in her.

"It's signed by the owner of the Bulls," Lew told them. "Look at the amount."

Her hands shaking, she opened the envelope. "Oh, my God."

Over her shoulder Millie said, "Wow. We'll be able to do even better than last year." She snatched the letter from Jacelyn's hands and reread it. "Um, Jacey, look who he copied in."

"Who?"

"The fund-drive coordinator."

She shook her head, knowing what Millie was going to say. "Don't tell me."

"It's our friend Mike Kingston." This from Lew. He frowned. "I thought you'd be happy about this, Jacelyn."

Get it together, girl. "I am."

"Why do you look like you're going to cry?"

"Long story, Lew." When his scowl deepened, she said, "I'm really pleased."

Pointedly, he looked at the folders. "We'll be able to reverse those stacks there."

Millie grinned. "Uh-huh. But the best thing is, it's ongoing. It's not just a Band-Aid for this year."

Jacelyn couldn't speak past the lump in her throat.

"Well, I'll leave you to spend all that money." He eyed Jacelyn. "This should take some of the edge off having the Bulls here and in the Sports Studies program, Jacelyn."

"Yes, of course it does."

Lew finally left. Millie retrieved her cell phone from her purse, then sat down beside Jacelyn. She held out her hand. "Here, try again. You have to thank him."

Jacelyn gave her a watery smile. By rote, she punched in Mike's cell. It rang one, twice, and on the third ring, he answered. "Yeah, Kingston here." His voice was rough, impatient.

"Mike, it's Jacey."

"Jacelyn?" A pause. "I didn't recognize the number when it came up."

Obviously that was why he had answered.

"I'm using Millie's cell phone."

"I see."

"We got the money and letter today from the Bulls. About what you did for the Outreach Program."

"Mmm."

"Thank you so much. This means a lot to me."

"I'm glad you're happy. Look, I gotta—"

"Please, talk to me. You haven't returned any of my calls."

A long pause. "I just don't think there's much more to say."

She glanced at her purse. "Maybe there is."

"What?"

"I…" She sighed. Now that she had him, she was tongue-tied. "I'm sorry about everything."

"All right. I believe that."

"I want another chance. With you. For us."

"No can do. I'm not settin' myself up for that kind of grief again."

"Mike, please."

"While I got you on the phone, you should know I turned down the offer to teach at Beckett in the spring, too."

"Oh, no. Mike."

"I gotta go. Apology accepted. We'll end on good terms. Goodbye, Jacelyn."

"Mike—" But the line went dead.

Millie took the cell from her and clicked off. "It didn't go so well?"

Jacelyn stared at the phone. "No. I guess the King doesn't believe in those second chances you were talking about earlier."

HIS WIDE RECEIVERS lined up before him, every single face stony. Mike addressed them. "We're gonna run today. Then catch some passes. Then run some more."

They exchanged looks. Marcus shook his head.

"You got a problem with that, Stormweather?"

Marcus glared at him. "No, sir. Can't see why we shouldn't be runnin' eight miles a day, particularly since we're in such bad shape."

Mike arched a brow at the sarcastic tone. "Add a hundred push-ups before the run."

"Aw, Coach," another player whined.

"And after," Mike put in. "Don't be such babies. I'll do them with you."

There was more grumbling as the guys left the locker room. Mike followed them out, led them around the track, did the push-ups and called them for a huddle.

They practiced a half hour longer than anybody else, and finally broke for the day. Furious with himself, he did another twenty laps around the field. Maybe if he tired himself out enough, he'd be able to sleep tonight. Her call this morning had set him back big-time. He'd just started *not* to think about her every damn minute. Just begun to forget the sweet rhythm of her voice and the sound she made when he was inside her. Then he had to go and take her call. Hell and damnation. He knew talking to her would throw him into another tailspin, so he'd erased all her messages without listening to them, and wouldn't have answered this morning if he'd known it was her.

After a scalding shower, he stomped into the office and found Marc sitting behind his desk, feet up, arms crossed over his chest. "Making yourself at home, Stormweather?" Mike asked, slipping on shorts and a T-shirt.

"Nope. I drew the short straw."

"For what?"

"To come talk to our Coach who turned into a maniac three weeks ago."

Mike gave him the sternest look the King could muster. "I could fine you for insulting a coach."

"Go ahead, it's better than having every wideout on the team quit. Think of it this way, you better listen to me or you might be bringin' Johnny Turk back up from the practice squad."

"Say what you gotta say, then."

"You've been working us too hard. We've won every game, only made a couple of fumbles or missed passes between the five of us, and we're in top condition. So what the hell's going on with you?"

He had to get it together. He was letting his anger at her interfere with everything. Exhausted from yet another fitful night's sleep, he sank into a chair. "It's personal."

"I figured that. I haven't seen Dr. Ross at any games."

"No."

"You through?"

"Yeah."

"She dump you?"

Please talk to me. "Nope. My choice."

Marcus's brows arched in surprise. "No shit? We were takin' bets she dumped you six ways to Sunday."

"Now that makes me feel a whole lot better."

Marc just stared at him.

"It's complicated. Look, I appreciate your honesty. I'll let up on the team. Tell the guys."

"Okay." Marc stood and crossed to the door. When he reached it, he turned back. "Anything I can do, Coach?"

"No, thanks. I'm fine."

"Yeah, right."

Mike stayed where he was, staring at the empty office. Damn it, how the hell did he get here? He never had women trouble. Usually, he could cut them out of his life without a backward glance. So long, it's been nice, have a good life.

But not with Dr. Jacelyn Ross. She'd gotten under his skin, bad. Which was why it had hurt like a son of a bitch to hear she'd even *considered* Neil Worthington's ultimatum to keep Mike away from Kyle. How dare she even *listen* to the accusation that he was a bad influence on her son?

Ironically, he and Kyle were closer than ever. The kid had come down with Eric for the Bulls' second home game, then they'd both come to Cincinnati for the away one. And Kyle was coming Friday night to spend the weekend with Ty. He'd even baby-sat the night of Mike's date.

What a fiasco that had been. Damn, he'd thought if he got interested in somebody else, things would be better. The woman, a friend of Tim Mason's wife, was nice enough, pretty enough, but she just wasn't…Jacey. He'd been rotten company and was embarrassed by it.

Then Eric had cornered him after the last game…

"She's miserable."

"Sorry to hear that."

"Then do something about it, man. This is my sister we're talking about here." He'd softened his tone. *"Cut her some slack, Mike. She had it rough after the public humiliation of what Neil did to her…then raising a son all by herself. Is it any wonder she doesn't change easily?"*

Hell. He stalked to the desk. The phone was right there. He could call her.

And do what? Change the fact that he'd never be sure she loved him for who he was? Never be sure she wasn't just a little embarrassed to be seen with him? Never be sure she didn't see him as an inferior species next to Worthington and Harrington and all the other academic types? No, he didn't want that kind of life. It'd kill him to love her like he did and have her be ashamed of who he was.

So to keep himself from picking up the phone, he kicked the wastebasket across the floor.

IN THE PRIVACY of the bathroom of her own home, Jacelyn dipped the stick in the urine sample and checked her watch. The directions said to wait four minutes. Four minutes to see if her life would be altered forever.

Exhausted, she dropped down on the toilet seat to wait. Her period was a whole week late. And she was never late. And she remembered, as if it had happened yesterday, that night after the Bulls' farewell party. She had gone to Mike's, and he'd taken her upstairs and made tender, exquisite love to her. But, with all those heightened emotions, they hadn't used protection. Oh, God, what had she been thinking? She wasn't eighteen. She was a grown woman.

What would she do if the little wand turned blue? There were alternatives to having a child, but none of those would be right for her. Besides, she couldn't quell the tiny bud of hope, flowering inside her. In her heart of hearts, she wanted to be pregnant with Mike's child. Then they'd have no choice but to work through the rift between them.

Well, time to face the music. Straightening, she rose and picked up the wand.

It wasn't blue.

She wasn't pregnant.

Tears came then. She sat back down and sobbed into her hands. After she quieted, she swore aloud, "Damn it," picked up the package and the wand and flung them into the trash. Son of a bitch. This was for the best. She was just tired. And frustrated.

Blindly, she made her way out of the bathroom and down the hall to her bedroom. It was four in the afternoon; lying on the bed, she tried to take pleasure in the warm September air coming in through the window, and the sounds of kids playing outside, but she couldn't. She tried thinking about Kyle…he was coming home at six for dinner. She was cooking for him. Hmm, she'd make something he'd like. She drifted off…

"Mom?" She heard the voice but turned away from it. "Mom?" Jacelyn felt a hand on her arm. "Mom, wake up."

Slowly, she opened her eyes. She could tell from the angle of the sun that she'd slept a long time. Flipping to her back, she saw Kyle standing over the bed.

"Hi, honey." The clock read six-thirty. "I'm sorry, I must have fallen asleep. I'll get up and cook now."

In the shadows of her room, he watched her. "Mom, what's going on?"

Oh, God, not now. She didn't want to talk about not going to the games, not seeing Mike, hedging about letting Tyler visit again. That's all Kyle wanted to discuss these days.

She sat up and leaned against the pillows. "Going on?"

He held something out she hadn't seen him carrying. "What's this all about?"

In his hand was the box to the early-pregnancy test kit. Oh my God. She swallowed hard, trying to gather her wits. She had to be a mother now, instead of a lonely woman who'd screwed everything up. At least she was good at one thing.

She scooted over. "Come sit down, honey."

He sat, clutching the incriminating box.

When she didn't begin right away, he said, "You told me just weeks ago that you believed you should really care about somebody before you had sex with them."

"I do believe that."

"Far as I know, you ditched Professor Hal and haven't been dating anybody. You spent most of the summer with me and Ty and Coach, anyway." He stopped suddenly and stared at her.

"Kyle, I—"

"Kay was right, wasn't she? About you and Coach. There *was* something going on."

She drew in a breath. "Kyle, really, this is a private thing for me."

"Hell, Mom, it doesn't work both ways? You can talk to me about sex, but I can't talk to you?"

"No, of course you can."

"You were…with Coach." Kyle held up the box.

"Well, yes."

"Why did you lie about it when I asked you?"

"For reasons I don't want to discuss."

"Did you care about him?"

"Of course I did." Jacelyn cleared her throat. "I do."

"What happened?"

"He went back to Buckland."

"So what? Millie and Gage are getting married. You and Coach could deal with his job, the distance, if you really wanted to."

"There were other problems, honey, ones I don't want to discuss with you. Those are private."

He gripped the box. "Just tell me one thing."

"What?"

"Am I gonna have a little brother or sister?"

Tears pooled in her eyes. "No, honey, it was a false alarm."

"Mom, look, if you're this upset, maybe you and Coach could…"

"No, we can't." Hell, she didn't want to put the blame on Mike, and she certainly didn't want Kyle to find out his father's role in all this. Kyle would believe the separation between her and Mike was his fault.

He sighed. "It's why you haven't been going to the games. Seeing him."

"Yes." She grasped his arm. "But I didn't lie to you before. I do believe what I said about sex."

He stood. Very adult now. "If you cared enough about him to sleep with him, you should be able to work this out." He started to walk away.

"Where are you going?"

"Out. I need some time to think."

"Oh, honey, stay and talk to me about this."

"No, I'll be back, though."

CHAPTER SIXTEEN

THE DOORBELL rang and Mike cursed. Damn it, why didn't everybody just leave him alone? He didn't get up; Tyler was staying with his grandparents because Mike had to leave tomorrow for a game in Oakland, and if anything was wrong, they would have called first. He sat where he was and nursed his beer in the glassed-in back porch and stared out at the treed lot. He wondered if Jacey would favor this spot where he'd built his house. Would she like the layout? It had tons of amenities, none of which meant dirt to him right about now. Damn it all. Could he feel any worse than this?

The bell sounded again.

"Go away," he mumbled at the intruder. But whoever it was didn't leave. They'd probably seen his car. Slowly, he rose and found his way to the front foyer. Peering through the glass side windows, he was shocked to see Kyle on the stoop. Mike whipped open the door. "Hey, buddy, what are you doing here?"

"I need to talk to you." He held something out. Mike looked down at his hand. In it was a box.

"What's that?"

"An early-pregnancy test kit."

"Aw, son, come on in." He showed Kyle into his house. Son of a bitch, all Jacelyn needed right now was to have to deal with a teenage pregnancy.

Leading Kyle to the back porch, he sat the boy down. "Want something?"

"Yeah, some answers." Kyle's tone was belligerent, almost angry. At him? It seemed so. But that didn't make any sense.

Mike sat. "How far along is she?"

"Holy shit. You *knew* she was worried about this—" he held up the box again "—and you let her go through it alone? What kind of man are you?"

"What are you talking about?"

Kyle's eyes narrowed on him. "What are you?"

"Kay. I presume she's pregnant. How far into it is she?"

"Kay's not pregnant."

"No?" He studied Kyle, glanced at the box. "Then what's that for?"

"This," Kyle said harshly, "is the pregnancy test kit my *mother* used today to see if she was having *your* kid."

"What?"

The boy spat out a four-letter word Mike had never heard him use before. "What was she, Coach, just another lay for you? Weren't your groupies enough?"

"Kyle, look, you got this all wrong."

"Do I? You had a freakin' date last weekend. I *baby-sat*. While my mother's been moping around for weeks." He crunched the box. "No wonder. You left her and she was scared shitless she was pregnant."

First things first. Mike gripped the boy's arm. "Kyle, is she pregnant?"

He shook his head. "No. She said it was a false alarm."

"Then how do you know about it?"

"I came home today and she was asleep. The house was a mess, so I decided to pick up for her. Take the garbage out like I do when I'm home. I was emptying wastebaskets and found this."

"But it was negative, you said?" That was good.

Then why was he so *disappointed?* Damn it. Nothing was feeling like it should.

"Does it even matter to you? You haven't called her, come to see her. No wonder she lied to me when I asked her before you left if something was going on with you two. She thought she was pregnant and you didn't even care."

Jacelyn had lied to her son about them? Another nail in the coffin of their relationship. Except...

Kyle stood and flung the box down. "Look, just tell me the truth. Did you dump her?"

Damn it all! What a mess. He couldn't tell Kyle the reason he and Jacelyn broke up—that she was so concerned about her son she'd made a deal with the devil. What could he say?

"It was my decision not to see her anymore."

Kyle shook his head. "My dad was right about you."

"Your dad?"

"He said you were just a dumb jock, out for yourself all the time." Kyle swallowed hard and his eyes were bright. "I thought you cared about us."

"I do, buddy."

He shook his head. "Not if you left Mom to deal with this all by herself. If you could do that, you're not the man I thought you were."

"Kyle, I didn't know she thought she was pregnant."

"Yeah, right. You probably didn't want to know."

"I'd have wanted to know," he said gently. *I'd have wanted her to be pregnant.*

"Sure." Kyle glanced upstairs to where Ty's room was. "Same thing happened to you before, didn't it? And you didn't marry *her*, either. You got a track record that speaks for you, Coach." He reached into his pocket. "Here, take these. I won't need them anymore."

Mike looked at Kyle's outstretched hand. In it he held the season passes. "Hey, don't do this. Come on. I—"

"What? Can you give me one good reason why you abandoned my mother?"

He couldn't. Not without implicating Neil. Which would in turn lay the blame on Kyle. And he wouldn't do that to this boy he loved like a son.

So he just stood there and watched Kyle walk out of his life. Earlier he'd thought he couldn't feel any worse than he did.

He was wrong. Now he'd lost them both.

JACELYN PACED the floor of her bedroom, watching the clock tick off the minutes. Her son had been gone for five hours. She'd called his cell phone several times. She'd called Eric, Kay, Millie, even Neil to see if he'd gone to them. She'd left Mike for last, promising herself, if Kyle wasn't back by midnight, she'd contact him.

The clock chimed twelve times and she picked up the phone. Oh God, what if he didn't answer because he recognized the number? He did. "Kingston," he said gruffly. He sounded wide awake.

"Mike, it's Jacey. I'm sorry to bother you, but I—"

Tears welled in her throat. "I'm looking for Kyle. He left here five hours ago, upset, and nobody's seen him since."

"He came to see me. He was upset when he got here, talked to me, then stormed out. I couldn't stop him."

"Oh, no."

"Did you try his friends? Neil?"

"Yes." Emotion clamored to get out but she had to be strong. "What if something's happened to him?"

"It's only been a few hours. He's probably just driving around. Do you want me to come up there?"

"I—what about Tyler?"

"He's with my parents. Look, I'm jumping in the car now. I'll be there in an hour."

Jacelyn hung up the phone. Kyle had gone to Mike, as he might have done to a father. *Please, God, don't let anything have happened to him.* In the time it took Mike to get there, she tried Kyle's cell again, and Kay and Eric both called.

When the bell rang, she opened the front door and threw herself into Mike's arms. "It's okay, sweetheart, I'm here. Hush." He eased himself into the foyer and shut the door. "Come on, let's sit down."

They sat on the family-room couch. Without preamble, she said, "He was so upset when he left here. I shouldn't have let him drive. But I thought he just needed some time to get his thoughts straight."

Mike squeezed her fingers. They were ice-cold. "I thought that, too."

"What did he say to you?"

Mike's gaze was somber. "He brought the pregnancy test kit. He's mad at me because I left you when you thought you were pregnant." He tipped her chin. "Why didn't you tell me?"

"I didn't suspect anything until last week when my period was late."

"Are you sure you're not pregnant, honey? Those tests aren't always right."

"Yes. I got my period an hour ago. If I'd only waited…" She swallowed hard. "I'm sorry he's so mad at you. None of this is your fault. It's mine."

"I—"

The phone rang and Jacelyn snatched it up. "Hello."

"Jacelyn, it's Neil. Kyle's here. He's upset with all of you and asking questions I can't answer." He drew in a breath. "Hell, are you pregnant?"

"No."

"He said something about a pregnancy test kit."

"Put Kyle on."

Muffled noises in the background. "He doesn't want to talk to you."

"I'm driving down."

"Now? It's after one."

"I don't care."

"Well, I have a packed day tomorrow, so get here fast."

Jacelyn hung up. "He's with Neil. I'm going to Ithaca."

Mike stood. "I'm driving you."

"No, Mike, you have a game tomorrow."

"The game's Sunday. The team leaves tomorrow. I'll meet them there. It doesn't matter anyway, Jacelyn. I have to see Kyle before I go. If I miss the game, I miss the game."

I have a packed day tomorrow...

"You are so unselfish."

He turned at the door. "I love Kyle, Jacelyn."

"I can see that."

On the way to Ithaca, they talked about Kyle's accusations. "Why didn't you tell him this was all my fault?" Jacelyn asked as they sped down the thruway.

"I think that's obvious. He'd blame himself for what's happened between us."

Again, she thought what a good man he was, how he unconditionally put Kyle's welfare above his own.

Coach says unconditional love is the most precious thing in the world...

He reached over and squeezed her arm. "Try to get some sleep. You're exhausted."

She dozed, and awoke when he shook. "We're in Ithaca. I need directions to Neil's place, honey."

In minutes they were there. Lights blazed from the clapboard house, and Mike and Jacelyn hurried to the door. Neil opened it before they knocked. "What the hell is *he* doing with you?" he bellowed.

"Not now, Neil." Her ex-husband stepped aside and they entered. "Where's Kyle?"

"Upstairs. You'll have to deal with this, Jacelyn. I have work tomorrow."

"Sure, Neil." She faced him squarely. "I need to know what you told him."

"Nothing. He mumbled something about you being pregnant. He said he didn't want to talk, he just wanted to spend the night. He's in the guest room."

Kyle didn't even have a room in his own father's house.

They heard noise on the stairs, then Kyle appeared in the doorway to the foyer. "Mom?" His gaze transferred to Mike. "What are *you* doing here?"

"Honey, we were so worried about you."

Kyle glared at Mike. "I don't want to see him."

"Kyle, Mike did nothing to you."

"No, but he did something to you. It's the same thing."

"Kyle, the reason I'm not seeing Mike is totally my fault."

"What do you mean?"

"I made some poor choices. I take full responsibility."

"I don't understand."

Neil checked his watch, then pushed away from the wall. "Oh, for God's sake, just tell the boy what happened."

"Neil…" Mike warned.

"I don't see what the big deal is." Neil faced Kyle. "Your mother had a fling with Kingston. She came to her senses when I pointed out what a bad influence he was on you. I convinced her to stop seeing him and to keep him away from you in hopes that *you'd* come to *your* senses and change your major back to music." He sighed. "There now, that clears the air."

Jacelyn watched openmouthed.

Mike stepped forward. "That wasn't exactly what happened, Kyle. Your mother and me not seeing each other isn't your fault."

"Isn't it? Dad just said it was."

Jacelyn groaned. "Kyle, honey, I won't let you take responsibility for this."

"Jeez, Mom, how could you think such awful things about Coach and still sleep with him?"

The stark words silenced everybody. The look on Mike's face told her Kyle had hit home.

Neil said, "You and your mother need to talk. I suggest you do that alone. I'm finding this conversation distasteful and embarrassing."

"You do need to talk to your mother," Mike added. "I'll head out. But before I do, I want you to know that the problems between me and your mother went a lot deeper than you changing your major. We aren't seeing each other for a lot of reasons, Kyle. We're really different, son. These things happen between people and it's nobody's fault." He squeezed Kyle's shoulder. "Especially not yours."

Mike turned to Jacelyn. "You should stay here and talk to him. It's too late to drive back. I'll take Kyle's car and he can ride with you in the morning. I'll leave it at your house and pick mine up."

"No, we're heading out. But you should drive Kyle's car." She wanted to say so much to Mike but she had to concentrate on her son now. "Thanks again." She gestured, her hand indicating Neil's house. "For all this."

"You're welcome." With a last squeeze on Kyle's shoulder, Mike took his keys and left.

Neil cleared his throat. "Well, I'm glad that's all cleared up."

"Nothing's clear, Neil, at least not to Kyle." She put her hand on her son's arm. "Come on, I'll explain it all to you on the drive back."

JACELYN COULD FEEL Kyle watching her across the car. He looked as though he wanted to ask how somebody so smart could be so stupid at times. "Let me get this straight. You and Coach hooked up. You liked him, and he liked you, enough to…you know. Enter Dad. He says it's Coach's fault I'm switching majors, and you agree to kick Mike out of our lives."

"Not exactly." She glanced over at him. "I agreed to consider it."

"Well, that's not as bad. Coach would still be pissed about it, though. Wasn't he?"

"Yes, but, honey, none of this is Mike's fault either. It's all mine."

Kyle laid his head against the seat. "Nah. From what I can piece together, it's mostly Dad's fault. Again."

"No, Kyle. I take responsibility for my own actions. I agreed to consider your dad's demands."

"Why did you?"

When she hesitated, he said, "Because you thought it was best for me."

"I had to think about that, honey."

"Hell, Mom, I'm almost twenty years old. I know my own mind."

"I guess you do."

"Why didn't Coach tell me the truth tonight? When I went to Buckland?" He shook his head. "I said some awful things because I didn't have the whole story."

"Why do you think?"

"He was protecting me, too. He didn't want me to think you two split up because of me."

"It's not your fault."

"No, it's Dad's, like I said. He came in and ruined everything."

"If my relationship with Mike was meant to be, honey, your father couldn't have ruined it."

Kyle was quiet. Then he asked, "Are you in love with Coach, Mom?"

Jacelyn sighed. Then she said simply, "Yes."

"I think he loves you, too. He tried to protect you tonight. Just like you did me."

She shook her head.

"What?"

"He was willing to miss the game in Oakland for you."

"He's so cool, Mom. You're crazy if you let him go."

"I've already lost him, honey."

"Well, to quote one of my favorite sports heroes, 'It's not over till it's over.'"

"What are you saying?"

"That there's still time to fix this if you really want to. You got choices, Mom. You gonna drop back and punt or you gonna go for it, fourth and goal?"

"I don't have any idea what that means."

"Think about it." He lay back and closed his eyes. "Oh, and Mom?"

"Yes?"

"He was willing to protect me just like you were tonight, right?"

"Uh-huh."

"Seems to me, then, you two aren't so different after all. In what counts."

Oh, God, could Kyle be right? On the entire drive back, she couldn't quell the thought. And the hope that sprang with it.

CHAPTER SEVENTEEN

MIKE FORCED BACK the urge to scan the stands, to look for Jacelyn. The players were warming up just before the game against Michigan started; he managed to keep his gaze from traveling to the team's friends-and-family section, but still he thought about her. He knew Ty would be there, along with Millie and her kids. And Kyle would come with Eric. Things were finally square between Mike and Jacey's son. Mike had driven up on Tuesday to have lunch with the boy. They'd sat in the Cyber Café and talked. Kyle had apologized for jumping the gun.

"Sorry about blaming you, Coach. It's just that where my mother's concerned, there's no question where my loyalty is."

"That's how it should be."

"Did I, like, you know, ruin things between you and me?"

"Nah, 'course not. We just had a small misunderstanding." Mike had taken out the passes Kyle had returned to him and slid them across the table. *"Can you make the game Sunday?"*

The boy's face had lit from within. *"Yeah, sure."* He'd glanced at the passes. *"There's still four here. Mom's invited?"*

"Um, yeah, I guess. How's she doin'?"

"She's sad." Kyle's expression had been hopeful. *"You should go see her while you're here. She's got office hours now."*

"Maybe…"

He hadn't, though. Twice he'd started up the steps to her office, but he'd walked away instead. She had to come to him. She had to make her choice clear. She had to decide on her own, without pressure from him, where *her* loyalties lay.

Absently, he watched the players warm up. He couldn't wrap his brain around the fact that she'd thought she was pregnant and hadn't told him. What did that mean? Would she have told him eventually? Would she have gotten rid of it?

Did you want more babies after Kyle?

Not at first. When it was too late, I wished I had, though.

She probably would have had his kid. Hell, he would have wanted her to have it. Truth be told, once the dust had settled, he wished like crazy she had been pregnant. That would have forced her hand.

Yeah, Kingston, and you never would have known, the rest of your life, if she'd truly picked you. Still, a baby with Jacey. A sister for Kyle and Ty. Being able to live together as a real family. When had Mike discovered that's what he truly wanted out of life?

The whistle blew and he knew he had to get his mind away from those crazy-making thoughts. What the hell? He needed to know if she was here, so he grabbed his binoculars from the bench and scanned the reserved seating section.

He found Kyle next to Tyler, both wearing team sweatshirts and Bulls' caps. It was the beginning of October, and today was warm.

Millie. Her boys. And several of the players' wives. Some brunettes wearing Bulls' shirts. Somebody with a football jersey that had his old number on it. Mostly everybody's face was obscured by the caps. Still, he'd have recognized Jacey if she was here. Damn it to hell, he thought, turning to the players. She hadn't come.

He was absurdly disappointed.

Jacelyn watched Mike pick up the glasses and scan the crowd. She wondered if he saw her. If he did, would he want her to be here? Over the past week, she'd started to call him innumerable times. But she'd stopped herself. She could tell when they went to get Kyle in Ithaca that she'd really hurt him. At first, she thought it best to leave it there. Then Millie and Kyle and Eric had been vocal about how wrong she was.

First her brother... *What's wrong with you, Jace? You love him, he's crazy about you and your kid. Where is your head at?*

Then Millie... *Damn it Jacey, wake up. He took all the blame for splitting so your son didn't get hurt. He drove up here then down to Ithaca, and was willing to miss a game for you guys. Do you have any idea what all that means?*

And finally a discussion with Kyle...
Coach was here today.
Her heart had plummeted. *He was?*
He didn't come to see you?
No, did he say he would?

Nope. Kyle shook his head. *Looks like the ball's in your court, Mom.*

Now, that expression she understood. She was going to have to make the move if she wanted Mike back in her life. And in the dark of every night for the rest of the week, she made her decision. She wanted him. And she was willing to fight for him. She patted her jeans pockets. Two things had come in the mail that week for her to use as ammunition.

The game took forever. Jacelyn got more and more nervous as the clock ticked down. She kept watching Mike, striding along the sidelines, yelling to the players, talking into the headset. All the while she wondered if he was going to forgive her for the doubts she'd had about him, for the misunderstanding about who he was, what he was, that she'd felt.

She glanced at the time. Five minutes to splashdown. Jacelyn was scared to death.

THEY'D WON. Mike should be happy. After returning to the locker room, after the cheers and pats on the back with the players, he took his time showering and dressing. As the scalding water beat down on him, he thought about the night ahead. He was planning to meet Kyle, Ty and Millie, Gage and her kids at an out-of-the-way restaurant for dinner.

Without Jacey.

He let loose a string of obscenities.

Stepping out of the shower, he dried off, dressed and still he lingered. For one thing, he didn't want to face any hangers-back who were looking for his autograph. Jeez, people were still after it. For another, he wasn't looking forward to pretending things were peachy keen in front of Jacey's friends and her son. Mike was miserable. He wanted Jacey with them, with him, in his life.

Then do something about it.

Oh, hell, watching from the stands wasn't cutting it. He was going to hike on back to the playing field and win this game. Plain and simple. Nothing more to it. Finally, he strode from the locker room, thinking about how he might go about getting his ladylove back.

The door slammed behind him with a heavy thud that echoed loudly in the area outside the locker room; it was empty, thank the good Lord. At least he didn't have to deal with rabid fans who wouldn't take no for an answer.

Then somebody stepped out of the shadows. "Hey, Coach."

Damn it. For a minute, she just stood there. The one who had been in the team family section, wearing the football jersey with his old number on it. Slowly, she approached him.

And Mike's heart began to gallop in his chest. He'd recognize that graceful sway of hips anywhere. When she reached him, she whipped off the cap and all that gorgeous blond hair spilled everywhere. "Hi."

He found his voice. "Hey."

She held up some papers. "Can I have your autograph?"

He stared hard at her, remembering that first meeting. "I, um, don't give autographs."

"Oh, please, just this once."

"I suppose it's for your son."

"Ah, no. It's for me." Then she said, wrenchingly, "For us."

"Ja—"

"No, don't say anything. Just open the top paper and sign it."

He looked down. And unfolded the document. It was his contract to teach at Beckett next semester. "Please, Coach, give it your John Hancock."

Drawing in a breath, he scrawled his name on the dotted line.

"Now the next one."

He arched a brow. "Two? Hmm. Don't know 'bout that. Maybe I'll sign it." He moved close enough to smell the take-me perfume she wore. "If I get something in return."

"You can have anything you want in return." Her tone was achingly sincere. "But look at it, please."

Mike couldn't help it. He leaned down and brushed his lips over hers. "I miss you so much."

Jacelyn grasped his shoulders. "I miss you, too."

He stepped back and opened the second thing, which was in some fancy envelope. An invitation.

You are cordially invited to attend the annual Beckett Holiday Ball held on November 11th at the Burgundy Basin Inn. You may bring a guest.

"The ball's an annual event," she explained softly. "I go every year." She swallowed hard. "So does every member of the Beckett faculty. And the mayor. And anybody who's anybody in Rockford."

A lump formed in his throat. "You want me to go?" He waved the other sheet. "As a faculty member?"

"No, as my escort." She held his gaze unflinchingly.

Reaching out, he traced the edges of the number on her football jersey. "Why, Jacey?"

She caught his hand and clasped it close to her heart. "Because I love you and I want a life with you." She brought his fingers to her lips. "I'm so sorry about everything."

Leaning in, he met her forehead with his. "Me, too. I didn't make any of this easy for you."

Jacelyn shook her head. "No, it was me. I was wrong."

Mike brought his hand to her lips. "Know what? I'm sick of all this blame. Let's deep-six it." He glanced around. "If it's all the same with you, I reckon I'd just like to start over again." He grinned. "Maybe pretend we just met, here, with you askin' for my autograph, like the last time."

She frowned. "All right, if that's what you want. Except that I don't sleep with guys I just met, and I was really hoping…"

He chuckled and pulled her close, his hand anchoring her to his body. "You got a point, darlin'. Maybe we'll just pick up where we left off."

"I'd like that, Coach."

"So would I, Dr. Ross."

So he took her in his arms.

HARLEQUIN *Super*ROMANCE®

A six-book series from Harlequin Superromance

WOMEN *in Blue*

Six female cops battling crime and corruption on the streets of Houston. Together they can fight the blue wall of silence. But divided, will they fall?

Coming in February 2005, She Walks the Line
by Roz Denny Fox (Harlequin Superromance #1254)

As a Chinese woman in the Houston Police Department, Mei Lu Ling is a minority twice over. She once worked for her father, a renowned art dealer specializing in Asian artifacts, so her new assignment—tracking art stolen from Chinese museums—is a logical one. But when she's required to work with Cullen Archer, an insurance investigator connected to Interpol, her reaction is more emotional than logical. Because she could easily fall in love with this man…and his adorable twins.

Coming in March 2005, A Mother's Vow
by K. N. Casper (Harlequin Superromance #1260)

There is corruption in Police Chief Catherine Tanner's department. So when evidence turns up to indicate that her husband may not have died of natural causes, she has to go outside her own precinct to investigate. Ex-cop Jeff Rowan is the most logical person for her to turn to. Unfortunately, Jeff isn't inclined to help Catherine, considering she was the one who fired him.

Available wherever Harlequin books are sold.

Also in the series:
The Partner by Kay David (#1230, October 2004)
The Children's Cop by Sherry Lewis (#1237, November 2004)
The Witness by Linda Style (#1243, December 2004)
Her Little Secret by Anna Adams (#1248, January 2005)

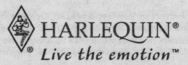

If you enjoyed what you just read,
then we've got an offer you can't resist!

Take 2 bestselling
love stories FREE!
Plus get a FREE surprise gift!

Clip this page and mail it to Harlequin Reader Service®

IN U.S.A.
3010 Walden Ave.
P.O. Box 1867
Buffalo, N.Y. 14240-1867

IN CANADA
P.O. Box 609
Fort Erie, Ontario
L2A 5X3

YES! Please send me 2 free Harlequin Superromance® novels and my free surprise gift. After receiving them, if I don't wish to receive anymore, I can return the shipping statement marked cancel. If I don't cancel, I will receive 6 brand-new novels every month, before they're available in stores. In the U.S.A., bill me at the bargain price of $4.69 plus 25¢ shipping and handling per book and applicable sales tax, if any*. In Canada, bill me at the bargain price of $5.24 plus 25¢ shipping and handling per book and applicable taxes**. That's the complete price, and a savings of at least 10% off the cover prices—what a great deal! I understand that accepting the 2 free books and gift places me under no obligation ever to buy any books. I can always return a shipment and cancel at any time. Even if I never buy another book from Harlequin, the 2 free books and gift are mine to keep forever.

135 HDN DZ7W
336 HDN DZ7X

Name	(PLEASE PRINT)	
Address	Apt.#	
City	State/Prov.	Zip/Postal Code

Not valid to current Harlequin Superromance® subscribers.

Want to try two free books from another series?
Call 1-800-873-8635 or visit www.morefreebooks.com.

* Terms and prices subject to change without notice. Sales tax applicable in N.Y.
** Canadian residents will be charged applicable provincial taxes and GST.
  All orders subject to approval. Offer limited to one per household.
  ® are registered trademarks owned and used by the trademark owner or its licensee.

SUP04R   ©2004 Harlequin Enterprises Limited

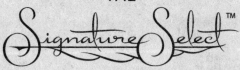
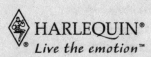

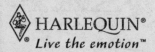

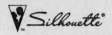

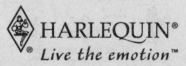